FLOWERS and CAGES

Hart of Rock and Roll Book Two

Mary J. Williams

ISBN: 0997616121
ISBN-13: 978-0997616125

Table of Contents

ABOUT THE AUTHOR

Writing isn't easy. But I love every second. A blank screen isn't the enemy. It is the opportunity to create new friends and take them on amazing adventures and life-changing journeys. I feel blessed to spend my days weaving tales that are unique—because I made them.

Billionaires. Songwriters. Artists. Actors. Directors. Stuntmen. Football players. They fill the pages and become dear friends I hope you will want to revisit again and again.

Thank you for jumping into my books and coming along for the journey.

HOW TO GET IN TOUCH

Please visit me at these sites, sign up for my newsletter or leave a message.
http://www.maryjwilliams.net/home.html
https://www.facebook.com/pages/Mary-J-Williams/1561851657385417?ref=hl
https://twitter.com/maryjwilliams05
https://www.pinterest.com/maryj0675/
https://instagram.com/2015romance/
https://www.goodreads.com/author/show/5648619.Mary_J_Willia ms

MORE BOOKS BY MARY J. WILLIAMS

Harper Falls Series

If I Loved You

If Tomorrow Never Comes

If You Only Knew

If I Had You (Christmas in Harper Falls)

Hollywood Legends Series

Dreaming with a Broken Heart

Dreaming with My Eyes Wide Open

Dreaming of Your Love

Dreaming Again

Dreaming of a White Christmas (Coming in December)

(Caleb and Callie's story)

One Pass Away Series

After the Rain

After All These Years

After the Fire

Hart of Rock and Roll

Flowers on the Wall

Flowers are Red (Coming in October)

Flowers for Zoe (Coming in November)

PROLOGUE

TRIED, CONVICTED, SENTENCED, and on his way to the state penitentiary, Dalton Shaw had learned two things. He wasn't as tough as he thought. And behind bars, there was no such thing as a guilty man.

The black eye and split lip Dalton sported proved that a cocky attitude didn't impress anyone behind bars. Especially a bruiser who had used up his last strike and was going away for life. It could have been worse. The guard could have broken up the fight after Wiley Malone had done permanent damage.

"I wanted to smash that pretty face into a pulp," Wiley growled as he was dragged away. "Next time, Shaw. There will be one. Count on it."

The odds that Dalton would wind up in the same prison as Wiley were better than even money. The judge who sentenced him made it a sure bet. Three years—less than one if he kept his nose clean. But it was a long time to watch his back.

"There are rules," Ryder Hart told him during their last visit before Dalton was relocated.

"What do you know beyond what you've seen on television?"

"I've done some research. So has Ashe. Zoe was the one who found you a tutor."

Ryder, Ashe, and Zoe. Dalton's bandmates. Friends. Family—a bond stronger than any blood relation. They were his lifeline and the only thing that had kept him sane. None of them had believed Dalton would do any significant amount of time. He didn't have a record as an adult and only minor scuffles as a minor. Beating the shit out of someone—no matter how well deserved—was serious. But hard time? It didn't make sense. Unless one added in the fact that Dalton's victim lived in a small town where his daddy's influence ruled. Dalton's lawyer had tried to get the trial moved out of the county, but the judge refused.

"I need a tutor to go to prison?"

Ryder nodded. Dalton knew his friend was trying to keep a positive outlook, but his dark eyes were shadowed with worry. "Jock Lowe. It isn't exactly *Miss Manners*, but there is a definite way to do things."

"Fuck that, Ryder. It's prison."

4

"And like you said, all we know is what we've seen on TV or in the movies. Forearmed is forewarned, Dalton. Listen to what the man has to say."

Dalton knew Ryder was right. But it seemed so final. Like a movie, he hoped for a last-minute reprieve. The sentence had been passed. Tomorrow the bus would take him to his new home.

How the hell had this happened? Dalton was twenty-two years old. The future had seemed so bright. *The Ryder Hart Band* had its first album coming out next month. The buzz was good—better than good. After years of barely scraping by, they were about to hit it big, and Dalton wasn't going to be there to share the moment.

"You need to hire a permanent replacement."

"Why? Are you planning on becoming a career criminal?"

"No, but—"

"Nobody can play the drums like you. It won't be the same, but we'll get by until you're out. Eight months—tops."

"What if it's longer?" The thought made Dalton sick, but it had to be said. "Things happen. The gray jumpsuit I'm wearing is proof of that."

"That's why we hired the tutor. He'll tell you how to avoid trouble." Ryder gripped his arm. "I'll never forgive you if you don't come back to us, Dalton."

"Time's up," the guard called out.

"I'm scared, Ryder." It was the first time Dalton had admitted it to anyone— even himself.

"We'll visit every week. Ashe, Zoe, and me." Ryder hugged him. "Stay strong, brother. More important, stay smart."

The next morning, the bus to the prison was filled to capacity. Wiley Malone sat near the front, glaring at Dalton as he walked past. The tutor Ryder hired had given Dalton a plan—a course of action—beyond watching his back and cowering in his cell. It wasn't foolproof, but it was something.

Ankles manacled, Dalton shuffled to his seat. The man he was chained to tripped, sending Dalton crashing into the side of the bus. His shoulder took most of the impact.

"Sorry."

5

Dalton shrugged it off. Thanks to Wiley, his body was already covered in bruises. What was one more?

"Don Fitzgerald." The man held out his cuffed hand.

"Dalton Shaw."

"I shouldn't be here."

Closing his eyes, Dalton sighed. *Here it comes*, he thought. Since his arrest, he hadn't met a single person who took responsibility for his incarceration. If he believed every story he heard, the criminal justice system got it wrong one hundred percent of the time.

Railroaded. Screwed over. Framed. Pick your term. When those doors locked them in their cages each night, the prisoners slept the slumber of the unjustly incarcerated. Some were tormented by the knowledge. Others accepted their fate. But go ahead and ask. Not one of them was there because they had done the crime.

"I'm telling you, man, I blame that bitch I married. Sure, the drugs were mine, but the police never would have found them if I hadn't been provoked into knocking the shit out of her. A man can only take so much lip, right? She made such a racket the neighbors called the police."

Dalton closed his eyes, picturing himself smashing Don's face into the bus window. He wondered if a broken nose would shut the asshole up. Probably not. There was one good thought. At least Don's wife was rid of her abusive husband for the next three to five years.

"What did they jack you up for?"

"They didn't."

Don frowned. "I mean what shit did they trump up on you, man?"

"I put a man in the hospital because he liked to use his wife as a punching bag."

"Huh?" Don looked more confused than before. "You ain't saying you did it?"

Don's exclamation of disbelief got the attention of half the bus. Dalton felt like an exotic animal on display. A rare species that the prisoners had heard whispered about but never observed in person.

"That's exactly what I'm saying. I did it." Dalton looked around. "And given the chance, I wouldn't hesitate to do it again."

6

CHAPTER ONE

"WHERE WOULD YOU be without me?"

"Are you serious?"

"As a heart attack."

There was a pause followed by a drawn-out sigh.

"Fine. You are a god on the drums, Dalton Shaw. Without you, the band would be shit. Sound like shit. Play like shit. And you, my friend, can eat shit. Happy?"

Grinning, Dalton spun his drumsticks like an old-time gunslinger, blew an imaginary puff of smoke from the ends, then holstered them in the loop of his jeans.

"Now I ask you, was that so hard?"

Ryder Hart shook his head. He wore his dark hair a little longer than usual these days because his fiancée had mentioned how sexy it looked. These days, if Quinn Abernathy liked something, Ryder was completely on board. Luckily for his friends and bandmates, Quinn was no Yoko. There was no danger of *The Ryder Hart Band* imploding. The group was as tight as ever—tighter. Quinn wasn't musically inclined, but she made Ryder happy. Which translated to his music—and his friends. The circle wasn't broken. It had expanded. Stronger. Unbreakable.

"Asshole." Ashe Mathison tossed a sweaty towel in Dalton's face.

"Jealousy is an ugly thing, Ashe. I'm a god. Remember that and act accordingly. Bowing would not be inappropriate."

"It's rock and roll, dipshit. We're all gods."

"Zoe!" In mock shock, Dalton put a hand over his heart. "Love of my life. What kind of language is that?"

"The kind I hear from your mouth. Every day."

"But I'm a man. Women—especially ones that look like blond angels—

shouldn't use such language."

The only thing that saved Dalton from a kick in the balls was the fact that Zoe Hart knew he was joking. They played together for seven years, known each other for over ten. Ryder was Zoe's brother by blood. Dalton and Ashe, her brothers by choice.

The years struggling to make it. Living on little more than dreams and determination. Crappy food, rotten hotel rooms. A bus that rattled along on its last legs. Personal triumphs and tragedies. Those things either brought them closer or broke them apart. *The Ryder Hart Band* had found their success. The records topped the charts. They played to sold-out stadiums. There was always someone trying to chip away at them. But it came from the outside. When they fought—which was inevitable—they kept it in-house. They never aired their dirty laundry.

The press weren't the enemy. However, as they had recently been reminded, stories about them sold tabloids. The band was notoriously close-mouthed about their personal lives. It wasn't that they harbored a ton of dirty little secrets. They simply preferred letting their music speak for them.

Dalton's past was a matter of public record. But the sordid details weren't. Last month a story claiming to *break the silence* caused a minor media frenzy. Ashe called it a forty-eight-hour wonder. It broke the internet, then was forgotten by the general public. Scandals were a dime a dozen and a story that happened seven years ago wasn't exactly breaking news. Especially when the *inside story* turned out to be nothing but rehashed gossip

Happily, the world moved on. Dalton, on the other hand, still dealt with the fallout. The *source* for the story turned out to be his brother-in-law. He had never liked his sister's husband, but Dalton had believed Norris Mayhue to be honorable. Finding out he was wrong had been a blow. Trust was an issue he and his friends took seriously. They had each other's backs—no matter what.

Before the tabloid hullabaloo, Dalton would have included his sister on

8

his short list of trusted confidants. Now, he wasn't sure. True, she had no control over what her husband did. But the ammunition Norris had accumulated—however ineffectual it turned out to be—had come from Maggie. Until Dalton spoke with his sister face to face, he couldn't be certain what had happened—and how much Maggie had known before the fact.

"When do you leave?"

Leave it to Zoe. She put on a tough, *I don't give a shit*, persona to the rest of the world. She would tease and bicker and throw as much crap as she took. But when it came to her brothers, she was as sensitive and caring as they came.

"Maggie isn't returning my calls."

"Is there a problem?" Frowning, Ryder set aside his guitar. "You spoke with your sister the day after the rags ran the story. Why go silent now?"

"I smell a rat," Dalton said. "Namely Norris. He's taken Maggie to visit his parents. I keep getting a message saying she'll call me as soon as they get back. Since we finished recording the new album, I thought I would take a few days and fly out to see her. What I have to say will go over better in person."

"There's no phone service in…? Where do his parents live?"

Reluctantly, Dalton met Ryder's gaze. "Arizona. Midas, to be exact."

"Hell, no." Ryder crossed his arms over his chest.

"Are you crazy?" Mid-drink, Ashe almost spit the mouthful of water across the room.

"Absolutely not."

Zoe stood in solidarity with Ryder. Even in heels, she was at least four inches shorter. Her hair was blond, Ryder's almost black. But there was no doubt they shared the same gene pool. The strong, stubborn chin. The set of their mouths. The shape of their eyes. And the way they barreled over any opposition with the sheer force of their will. That determination had kept Dalton going through the darkest months of his life.

9

"It's only a place," he reminded his friends. Then singled out Ryder. "Like Chicago."

Ryder's eyes narrowed. Not too long ago, referencing Ryder's hell on Earth would have gotten Dalton a punch in the face. Change can take a lifetime—or it can happen in a blink of an eye. In Ryder's case, it was a little of both. He had always been strong. Loving Quinn made him stronger. His demons hadn't disappeared. But, according to the man himself, they were no longer lurking around every shadowed corner, waiting to pop out without warning. Quinn was the light. Dalton wondered what it was like to feel that way about someone. He wondered if he would ever know.

"I will admit that I may have given one city more power than it deserved," Ryder said calmly, though there was a tell-tale tightening of his jaw. "Arizona is bad enough, Dalton. But Midas? Is that an unhappy coincidence or is Norris trying to fuck with your head?"

"Maggie met Norris there while I stood trial."

Ryder and Ashe exchanged surprised looks. "You never told us that."

"I just found out." Dalton ran a hand over his head, tugging at his hair. "I don't know why we get so hung up on this crap. Like I said, it is only a place. It's not as though I'm planning on a return trip to the state pen."

Dalton had been arrested and stood trial in Midas. Not too far away, he did his time in Goodyear. The irony of the name was never lost on him. *Goodyear?* The fucked-up year was more like it. He had learned a lot. Had more than a few sleepless nights. Took his share of lumps. And wouldn't wish the experience on any but his worst enemy. Hell, for his worst enemy, Dalton's wishes were much darker than eleven months behind bars.

Now, he was pushing thirty. He could look back without breaking into a sweat. Dalton had served his time. Worked off his parole. He was an upstanding citizen. He voted on Election Day and paid his taxes. The only visible proof of his time in prison was the tattoo located on his back—just below his right shoulder blade. The image of a chained tiger breaking free of its bonds had seemed symbolic at the time. Now, Dalton

10

thought it a bit pretentious. But it was part of him. A reminder that no matter how good his intentions, bad shit happened.

Time—and good friends—had settled Dalton but he hadn't lost his edge. It was there in the way he played his drums. Controlled chaos, as one critic put it. That chaos was born in frustration. Fueled by anger. Pushed by fear and ambition. None of those factors were relevant to the man he was today. But the passion for the music? That would never die. It kept the songs he wrote fresh. It made his performances focused. It gave his life purpose.

It was a good life. Damn good. However, until this crap with his sister and her husband, Dalton hadn't realized that he had some unfinished business.

"Why do you need to do this?"

It didn't take any thought to answer Zoe's question. Dalton looked at Ryder.

"I have a few demons to chase out of the shadows."

A half smile formed on Ryder's lips. Without a word, he shook his head.

Zoe stepped forward. "I'm going with you."

"No, you aren't."

"Yes, I am."

"Do you want to add fuel to the rumors that we're sleeping together?"

The rumors ebbed and flowed. Sometimes it was Dalton and Zoe. Sometimes Zoe and Ashe. Occasionally, it was all three of them.

"When have I ever cared what people think?"

"Don't worry. I have this."

"Jesus, Ashe," Dalton laughed. "If I'm not fucking Zoe, I'm fucking you. I love you, man. Let the rumor mill grind someone else's ass for a little while."

"I'm hurt," Ashe pantomimed wiping away a tear. "Am I not good

11

enough to be your imaginary lover?"

"If I flew that way, you would be at the top of my list."

"Thanks a lot," Ryder snorted. "What am I, chopped liver?"

Dalton rolled his eyes. Women loved Ryder. Men loved Ryder. Gay. Straight. Everyone in between. Hell, their manager, Alden Christopher carried a torch bright enough to light up one of New York City's smaller boroughs. All kidding aside, Dalton wasn't going to jump on the bandwagon that fed Ryder's ego.

"You're too pretty."

Frowning, Ryder stroked his chin. "You think so? Maybe I should have kept the beard."

"Are you saying I'm *not* pretty?" Ashe tried his best to appear concerned.

For the first time in weeks, Dalton laughed. Full-on, from his belly, no holds barred, laughed. His friends. How had be gotten so lucky?

"When are you leaving?" Zoe asked, her blue eyes direct as always.

"First thing in the morning."

"Take the plane."

"I don't think so," Dalton said, shaking his head.

Ryder loved their private jet, using it whenever he got the chance. Dalton appreciated the convenience when they were on tour, but whenever possible, he preferred to keep his feet on the ground. Or in his brand new sports car. He didn't want to hear statistics. Flying was safer than driving. Tell that to his stomach.

Besides, in a car, Dalton was in charge. Behind the wheel, he controlled his destiny. Midas was a six-hour drive. Less, depending on traffic. He didn't know how long he would be there. A day or two. Maybe a week— though that seemed like a stretch. Dalton liked the idea of having a car at his disposal—*his* car.

Dalton wasn't particular about many things. He could play any drum set. From crap to high end, Dalton could make them come to life. Home was better, but when he was tired, any bed would do. However, there were three things on which he would not compromise.

Drumsticks.

Dalton had his custom made. They fit his hands perfectly. The right length. The right weight. He carried a set wherever he went. When Dalton played, his sticks were essential.

Shoes.

Dalton was not a fashion plate—he left that to Zoe. A good haircut. Clean jeans, a soft t-shirt, and whatever jacket happened to fit the weather. Labels didn't matter. He didn't care about the price. Cheap. Expensive. As long as his clothes were comfortable, that was all that mattered. However, when it came to what he put on his feet, Dalton liked high end and custom made. Not flashy. The black boots he wore today were simple in design. Classic. They cost more than his first car—and were worth every penny. The fit was perfection. A man had once told Dalton, *if your feet feel good, you feel good*. Words of wisdom never to be forgotten.

Last, but not least, alcohol.

Bourbon was his drink of choice. Dalton rarely indulged. He grew up with a mother who liked her hooch the way she liked her men—cheap and plentiful. Sylvia Shaw began most nights with a bottle of vodka— economy size—and the first guy she could pick up. The next morning she reeked of both. It was a sad picture Dalton had carried with him all his life. He drank in moderation. And then, only the best.

As for sex? There was a time when it looked as if Dalton would follow in his mother's footsteps. After a gig, he used to screw hard, fast, and indiscriminately, letting his dick dictate his actions. On occasion, it got him in trouble. One time, it landed him in prison. Lesson learned. He hadn't fallen into his old pattern after he served his time. There was sex. Plenty of it, thank you very much. However, Dalton had developed a discerning palate. Quality over quantity.

Speaking of which. Dalton had a date with a lovely tax accountant. She had legs that went on for days and smelled like a meadow after an April rain. He couldn't think of a better way to kick off a trip he wasn't looking forward to than a night spent in the arms of a beautiful brunette.

"Keep in touch." Ryder pulled Dalton in for a hug. "Call me—every day."

"What am I, twelve?" Dalton grumbled.

But Dalton knew he would do as his friend asked. Ryder took his job as leader seriously. He was a rock. And truth be told, Dalton would have been disappointed if Ryder hadn't shown his usual concern.

"Take care." Zoe took Ryder's place. She wasn't as naturally demonstrative as Ryder. One of her hugs was to be savored.

"You know I will." Pressing his luck, Dalton kissed Zoe's cheek. When she simply hugged him tighter, he *knew* she was worried about him.

Ashe gave his hand a firm shake. "If you need us—need anything—just say the word. You know we'll be there."

Dalton *did* know. *This* was his family. Professionally. Personally. They had his back. Not everyone had one person he could count on like that. Dalton did—times three.

"We have a charity gig on the fourth of September."

Dalton didn't need reminding. The money went toward helping children. Abused children. It was a problem that had touched them all—some more than others. Knowing Dalton would never miss the concert, Ryder gave his friend a time frame to follow. A week from today. Seven days was more than enough time to deal with his family drama, exorcise his demons, and get back to Los Angeles—to them—where he belonged.

Nodding, Dalton grabbed his bag and slung it over his shoulder. Looking around the room—seeing the love and concern—he smiled.

"See you in September."

CHAPTER TWO

THERE WAS SOMETHING about a stretch of highway at dawn. Deserted, it felt like his personal roadway—built for him and him alone.

Dalton set out from Los Angeles just as the sun began to light the morning sky. He felt loose, relaxed and satisfied.

"If you stay, I'll fix you my famous waffles," his bedmate purred.

With genuine regret, Dalton slid from the warm bed. He liked the woman. Becky was fun, smart, and knew her way around a man's dick. But he wasn't interested in more. There was something terribly intimate about a morning after breakfast for Dalton, almost as intimate as being inside her welcoming body.

"I have to get on the road." Zipping up his pants, Dalton leaned over, brushing his lips across hers. "Thank you for last night."

"Will you call me when you get back?"

Well, shit. It would have been so easy to tell Becky yes, though Dalton knew the answer was a resounding, *I doubt it.* It might seem cold. However, in his book, raising false hopes was worse than brutal honesty.

"It was fun, Becky. But no. I won't be calling."

"Fuck you." In a huff, Becky rolled away, presenting Dalton with her back.

It wasn't the first time those words had followed him out a woman's front door. He doubted it would be the last. At least Becky had been satisfied with cursing him. Now and then, breakables were thrown at his head. It seemed with some women, when it came to post-coital goodbyes, honesty was better in concept than practice. They claimed to want the truth, but only when that truth matched their expectations.

Dalton didn't understand that kind of thinking. However, a few bad experiences hadn't changed the way he conducted his life. More often than not, when he was upfront with his bed partners, it worked out fine.

Thankfully, Becky, and the pottery tossers, were the exceptions, not the rule.

It hadn't taken Dalton long to shake off what he considered a minor blip in an otherwise fine evening. He thought he and his sex partner were on the same page. If she expected more, that was too bad. Dalton had enough problems waiting for him in Arizona.

For now, there was nothing but open road. Hitting a button on the dashboard, Dalton smiled when Hank Williams filled the car. Classic. Mournful. Brilliant. The country legend had been one of his first big influences. Though stylistically, Dalton had gone in a different direction, it was the love of old time country that had drawn him, Ryder, and Ashe together.

Sometimes it felt like a lifetime ago. Or, like this morning, a blink of the eye. They were three kids—teenagers. Dalton could remember the feeling of desperate ambition. Ryder and Ashe understood. They met in a bar just outside of Chicago, each having traveled down very different paths.

Dalton had been wary. He had joined—and quit—three different bands in the past year. This felt different. And it was. Their styles meshed from the first jam session. Ryder's lead vocals were strong and distinctive. Ashe could play any instrument, but his specialty was keyboard and saxophone. Dalton added the beat. It was three years before Zoe joined the band—the added spark that sent them from locally in demand to international superstars.

They were *so* young. Cocky idiots who believed they were destined for greatness. Dalton opened the window, breathing in the cool morning air. Only time could judge such things. When it came to *The Ryder Hart Band* and the music they made? It was too soon to tell. But whether he and his friends left a lasting legacy or drifted away into oblivion, they were having a hell of a good time getting wherever it was they were going.

THERE WERE DAYS when sweat poured down Colleen McNamara's body. When she smelled like someone had dipped her in gasoline and

16

there seemed to be more motor oil under her fingernails than in the car she worked on. Days when her boss bellowed for her to speed it up. When she arrived at the garage at the crack of dawn, leaving well after the sun had set.

It was on days like that—like today—when she wondered if her mother had been right. The very thought sent a chill down her overheated spine. But there it was. Perhaps Colleen should chuck her job at *Dole's Auto Repair* and apply for beauty school. In less than six months, she could be elbows deep in hair spray and permanent wave solution.

No more dirty garage floors, stifling heat, or permanently stained coveralls. Colleen could trade it all for air-conditioned comfort surrounded by pink... everything. From the salon curtains, the tiles on the floor, and her mother's hair. Pick a shade. Everything inside the *Cut and Curl* looked like an advertisement for cotton candy.

And that was the problem. There was nothing frilly or sweet about Colleen McNamara. And, for the love of God, she hated pink.

"Move your ass, Mac."

"If you say that one more time, Dole, I swear I will shove this spark plug up your ass."

"Shit," Dole huffed. "Is it that time of the month again?"

Because Colleen respected her tools, she carefully set down her screwdriver before calmly turning toward her lunk-headed boss.

"Funny, I was about to ask you the same thing."

"Men don't get PMS, girly."

"Then why are you bloated and bitchy?" Colleen looked him up and down. The beer belly. The bloodshot eyes. The nose that would have put Rudolph out of his reindeer job. Shaking her head, she heaved an exaggerated sigh. "Oh, that's right. It isn't PMS. It's Wednesday. And Thursday. And Friday. And..." Colleen trailed off. She made her point, no need to run it into the ground.

"You better watch your mouth, Mac."

17

"And if I don't?"

His face the shade of an overripe eggplant, Dole took a threatening step in her direction. Colleen simply raised an eyebrow, crossed her arms over her greasy coveralls, and planted her feet as if to say, *take your best shot. I dare you.* Dole didn't dare. It wasn't that he had a problem with knocking women around. His wife knew what the back of his hand felt like. He fantasized about putting Colleen in her place—on her knees, sucking his dick.

There was one major problem. Dole wasn't certain he could take her down. He outweighed her by two hundred pounds—at least. But it was ninety percent blubber. Before his first cup of coffee—which he chased down with a box of *Entenmann's*—Dole was already four cigarettes into his first pack of the day. There was always someone hanging around the garage. It was bad enough that Colleen spoke to him like he was trash under her feet. He would never live down the humiliation of her besting him physically.

"I'm still your boss," Dole muttered. Sending Colleen one last glare, Dole shuffled back to his office.

Colleen waited until Dole was out of sight before returning to work. She knew that she intimidated the hell out of him. But she never made the mistake of turning her back on him when he was angry. If that mass of man fell on her, it would be game over.

With a sigh, Colleen lay down on the old wooden dolly, rolling herself under a jacked-up Blazer. This was her job, and she needed it. It would be smart to keep her mouth shut, but sometimes she had to let off steam or explode.

Dole was an uneducated, misogynistic pig whose father, the original Dole of *Dole's Auto Repair*, had left him a thriving business. Five years later, he had all but run it into the ground. Then Colleen came along. It didn't take long for word to spread. She had the magic touch. And that touch was going to get her out of Midas—soon. The stash of money she had been saving since her first job sweeping hair at her mother's salon was almost where it needed to be. Barring a disaster, in less than a year,

18

Colleen would be gone from Midas.

Unfortunately, there always seemed to be some kind of disaster. Six years ago, Colleen had her bags packed when her mother had been diagnosed with lung cancer. Two packs of Camels a day finally caught up with her.

Unpacking her bags, Colleen did what anyone would have done—she stayed. The beauty parlor needed a manager, and her mother needed a caretaker. Months of radiation and chemotherapy followed by a long recovery of her general health and the cancer was gone. Thank God. But so was Colleen's money. Bills had to be paid.

More determined than ever, Colleen started from scratch. She worked with single-minded devotion. Long hours putting up with Dole and crap equipment. Doing jobs on the side. It had finally paid off. Colleen could see a future away from Midas. Where didn't matter as long as it was bigger and better. In other words, any place but here.

Colleen rolled out long enough to turn up the volume on the old radio. For a second, she closed her eyes, letting the song and its pounding rhythm soothe her mind. Soon, she promised herself. Closing her eyes, she pictured her favorite fantasy. Behind the wheel of her restored fifty-five T-Bird, the wind blowing through her dark red hair. Straight ahead was an old sign. Faded, bent on the tips and riddled with bullet holes, it was the most beautiful sight on Earth.

Two words that made her heart beat with hope. *Leaving Midas.*

SMOKE ROLLED FROM under the hood of Dalton's Porsche. Then the car coughed. Sputtered. *Shit.* The car was practically brand new. If it couldn't survive a little six-hundred-mile road trip, what good was it? Naturally, it had to happen as he pulled into Midas. The sense of doom and gloom that began its descent over him about an hour ago grew heavier.

Was this a sign? A portent of things to come? There was no law that said Dalton had to stay. He could call a tow truck. Phoenix was about fifty miles east. Civilization beckoned.

As his car limped along, Dalton glanced to his right. *Dole's Auto Repair*. Now *that* was a sign.

Unless things had changed, it was the town's one garage and not equipped to deal with a high-performance sports car. However, it was conveniently located—right in front of him, to be exact. At this point, he didn't have an option. Dalton had come all this way to see his sister—and exorcise of a few old ghosts. If he had to do it in a borrowed car, so be it.

Dalton stopped beside the one gas pump. If he were lucky, the problem was a dry radiator. But in his experience, Midas and luck did not go hand in hand. Then again, he wasn't the same man he once was. Perhaps Midas had changed, too.

As soon as the thought popped into his head, Dalton broke out laughing. Who was he kidding? Deep down he was the same. A little more polished but there were enough rough edges left that the old Dalton would have easily recognized the new one.

And Midas? The town looked exactly the same. Scratch that. It looked like an older, dirtier, more rundown version of the old, dirty, rundown town from seven years ago. Back then, the place needed a makeover. Now, it needed a bulldozer. Time changed everything. Not always for the better.

The longer Dalton waited, it became apparent nobody was coming to find out if he needed help. He could sit in his car until hell froze over— or in this case, Midas—or he could move his ass and search it out on his own.

There was no preparing himself for the blast of inferno-like heat. Great, another hell reference. Dalton needed to change his attitude. He wasn't here by force. It had been his decision. Yes, it was hot. He had sweated through worse. The last time being a July concert in Texas. By the end, there was a pool of sweat under his chair the size of a small lake— though hot and much saltier. If he could survive that, he could manage to walk twenty feet from his air-conditioned car to the open door of the garage.

Admittedly, neither Los Angeles nor Texas carried the added memory of having his face shoved in the scorching dirt while two police officers held him down and another cuffed his hands behind his back. Only Midas had that particular distinction.

Shaking the image off, Dalton adjusted his sunglasses, pushing them up the bridge of his nose. Half a dozen steps and his black boots were coated with dust, dulling the shine of the expensive leather. The sight didn't help to raise his spirits. The sound of a bell ringing was a welcome distraction. A short, solidly built young man—Dalton would have guessed him to be in his late teens—exited the office, a can of Coke in one hand, a set of keys in the other.

"Excuse me," Dalton called out. "Is there a mechanic on duty?"

Without breaking stride, the kid jerked his head toward the right. "You'll find Mac in there."

It wasn't the rudeness that surprised Dalton. It was the utter lack of curiosity. Midas was a small town. How often did a stranger in an expensive sports car engage this guy in conversation? There was money in the area. But that was on the north side of Midas. Those families didn't frequent places like *Dole's Auto Repair*.

Wiping the sweat from his upper lip, Dalton's stride ate up the few feet between him, the open garage door, and a merciful patch of shade. Music was the first thing that greeted his entrance, a song he recognized immediately. *Wild Jasmine*. After all the years of success, it still gave a Dalton a thrill when he heard his band on the radio. It wasn't that long ago when it happened for the first time. The four of them swore they would never take it for granted. And they never had. An extra jolt came from the fact that the song was one of his. A rare solo effort. His words. His music. Ryder's voice. Dalton grinned. It was a good thing. If it had been left up to him to sing lead, the band would have died a quick, painful death.

No, Dalton was happy to play his drums, harmonize, and on occasion— find writing gold.

The heat wasn't much better inside the garage. But without the sun pounding down on him, Dalton felt a bit of relief. Looking around, he

21

wasn't impressed—or encouraged about the fate of his car. To call the place a mess would have been kind. The floor looked like a graveyard for broken parts. And they hadn't been buried with dignity. Tossed in every direction, it was chaos layered in dirt and grease. The work bench was a bit better. He could see where someone had tried to organize the tools, but it was haphazard at best. Shiny, well-maintained wrenches, and screwdrivers warred with the rusty and dented—and it appeared to be a losing battle.

Shaking his head, Dalton's gaze stopped on a pair of scuffed work boots that peeked out from under a dark gray SUV. The rest of the person's body was hidden from view, but Dalton assumed he had found the mechanic. Bending down, Dalton raised his voice to be heard over the music.

"Are you Mac?"

The thunk of metal hitting flesh was followed by a string of curse words that had Dalton raising his eyebrows. Not for the severity, or impressive variety, but because it was obvious the mechanic with the foul mouth was a woman.

"What is wrong with you?" The dolly shot out from under the vehicle. Before it came to a stop, she was on her feet and in Dalton's face. "Never—as in do not ever—yell at someone who is working on heavy machinery. I could have been seriously injured."

Fascinated, Dalton watched as the redheaded fury began pacing. She came to about his shoulders. Slender, though it was hard to tell. The baggy coveralls hid her shape from his view. Green eyes flashed his way. He thought she was pretty. Maybe beautiful. The grease smudged on her chin and forehead didn't enhance—or detract. But it did highlight the fact that her skin was a lovely pale shade of cream.

"Look at that," she shoved her thumb at Dalton. "Ouch! I could have broken the bone. What good is a mechanic with a broken thumb? I need this job, mister. Money doesn't grow on trees, you know. Food. Rent. A basic quality of life. They all take the green stuff. Moolah. Dinero. Capisce?"

Dalton stared—dazzled and tempted. She was spectacular and so full of life, he wanted to reach out to find out if the vibration she sent through the garage intensified when he made contact.

"Do I know you?" She moved closer, then quickly seemed to dismiss the idea. "No, I wouldn't forget meeting you."

Was that good or bad? Dalton couldn't tell. But he knew he wouldn't have forgotten either—and it was *all* good.

She stopped, hands on hips, her head tipped to one side and glared. "Well, don't you have anything to say?"

"Plenty. But I was waiting for you to wind down." When her green eyes grew wide, and her lips twitched, Dalton knew he was going to like this woman.

"Let me think." Pursing her lips, she thoughtfully tapped her chin with her index finger. "Yes. The wind down is complete. So tell me, gorgeous, what was so important it was worth risking my life and livelihood?"

"I hate to set you off again, but don't you think that's a bit of an exaggeration?"

"Hello." She shoved her thumb at him again.

"I could kiss it and make it better."

She looked him up and down. "Mm. I'll bet you could. Unfortunately, I don't have time to play."

Too bad, Dalton thought with regret, *neither did he*.

"Are you Mac?"

"I'll answer to it. I prefer Colleen."

Colleen. It suited her. Dalton would have loved to find out what Colleen had on under those coveralls. Damn bad timing.

"My car started smoking just as I reached Midas."

"Okay. Where is it?"

"Out front."

"Let's take a look."

Dalton fell in step with Colleen. He didn't want to offend her, but he had to ask.

"It's a Porsche. Have you ever worked on one?"

"Nope." Stopping when she got her first look at the gleaming silver body, Colleen let out a low whistle. "You poor baby."

"I'm fine," Dalton assured her. "It's the car."

"I meant the car." Colleen ran her hand over the sleek hood. "What did he do to you?"

Laughing at himself, Dalton had to admit he wasn't used to an inanimate object getting all the attention. Ryder was the face of the group—and that was how Dalton liked it. But that didn't mean he faded into the background. He lived the life of a rock star. Money. Beautiful women. His life lacked neither. And the perks? There was no such thing as needing reservations. From restaurants to hotels. If Dalton Shaw wanted in, he was in. Though he could remember when that hadn't been the case, enough years had passed that it had become the norm.

"I didn't *do* anything. The car betrayed me—not the other way around."

"It's a car, hotshot. It wasn't programmed for betrayal. If something happened, it's on you."

Colleen reached into the driver's side, popping the hood. Dalton was no longer worried about her competency. Good or bad, he was dying to see her at work. He could always replace the transmission—or whatever. Watching her red hair gleam in the brutal sunlight. Seeing the way her coveralls stretched over her ass—her very shapely ass—as she checked under the hood was worth the price.

"It's probably the radiator." Dalton leaned in.

Colleen snorted. "You wish. See this?" She held up a handful of wire. Between the charred ends and a smell that was something between burned rubber and freshly tarred road, there was little doubt she had found the source of the problem.

"That doesn't look good."

"You have to love a man with a flair for stating the obvious."

Inexplicably, Dalton felt a blush rise up in his cheeks. In this heat, at his age, and with his experience, he wouldn't have thought it possible. Thank God his already flushed skin made it impossible to detect.

"The car is practically showroom new. That," he nodded toward the

24

wires, "should not have happened."

Dalton wanted to add that it couldn't be his fault, but he held his tongue. *Obvious* was bad enough. He refused to sound petulant.

"You're right." Colleen tested another connection, tugged on a hose, then pushed him back before closing the hood. "Do you want the technical term or would you like me to dumb it down?"

"Throw me the tough stuff. Maybe I'll learn something."

"This," Colleen patted the car, "is what we professionals call a big, juicy lemon."

"Lemon is technical?" Frowning, Dalton rubbed the back of his neck. "What's the dumbed-down term?"

"Lemon," Colleen grinned, showing off her straight, white teeth.

Dalton wondered if the heat melted his common sense, but he liked Colleen. Her sassy mouth and easy smile appealed to him beyond the desire he normally felt for the opposite sex. *Lust* was easy. *Like* was another thing entirely. It could lead to something rare. Something he had neither the time nor inclination to explore—friendship. With surprising regret, Dalton pushed the thought aside.

"Do you think you can fix it?"

"Maybe." Colleen shaded her eyes. "But why bother? Have the dealership replace it. Or get your money back. I can probably get it running. But it's just a matter of time until something else goes wrong."

"I don't suppose there's a place in town where I can rent a car?"

"Are you passing through?"

"No. I'll be in town for a few days."

Eyes narrowed, Colleen nodded as though coming to an important decision. "Would a classic Thunderbird do?"

"Are you kidding?" Dalton had almost purchased a T-Bird before deciding a new car would be more practical. "Where do I go?"

Colleen took a set of keys from her pocket. "One hundred a day—in advance. Plus a thousand-dollar security deposit."

"What year is it?"

"Fifty-five. Everything is original. "

It sounded too good to be true. "How can you be sure?"

"Because I restored it myself." Colleen looked at him, her gaze steady.

Dalton figured he could change his mind if the car turned out to be a piece of junk. But he doubted that would be the case. He didn't know why, but he was certain Colleen wouldn't have offered if it were. A person didn't restore a car overnight. She had to put in a lot of time and effort. Which meant she wouldn't rent it to him unless she really needed the money.

"Well? What do you say?"

"A classic T-Bird?" And the chance to help Colleen? "I say hell, yes."

IN THE OFFICE, Dole peeked through the slats of the window blinds. He looked hard, unable to believe his eyes. But there was no mistaking the tall, dark-haired man. Dalton Shaw had come a long way. Rich and famous—the son of a bitch.

Grabbing the phone, Dole punched in the number he knew by heart—a number he hadn't used in years.

"Hello."

"It's Dole. Dole Wharton?" When there was no answer, he added, "From the garage at the end of town?"

"I know who you are. What do you want?"

Dole wasn't the sharpest tool in the box, but he recognized contempt when he heard it. Knowing his next words would knock the stuck-up bastard on his ass, Dole felt a surge of glee.

"You'll never guess who's back in Midas."

CHAPTER THREE

COLLEEN RESTED HER hands on the tile. Head bent, she sighed with pleasure, as the stream of water rushed over her tired body, washing a day's worth of dirt and perspiration down the drain. There were times when she thought nothing was better in the world than indoor plumbing. Books made traveling back through time sound romantic—especially when a sexy Scot waited on the other side. Nope. Colleen wasn't going anywhere that didn't have hot and cold running water. A bath in a cool lake did not equal the sheer delight of standing under a fully pressurized shower.

Besides, outside the pages of a novel, that Scot would have smelled to high heaven. Oral sex with a man who hadn't washed his dick in who knew how long? If at all? Colleen shuddered at the thought.

Reaching for her one indulgence—an expensive body wash that left her smelling like wildflowers instead of motor oil—Colleen lathered her body starting at her feet and slowly working up. Not surprisingly, her thoughts turned to a certain sexy man who she would have bet a month's pay washed his privates on a daily basis.

Colleen laughed. Dalton Shaw. Who expected a famous musician to pull his outrageously expensive sports car into the parking lot of *Dole's Body Repair*? Things like that just didn't happen. Add her sore thumb, the heat, and her frustration with life in general to the surprise factor. Was it any wonder she hadn't recognized him?

Not that those things kept her from flirting. She had been distracted—not dead. It had been awhile, but Colleen recognized the zing—the zip of awareness—immediately. And felt his interest in return. Strangers were in short supply around Midas. Ones who looked like Dalton? Colleen smiled, turning her face to the spray of water. Nobody looked like Dalton—stranger or otherwise. His short dark hair and that crazy, sexy beard. On top of a long, lean body. It made Colleen tingle when she thought that not long ago, he stood close enough to touch.

The entire episode had been odd—and exhilarating. The fact that Colleen had offered to rent Dalton her car—her baby—said it all. Nobody touched the T-Bird except Colleen. From the moment she polished the final piece of chrome, it had been off limits. Maybe it was the heat. Or her hormones. Or finding out the man standing less than three feet away was a certified superstar. She preferred to think it was the promise of some easy money. Whatever the explanation, she had promised Dalton Shaw the use of her car. He hadn't given her time to change her mind. He had taken out his wallet, removed a wad of cash that made her jaw drop, and peeled off two thousand dollars without a second's hesitation.

Colleen hadn't expected things to move that quickly. Who carried that kind of cash around? She thought he would need to visit a bank—fifty miles down the road in Phoenix. Faced with handing over the car keys, a case of nerves hit her—hard.

"I understand." Dalton had smiled. It was a killer smile. "All you have is my word—"

"And your money," Colleen added, fanning herself with the stack of hundreds.

"And my money. If you need more, that's not a problem."

They stood in one of the few patches of shade. Though Colleen always covered her car with the protective tarp, this spot under an old, ragged strip of awning was unofficially hers. No one bothered her baby back here—not if they knew what was good for them.

"It isn't the money." Colleen laughed to herself. She was fairly certain it was the first time that combination of words had left her mouth. "I know it's just a car, but..."

"I understand. You put a lot of yourself into restoring it. Not simply your time and effort. Your heart. And a bit of your soul."

"Yes." Colleen was surprised that Dalton understood—nobody else did. Not her mother. Not her friends. It took a stranger to see what she hadn't been able to put into words. *Her heart and a bit of her soul. How did he know?*

As though he heard her thoughts, Dalton answered. "It's a little like writing a song. There is always a bit of me in it."

Colleen wasn't proud of what happened next. It made her seem like one of those women she always ridiculed. Dalton reached up and removed his sunglasses. That was all it took. When he turned his blue eyes her way, every last bit of doubt melted away. It was crazy and illogical and so not her. But there it was. Proof that Colleen McNamara was no better than a giggly, empty-headed teenager. A sexy smile and a pair of the deepest blue eyes God ever created, and she was putty.

Five minutes later, Dalton drove away. He had been the one who insisted on signing a quickly put-together receipt—something that had flown out of Colleen's mind.

Turning off the water, Colleen stepped from the shower. She didn't think Dalton Shaw was about to abscond with her car. In all likelihood, he would return it without a scratch. However, if something *did* happen to her sweet ride? It was exactly what she deserved for turning into a huffing, puffing, blithering fangirl.

Standing in front of the bathroom mirror, Colleen dramatically clasped her hands to her chest, her eyelashes batting wildly.

"Dalton Shaw," she gasped at her reflection. "Take my car. Take my common sense. Take me!" With a sneer, she stuck out her tongue and sent herself a big, wet raspberry. "Idiot."

Shaking her head, Colleen wrapped her hair in a towel. Yes, it was foolish. And maybe she would regret her decision. But damn, she laughed. Alone in her apartment, with no prying eyes to judge or mock, she could admit one thing. *Dalton Shaw has the bluest eyes.*

THE NORTH SIDE of Midas, Arizona bore little resemblance to the place where Dalton's car died an ignominious death. Technically, they were same. They had the same city government headed by the same mayor. The aquifer provided water to all the residents—rich and poor.

29

And the same brutal sun beat down on every home. That was where the similarities ended.

The privileged class in Midas wasn't large. In a town of fewer than ten thousand residents, the poor far outnumbered the rich. However, those who had money had a shitload of it. And with money, came power. Power that reached far beyond the Midas city limits all the way to the governor's mansion, the United States Senate—and beyond.

Dalton had come to Midas, a cock-sure twenty-two-year-old man. He had left in chains. Less certain of himself, but he had discovered one thing. Right didn't matter when wrong had the face of a rich man's son. That bit of knowledge had come at a hefty price. Almost a year of his life.

Though Dalton wouldn't say that prison had been an experience he would recommend, it had taught him a lot about himself. His reward—if he believed in that kind of thing—had been a damn good life. Friends. Success. Money. As Dalton crossed the line between the south of Midas and the north, he didn't feel the dread he had expected. He was no longer a nameless, faceless nobody.

One Tweet. A single Facebook post. A hint on Instagram. That was all it would take to have the social media world descend on this sleepy little Arizona town. Fame—Dalton's kind of fame—came with power. Power he wasn't afraid to wield.

Dalton turned onto a pretty little street. Tree-lined, the grass in every yard was green and meticulously manicured. Cookie-cutter houses lined up like good little soldiers. Stamped with bland conformity, the colors didn't vary beyond a shade of beige. Not too dark, not too light. The same porch with the same front door with the same windows. Not too big, not too small.

As he pulled into the driveway of the one marked with a black two-sixteen on the curb, Dalton wondered if this were the inspiration for *The Stepford Wives*? The thought sent a chill down his spine. His sister was in that house. At least, he *hoped* it was still Maggie.

Laughing at himself, Dalton turned off the engine. Colleen's car—that was how he thought of it—drove like a dream. The engine hummed—quiet but powerful. She had restored the interior with meticulous care. If he didn't know better, Dalton would have sworn the car sat suspended in time for the last sixty years. Colleen wasn't good. She was a master. If she decided to restore cars full-time, she could make a fortune.

"Dalton?"

Maggie ran from the house, waving. Taking a deep breath, Dalton exited the car. Opening his arms, he greeted his sister with a warm hug. He tried to feel the connection—the bond between siblings—but it wasn't there. It never had been. Dalton found it sad because he knew how special a brother/sister relationship could be. He saw it between Ryder and Zoe. Unconditional love. A blood bond that nothing could sever.

Sadness and guilt were the two emotions he associated most with Maggie. Sadness that they would never be close. And guilt that Zoe—his friend and bandmate—was the true sister of his heart.

"I'm so glad you're here." Maggie held onto Dalton's arm. "Come inside. We'll have a long talk and catch up."

They were going to have a long talk, all right. Something was going on, and Dalton wanted answers. However, getting them from Maggie wasn't easy. In so many ways, she was like their mother. Beautiful in a wistful kind of way. The soft, flyaway blond hair, the pale blue eyes. The slight build that ran toward brutally thin. And the ability to pretend the world was perfect even as it crumbled into a million irrevocably broken pieces.

Dalton couldn't help his mother. No one could have. But he tried with Maggie. When they were younger, that meant chasing away bullies. Someone always seemed to be after her and—according to her and her tear-filled eyes—it was never her fault. Dalton hadn't asked a lot of questions. If someone pushed his sister—he pushed back. In his mind, that was what older brothers did. Older and wiser, Dalton understood that Maggie brought trouble on herself. Like their mother, she enjoyed the drama. Knowing that Dalton would clean up after her gave Maggie added courage to cause mischief and mayhem.

31

After Dalton had left home, he sent a check whenever he could—guilt money. Maggie was upset at first, but soon she found a succession of boyfriends who—for a short time—were willing to play protector. It was a race to see which would happen first. They either grew tired of her games or Maggie decided she wanted a new toy to play with.

Dalton had been in prison three months when Maggie wrote him with two pieces of news. Their mother had died—her liver finally gave out. And Maggie had gotten married. She didn't give him many details. Simply that his name was Norris Mayhue, they were moving to Buffalo where Norris had an amazing job waiting, and that she was blissfully happy.

Dalton hadn't expected the marriage—or Maggie's bliss—to last long. Last month, Maggie and Norris celebrated their seventh wedding anniversary. Maggie always sounded happy, but with his sister it was hard to tell. As long as Dalton continued his practice of sending money every month—the amount had increased dramatically over the years— she kept her problems to herself.

"We need to talk, Maggie. Someplace private."

"Don't worry about it. Tilly and Sly are never here. They belong to the country club. If it isn't golf, it's tennis. In the evenings, they usually eat in the dining room and play bridge until after midnight." Maggie giggled. "The perfect in-laws. I haven't seen them more than five minutes at a stretch since we got here."

The house looked comfortable. Too much seventies avocado for Dalton's taste, but to each his own. The sofa was a riot of flowers, the pattern carrying over to the curtains. Wall-to-wall carpet—not a sliver of hardwood to be seen—covered the floor. It was clean and neat. And made Dalton grateful for his dark oak and stainless steel.

"Would you like a glass of ice tea?"

Maggie would have continued to the kitchen if Dalton hadn't taken her arm and led her to the sofa.

"I'm fine. Sit and catch your breath." Dalton took the chair opposite.

32

"Where is Norris?"

"Looking for work."

"At this time of the day?"

"It's all about networking. Especially in a small town."

Dalton frowned. He thought this was a social visit. The fact that Maggie's husband needed a job was a surprise. Searching his brain, Dalton tried to remember what Norris did for a living. Hardware store manager? Or was it a feed store?

"Was he laid off?"

"No." Not meeting Dalton's gaze, Maggie picked at a loose thread at the seam of her blue cotton skirt. "He decided working at the *Tool Shed* had become a dead end. And those Buffalo winters." Maggie shuddered. "Norris decided it was the right time for a change. A fresh start is exactly what his career needs."

"Is that why Norris sold the story to the tabloids?"

"He didn't mean any harm, Dalton," Maggie said earnestly. "He wanted a little extra cash for the move."

"By selling me out?" Dalton felt a wave of bitterness.

The story didn't matter. Most of it was a matter of public record. It was the betrayal that rankled. Norris had married Maggie knowing that Dalton was serving time. At the time, it was a big story in Midas. One of the reasons they moved across the country was to leave the notoriety behind. Norris wanted a quiet life where nobody knew about Maggie or her jailbird brother.

Not that any of that stopped Norris from taking Dalton's money.

"I know the money was to keep us quiet, but—"

"That's bullshit, Maggie." Dalton wouldn't let his sister rewrite history. "I hoped you—and Norris—would respect my privacy. But the money was a gift. My way of helping out. It was never meant to be a bribe."

"I'm sorry," gasped, her eyes wide with what looked like concern. "That isn't what I meant. Honestly. It's just that things have been tough—financially speaking. The story gave us a little boost. Please try to understand."

"All you needed to do was call, Maggie. Have I ever turned you down when you needed something?"

"Norris…" Maggie blinked, trying her best to summon up a tear. Dalton had seen their mother do the same thing more times than he could remember. "He's a proud man, Dalton."

Not too proud to sponge off his parents. Or Dalton. The cash Norris received from the tabloid story was pocket change. He could have easily gotten more. A lot more. Suddenly, Dalton had a sickening thought.

"Is there more to come, Maggie? More stories?"

"I—" Maggie reached out, taking Dalton's hand. "Would it be so bad?"

"That answers my question."

Dalton wasn't worried about the truth. There were no deep, dark secrets that would destroy his world. But the tabloid rags weren't interested in the truth. With Norris feeding them information—real or made up—the embellishments could go on for months. It would be annoying. Possibly embarrassing. None of that would matter if Dalton were the only person affected. He had friends—his true family—back in Los Angeles. They would weather it together as they did everything else. But why should they have to?

"How much to kill the stories?"

"I don't know."

Dalton had to hand it to Maggie. The way she wrung her hands and bit her lip. He could almost believe she felt something bordering on distress.

"Have Norris call me." Dalton needed some fresh air. "And make certain he does it soon. Tomorrow at the latest, Maggie."

"I will." Maggie followed him to the door. "I'm sorry, Dalton."

Taking a deep breath, Dalton met his sister's gaze. "So am I."

34

Dalton didn't know what he felt. Anger? Damn straight. But more at himself than Maggie. He should have taken his friends' advice and stayed in Los Angeles instead of dragging himself to fucking Arizona. He had convinced himself that he had to see his sister's face when he asked his questions. All he got for his troubles was a broken-down car and a splitting headache.

The best thing would be to check into the only decent hotel in town. Take some aspirin and settle in for the evening. With any luck, Norris would grow a pair and call him tonight. He could be done with this mess and on his way back to civilization.

That would be the best thing to do. Or he could say the hell with what was best and make the most of a royally fucked-up situation. Dalton ran a hand over the soft leather armrest, a speculative smile playing across his lips. He knew what his friends would say. Ryder would urge caution. Ashe would do the same—while encouraging him to have a little fun. Zoe would simply shake her head and call him an asshole whose brains were located in his dick.

They would all be right.

Picking up his phone, he scrolled through his contacts, stopping on the last—and newest number. Dalton paused, but only for a second. Hitting the keypad, he waited.

"Hello?" The sound of Colleen's voice told Dalton everything he needed to know. He felt his shoulders begin to relax. Calling her had been the right decision.

"What are you doing for dinner?"

"Having it with you."

Dalton grinned. Definitely the right decision.

CHAPTER FOUR

DRESSING FOR A date with a rock star was no different than dressing for a date with a farmer. Or a lawyer. Or a park ranger. Or... Colleen chuckled. She had her first date at the age of fifteen. Eleven years later, the variety of her suitors was impressive for a small-town girl. Men liked her. And she liked men. She enjoyed the conversation. Sometimes, if the chemistry were right, she enjoyed the sex.

The full-length mirror on the back of her bedroom door didn't lie. Colleen looked good. She was a woman comfortable in her skin—flaws and all. Did that mean she wouldn't have changed something if the genetics gods had given her a menu of options? Sure. Who wouldn't? But she liked her body. It was strong and resilient. It allowed her to work long hours without breaking down, and her legs looked damn fine in a skirt.

Doing a final twirl, Colleen gave herself an approving nod. She didn't dress up often—unless her date sprang for a night in Phoenix. However, she enjoyed putting on the ritz. Not to impress Dalton, but herself. He had traveled the world. Beautiful women threw themselves at him—literally. Colleen smiled when she pictured Dalton stepping over bodies on his way to a waiting limo. Inside? Gorgeous females draped in satin and silk.

No, she wasn't trying to compete. She simply wanted to look her best. And if Dalton's killer blue eyes flared with appreciation? Win/win for Colleen.

Dalton's call had been a surprise. A very pleasant one. Colleen had already slipped into her favorite around-the-house shorts and t-shirt, debating whether to heat up the oven for a pizza or stay cool with a sandwich. Not the most exciting evening, but it suited her mood.

When the phone rang, Colleen debated ignoring it. What was voicemail for if not to avoid family and friends? But at the last minute, she gave in. Seeing it was Dalton perked up her mood considerably. Until she remembered that he was in possession of her prized car. If he had totaled her baby, there would be blood.

36

"Hello," Colleen answered cautiously.

"What are you doing for dinner?"

A tingle of anticipation zipped through Colleen's body. Zing. Zip. Zowie. The pizza could stay in the freezer for another less-promising evening. What was she doing for dinner?

"Having it with you."

Glancing at the clock, Colleen realized that Dalton was due at any second. Slipping on a pair of strappy sandals with wonderfully high heels, she walked to the bathroom. She wasn't a frilly girl, but feeling feminine came in many forms. Besides, there was as much power to be found in a pair of high heels as scuffed up work boots.

Leaning close to the mirror over the sink, Colleen did one final survey. Makeup? Good. All she used was a bit of powder, some mascara, and a touch of color on her lips. Hair? The dark auburn tresses hung in natural waves across her shoulders. She rarely found the need—or the patience—to do more than a wash and go. There had been plenty of time for it to dry. With a quick flick of her comb, she was ready to go.

The sound of the doorbell put a smile on Colleen's lips. Feeling like a kid about to open a beautifully wrapped package, she hurried to the door. Humming, she reached for the knob and burst out laughing.

"Is it me?" Dalton checked his fly. "All zipped up. Though if that made you laugh, my ego would be in shreds."

"Come in." Colleen moved to the side. "I was laughing at myself, not you. Though I hope your ego could withstand a chuckle or two."

"Trust me, no man wants to hear a woman chuckle at his… zipper."

Sexy. Gorgeous. And a self-deprecating humor that was hard to find— and completely irresistible. Dalton Shaw just went from yummy to mouthwatering.

"I don't do sex on a first date."

"Me neither."

Colleen crossed her arms and waited. Dalton looked as if he planned on waiting her out, then, to her delight, he grinned.

"Honestly. I will admit to screwing around—in my younger days—with women I just met. But if it's a date? Nope. I save myself for at least the second or third."

"In your younger days, old man? What are you? Twenty...?"

"Nine."

Colleen gasped. "Decrepit."

"Thirty is old man territory for a rocker."

Slowly, she circled Dalton, checking him out. What she saw was so far from an old man it wasn't funny. His long legs nicely filled out the faded denim of his jeans. Add a trim waist. A flat stomach. And those arms. Dalton's t-shirt wasn't tight in a *look at my amazing body* kind of way. However, the sleeves circled his biceps, emphasizing the size and shape.

Old? Hardly. There wasn't a man alive—at any age—that would balk at trading bodies with Dalton Shaw.

"You're practically falling apart in front of my eyes."

Because she couldn't resist, Colleen rested her hand on Dalton's upper arm. She didn't squeeze. It was more of a pet. *Nice kitty*. Meeting his gaze. *Oh, my*. Colleen swallowed. More like a big, dangerous, full-grown panther.

"Like what you see?" Dalton purred.

"Yes." What was the point of lying? Dalton knew when a woman was interested.

"We could skip the date."

"Food or sex?" Colleen licked her lips, drawing Dalton's attention.

"That's right."

Dropping her hand, Colleen stepped back. It wasn't easy, but it seemed like the right move.

"Food?" Dalton asked with a sigh of regret.

It was the glint of good humor in his eyes that almost changed Colleen's mind. If he had pushed his advantage, the evening would have ended quickly. Most likely with Dalton in the hall clutching his balls. The fact that he wanted her but was willing to let her set the pace? If she were so inclined, Colleen would already be half in love.

38

"It is chicken fried steak night at *The Sidewinder*."

"*The Sidewinder?* I don't remember it."

"Have you been to Midas before?

Dalton waited while Colleen picked up her purse and set the lock on the door. Holding out his arm, he nodded.

"We had a gig here about seven years ago."

"I—" Colleen stopped in her tracks.

"You...?" Dalton's face didn't betray any emotion.

"I spent that summer in Phoenix taking classes. By the time I got back, you were gone."

"Up the river." Dalton patted her hand. "In the big house?"

"I think you were standing trial."

"Ah, yes," he nodded. "Good times."

"Sarcasm or bitterness? Sometimes it's hard to tell the difference."

Dalton stopped beside the T-Bird. To Colleen's surprise, he burst out laughing.

"That was a joke?" When she nodded, Dalton threw his head back and laughed again—harder and longer.

"That was my first attempt at prison humor." Colleen figured she might as well push her luck. "Are all ex-cons so jovial about the subject?"

Wiping the moisture from his eyes, Dalton let out a sigh.

"Hell if I know. But I wouldn't test the theory. I met some mean bastards in the pen. They hit first. Gender doesn't matter."

"I knew a guy like that. Gender *did* matter. He gave a new meaning to women and children first."

That drove the smile off Dalton's face. Carefully, he cupped Colleen's face in his hand, his thumb lightly caressing her cheekbone.

"Has someone hit you?" Dalton's look was a breath-catching combination of tender and fierce.

"No," Colleen reassured him, her hand gripping his wrist. "I had a friend in high school. Her father knocked her mother. And her sister. And her.

39

Then she picked a boyfriend with the same habit."

"What happened to her?"

"She married the bastard and moved to Albuquerque. Last I heard she had two daughters. In a perfect world, her boyfriend changed when he became a husband and father."

"The world isn't perfect."

"No."

Colleen felt a stinging at the back of her eyes. She wasn't going to cry, but it became a close thing when Dalton gathered her near.

"I don't hit women. I would never knowingly hurt a child. But, Colleen?" Dalton lifted his head, looking her directly in the eyes. "The crime I stood trial for? I was guilty."

Colleen waited for Dalton's revelation to change the way she felt, but it didn't happen. His arms comforted her. She felt protected—safe. She believed he had a dangerous streak. She didn't doubt his words. He had been guilty. Colleen wasn't foolish enough to trust her instincts completely. She didn't know this man and her hormones were on high alert—wanting him could be clouding her judgment. Dalton could turn out to be one of the bad guys. But for the moment, she didn't think so.

"Do you want to talk about it?"

Smiling, Dalton shook his head. "You never say what I expect."

"That, my friend, is a compliment of the first order." Brushing her lips against his, Colleen moved away before either of them could take it further. Caution was never a bad thing. "Let's go to dinner. I lost my appetite. Now it's back."

Dalton helped her into the passenger seat. As he walked around the car, Colleen marveled that it didn't feel odd to sit here while he sat behind the wheel. Maybe today's heat had fried a bit of her brain. Or it might have been Dalton. Either way, she buckled her seatbelt and relaxed.

"Chicken fried steak?"

"And a frosty margarita."

It sounded like heaven. Or as close as she could get in Midas, Arizona.

THE SIDEWINDER WASN'T exactly jumping, which was fine with Dalton. He wasn't worried about someone recognizing him. It happened all the time. But that was for his music. His arrest had been big news in Midas. It had been carried out in a very public manner. Dalton had no idea where all the police cars had come from. The flashing lights lit up the night sky. That was not something quickly forgotten.

"This used to be a dentist's office," Colleen informed him as their waitress showed them to their table. "Dr. Painless. He lasted less than a year."

"I wonder why?"

"I know. Dr. Feelgood is a cliché, but the curiosity factor alone would have pulled in a few patients."

They gave their drink orders. The waitress left, giving them time to decide on their meal.

"I don't know why I'm looking. I always have the special."

Dalton peered at Colleen over the top of his menu. "Wednesday chicken fried steak."

"Thursday spaghetti and meatballs. Friday varies. Usually some kind of fish." Colleen wrinkled her nose.

"Not a fan?"

"It's always deep fried. I want my sole grilled, not covered in crispy grease."

Dalton could relate. There was a place for fast food. Sometimes it was a necessity. But there was no substitute for beautifully prepared food made with the freshest ingredients. It was one of the many joys of having the money to travel where he wanted and do it first class all the way.

"There is a place on the coast of Italy that serves a Fillet of Sole Ponte Vecchio. It is one of the five best things I have ever eaten."

"You keep track?"

"I do when it's that good."

"I want to travel," Colleen said with a wistful sigh.

41

"To Italy?"

"Italy. France. Seattle. New York."

Smiling, Dalton thanked the waitress as she set their drinks on the table. He took a sip of his beer before he could do something stupid like give into a sudden desire to invite Colleen on the trip he planned before leaving Los Angeles. Two weeks in Greece. Not the touristy places. He had marveled at the Acropolis years ago. This time, Dalton had rented a boat. Not too big, but one that had a full crew so he could sit back and enjoy as they sailed around the different islands. Ashe planned on joining him for a few days.

The two men would undoubtedly find the time to romance some local beauties. But the idea of seeing Colleen in a tiny bikini, her red hair gleaming in the Mediterranean sunlight, held a great deal of appeal. It wasn't practical. It wasn't going to happen. But it was a nice image.

Dalton's favorite meals were ones that were drawn out by good conversation. To his delight, Colleen turned out to be a lively, opinionated companion.

"I don't want a handout." Colleen waved her fork for emphasis. "I want fair pay for work well done. Dole thought he could get away with agreeing to one salary and giving me another. He quickly learned otherwise."

There was something about a strong, confident woman that got Dalton's blood pumping. Sweet and docile was fine for a change of pace. But give him a woman like Colleen any day.

"I would have loved to witness that confrontation."

"It was short but not very sweet. Dole can do the basics. Change the oil. Fix a flat. But those things don't keep the lights on. Or provide his wife, Selma, with enough cash to buy fripperies in Phoenix."

"Fripperies?"

"Dole's word, not mine," Colleen said. "I have no idea what they are, but she seems to need a lot of them."

"Are they like thing-a-ma-jigs?"

"No. Probably more in the neighborhood of do-dads."

As though the difference was of deep importance, Dalton nodded, barely managing to keep a straight face. When his twinkling eyes met hers, they both burst out laughing.

"Dole must have come to his senses, or you wouldn't still be working there."

"I get a fair wage," Colleen shrugged, taking a bite of her chicken fried steak.

"Stop me if I'm overstepping your boundaries—"

"Boundaries?" she interrupted with a quiet snort. "Did we set those?"

"Not verbally. But everyone has a line that shouldn't be crossed." Dalton certainly did.

"You see before you an open book." Colleen took a drink of the margarita she had nursed through the meal, pushed her empty plate to the side, and then rested her elbows on the table. "Shoot. What do you want to know?"

"What are you doing in Midas, Arizona?"

"I like how you make it sound like the filthiest curse word ever."

"Well..." Dalton shrugged.

"Which begs the question, what are *you* doing here?" Colleen put up a hand before he could think of a suitable answer. "Never mind. Besides, you asked first. Do you want the long version, or should I *Reader's Digest* you?"

"I don't have any place to be. How about you?"

"This is Midas, Arizona," Colleen grinned, copying Dalton's tone. "You are the only game in town. No offense."

Dalton wasn't the least bit offended. He was intrigued, entertained, and not surprisingly, aroused.

"Then I vote for the long version," he said, settling back.

"I wasn't born here. The whys and wherefores are more my mother's story than mine. My father had left before I was old enough to care. After years of barely getting by working as a beautician, Mom remarried. Evan Crawford."

"How old were you?"

"Thirteen. Before I could blink, we were on our way from our home in Kansas to a shiny new life in Arizona." Colleen sighed. "Little did my mother know she was trading one dead-end town for another. But at least she had a husband."

"What happened?"

"Surprise, surprise, step-daddy wasn't the man he made himself out to be." Dalton heard the trace of bitterness in Colleen's voice. "He couldn't work—bad back. Mom got a job at the local beauty salon. And three months later, her husband, along with the little money she had saved, skipped town."

"Bastard."

"The crazy part is, he made Mom happy. She was a different woman than the one I grew up with. She smiled and laughed. Working wasn't a problem—she liked her job. When her marriage collapsed, so did she." Colleen gave a philosophical shrug. "Nothing good lasts long in Midas."

"You have."

Obviously pleased by his comment, Colleen's lovely green eyes widened. "That may be the best line ever."

"It wasn't a line," Dalton assured her.

"That's what makes it so good."

Dalton slid his hand across the table until the tips of his fingers brushed Colleen's. A bit of comfort and encouragement.

"I wanted to leave, but Mom wouldn't hear of it. For better or worse— you have to love the irony of that—this was now our home. After a few weeks, she started to come out of her funk. She dragged herself to work. Eventually, she bought the salon. She got married last fall. So far, so good."

"That covers your mother. What about you?"

"I guess that was the point, wasn't it?"

"Not that I was bored." Dalton's index finger lightly tapped hers. "But yes, that was the point."

"There isn't much to tell. I like engines, and they like me. I've always had the knack. Back in Kansas, a repair man told Mom our refrigerator couldn't be fixed."

"You fixed it?"

"I am proud to say that refrigerator brought us fifty dollars. A neighbor bought it before we left town."

Beautiful, funny, and talented beyond Dalton's comprehension. He knew what a spark plug looked like, but that was where it ended. They could have used Colleen in the early days. Calling their first tour bus unreliable put it mildly. More often than not, the money they earned from a gig was put right back into their transportation. Colleen would have saved them a fortune in repairs.

Over the next hour, Colleen explained how close she had come to leaving Midas. Her mother's illness. And starting over again.

"I've seen my last Midas summer," she said with a firm nod. "If I lose it all tomorrow, nothing is keeping me here."

"Where will you go?"

When Colleen hesitated, Dalton wondered if she had reached the edge of her boundaries. Then she continued—cautiously.

"I've never told anyone."

"I won't be offended if you want to keep it to yourself." This time, when his hand moved, it was to take hold of hers.

"I'm afraid." A burst of air rushed from Colleen's lungs. "That's something I never admit—not even to myself."

"Change is scary."

"I want a change," Colleen said, her eyes burning with emotion. "I want different. But..."

Dalton's grip tightened. "Tell me."

"What if I'm not supposed to get out of here, Dalton? What if this is it for me? Day after day of working for Dole. My mother says I should get married. Have a few babies. That will make me happy."

"What did you say?"

45

"If I weren't afraid of hurting her feelings? *How did that work out for you, Mom?* Instead, I smiled, nodded, and mentally crossed off another day."

"You'll get out, Colleen."

Colleen stared at some invisible point over Dalton's shoulder. When her gaze returned to his, the emotion was there, but it had dimmed considerably.

"I should have left when I was eighteen. But Mom begged me to stay one more year while she got the salon on firmer ground. Then I decided to take some classes in Phoenix. I'm glad I did. I learned a lot. That was when I started refurbishing the Thunderbird. I found it dirt cheap. I promised myself as soon as I finished, I was out of here."

"Your mother became ill, Colleen."

"And now she isn't." Earnestly, Colleen sat forward, both hands gripping his. "It has to happen this time."

"Breathe," Dalton urged. "That's right. In and out. In and out."

Gradually, Colleen's shoulders relaxed and the death grip on his hand loosened.

"That wasn't the least bit embarrassing," Colleen cringed. She tried to pull away, but Dalton held on. "Was that a panic attack? Great. Mental instability. Just what I need."

"You aren't unbalanced," Dalton said with calm certainty. He knew what that looked like, and Colleen didn't come close to qualifying. "You needed to vent, which you did quite nicely."

"Thank you for listening." Taking another deep breath, she smiled— genuinely smiled.

"Better?"

"Much."

"Good." Lifting her hand, Dalton kissed the back. "Ready to finish?"

"First. Do that again." When he lightly brushed his lips across her fingers, Colleen sighed. "That's nice."

"Second?" Dalton let her take back her hand.

Colleen frowned, then her smile brightened her entire face. "Right. Second. Am I ready to finish what?"

"You were going to tell me your dream? What will you do when you leave Midas, Colleen?"

Dalton thought he knew the answer, but he wanted to hear the words from her.

Colleen's smile turned into a grin. "I am going to be the best damn classic car restorer in the country. Eventually, the world."

It made perfect sense. Dalton knew first hand that Colleen had the skill to make her dream come true.

"I would say it's a sure bet."

"You think so?"

"My money is on you."

"WHAT IS HE doing in Midas?"

"Having dinner." The second the words were out of Drum Anders' mouth, he wished them back.

There was a long pause. "Was that an attempt at humor?"

More like sarcasm, but Drum wisely kept that to himself.

"No, sir. It's a fact. Shaw spent the afternoon visiting his sister. Then he checked into *The Midas Manor*. After picking up Colleen McNamara, they drove to *The Sidewinder*. Dinner, drinks, and conversation, sir. That's all there is to report."

"After seven years, Dalton Shaw chooses now to show his face in this town again?"

"It could be a coincidence. Like I said, the first thing Shaw did was visit his sister."

"You don't get to my position in life believing in coincidence. Keep an eye on him. Perhaps you're right, and I have nothing to worry about."

"I'll call if he does anything out of the ordinary."

"You'll call if all he does is scratch his ass. I will decide what's important and what isn't. I want everything documented. Understood?"

47

"Yes, sir."

With a resigned sigh, Drum took another picture. Same angle. Nothing new. For everyone's sake, he hoped this ended soon. The last time Dalton Shaw came to Midas, he was a two-bit drummer in a struggling band. Now, he was a world-famous rock star. He could go anywhere in the world. Why here? Unless his boss was right. Was Shaw going to cause trouble?

Raising his phone, Drum caught Shaw kissing Colleen McNamara's hand. She was a good-looking woman but hardly worth coming to this shithole town. There had to be more to it than sex.

Because he messed with the wrong family, Dalton Shaw had been railroaded. He was sent to prison for doing something that in any other part of the country would have gotten him a medal. Or at the very least a suspended sentence. Was his return a coincidence? Or was he back for revenge?

CHAPTER FIVE

IT HAD TO be the oddest date Colleen had ever been on. It was also the best. They began the evening relative strangers with little more than an instant attraction between them. Now? The connection had grown to something bigger, better—and a bit frightening. Sharing her inner-most thoughts and dreams went beyond the casual. To what, she couldn't say.

However, Colleen knew one thing. She liked the feeling—whatever it was. She *liked* Dalton Shaw. And there weren't many people she could honestly say that about.

"I'm surprised we made it through dinner without someone recognizing you."

Dalton helped Colleen from her seat. It was a little gesture but not one she saw every day. Or, thinking back, ever. The man turned out to be a big, sexy anachronism—in the best sense of the word.

"You mean because I'm a celebrity?

Colleen took Dalton's proffered arm as they walked toward the exit.

"You're a rock star. Celebrity is something else. Like a Kardashian or one of those *Bachelor* people."

"I appreciate the distinction." Dalton paused outside the restaurant, scanning the parking lot before moving to the car.

Feeling she missed something, Colleen frowned. "Is there a problem?"

"I hope not."

With what seemed to her to be undue haste, Dalton hustled Colleen into the car. Before he could start the engine, she stayed his hand.

"Do you want to explain?" Deciding that was too easily shot down, Colleen amended her question to a statement. "Tell me what's going on, Dalton. You were relaxed and easy during dinner. Now you're as tense as a dog anticipating a thunderstorm. No clouds. No lightning. So what changed?"

Dalton gripped the steering wheel, his knuckles showing white.

"How hard would it be for you to trust me?"

"Do you want money? Or a vital organ?"

Colleen wasn't certain, but she thought the sound Dalton made was close to a laugh.

"No on both."

"Do I have to lie, cheat, or steal? Because I'm fine with two of those—for the most part. The third is tricky but on occasion? Sure."

"When are you okay with stealing?"

"*Ocean's Eleven*. I didn't like the casino owner. Of course, they lost all their money, but not until the sequel."

"What the hell are you talking about?"

Colleen had no idea. But it made Dalton smile.

"I trust you. Up to a point."

Dalton nodded. "Smart woman." He started the car, cautiously pulling out of the parking lot. "I want you to take the T-Bird back to your place."

"Are you leaving town sooner than expected?" Colleen thought that would be a damn shame. "I tinkered with your car, but even if I get it running, I wouldn't suggest trying to drive it back to Los Angeles."

"I'm not leaving town. Not yet. And I'm holding you to the rental agreement. I don't want to leave the car in an unprotected parking lot."

"Because...?"

"This is where that trust part comes in. Can you cut me some slack?"

"Slack equals patience. That has never been my strong suit." However, if Dalton thought her car was in danger, she wouldn't push. At least, not tonight. "I can put a few pieces together. Does this concern what happened to you seven years ago?"

"Yes."

"Will you tell me the whole story?"

"Probably."

"Is probably the best I'm going to get?"

"Yes."

Suddenly Mr. Chatty morphed into the monosyllabic man. It should have

50

been funny, but Colleen didn't feel like laughing.

"Stay at my place."

"No."

"Damn it, Dalton. My apartment comes with a locked garage. I have double bolts on my front door. My car and you will be safe."

"I'll stay if I can share your bed."

"Okay."

"We won't get much sleep, Colleen."

"I know."

This time, when Dalton laughed, Colleen heard it loud and clear.

"Jesus. Really, Colleen? You would have sex with me? Why?"

"I'm worried about you. If you're in my bed, I know you'll be safe."

"I appreciate the thought, but no. I'll be fine in my motel room."

Colleen wondered about men. Ninety-nine percent of the time they seemed to think with their dicks. Until a woman wanted him to. Then he decided to exercise that one percent of his brain that mostly lay dormant.

"It isn't as though it would be a hardship. I planned on us having sex by the weekend. What's wrong with speeding up the timetable?"

The streetlights illuminated the interior of the car enough to allow her to see Dalton's face and his bemused expression. Deciphering his thoughts wasn't as easy. He pulled the car to a stop outside the motel. Within a minute, he was out of the driver's seat and Colleen replaced him. When she rolled down the window, he leaned down.

"Drive straight home, lock your doors, then give me a call."

"One of the few good things about living in Midas is the lack of crime."

Giving her another enigmatic look, Dalton stood back.

"Lock your front door, Colleen. Then call me."

"Fine. But you first." Colleen motioned toward the door to Dalton's room. "You're making me nervous. I'm not leaving until you are safely inside."

Dalton looked as if he might argue. His blue eyes narrowed. But to her

51

surprise, he nodded.

"The car doors are locked. Roll up your windows. And Colleen?" he said as she began to comply.

"Yes?"

"Thank you for trusting me."

"You're welcome. Dalton?" Colleen called out as he entered the motel.

"Yes?"

"Don't make me regret it."

DALTON WAITED FOR Colleen to call. She didn't play games. Fifteen minutes after she pulled out of the parking lot, she checked in.

"We should exchange passwords. Or a secret knock," Colleen said the second he answered.

"That won't be necessary." Dalton knew he overreacted, but he'd had a strange feeling since leaving the restaurant. He would risk looking foolish if it meant keeping Colleen safe. "Are you free for lunch tomorrow?"

"I usually work straight through. Why don't I pick you up around eight o'clock? I'll drive us to the garage, and you can have the car for the rest of the day."

"That's a plan."

"Good night, Dalton."

"Good night."

Dalton turned the air conditioner on high before stripping off his clothes. The water pressure in the bathroom wasn't great, but it was good enough for a cool shower. After drying off, he stretched out naked on the bed before calling Ryder.

"It's about time," Ryder answered after the second ring.

"Hello to you too."

"Everybody is here. Just a second while I put you on speaker."

Everybody included Ashe, Zoe, and Ryder's girlfriend, Quinn Abernathy. She was new to the group, but Ryder trusted her implicitly. That was

52

good enough for Dalton.

"How's it going?" Ashe asked after everyone had said hello.

"It started off great. The drive was relaxing. About ten miles short of Midas, my car went to shit."

Dalton explained about the smoke and how he barely made it into town before the car gave up the ghost.

"You're lucky you found a garage," Ryder said.

"What are you doing about transportation?" The question came from Zoe.

"The mechanic had a car to rent."

Dalton didn't go into detail about Colleen. Or that there even *was* a Colleen. At this point, what was there to say? Except that he met a sexy redhead who made him laugh. In all likelihood, that was as far as it would go. If he and Colleen became lovers—a hope, not a certainty—it was nobody's business but theirs.

As a group, Dalton and his friends shared almost everything. There were no secrets. Trust was rock solid. However, when it came to his—or anyone's—sex life, they respected each other's privacy.

"Did you speak with your sister?" Ashe asked.

"I suppose you could call it that."

It helped to share the details of his meeting with Maggie. Talking it out clarified things in his mind—at least as much as possible.

"It sounds like a muddled mess." The concern in Ryder's voice was to be expected. He took his responsibilities as leader seriously. He didn't like to be so far away and powerless.

"You know Maggie. Vague is her middle name. Unless Norris has some earthshaking revelation to impart, I plan on cutting them off for good."

"Hallelujah," Zoe called out. "It's about time. Maggie's big-eyed wounded doe routine makes me gag."

"She *is* my sister, Zoe." Dalton couldn't defend Maggie, but he wasn't going to trash her either.

"Anything else?"

Dalton didn't have to ask what Ryder meant.

"Nothing concrete. Tonight at dinner, it felt as though someone was watching me. But..." Someone was always watching. Fame—and all its perks—meant a certain loss of privacy. Dalton was used to it and barely noticed anymore. However, while he was in Midas, his radar was on high alert.

"What happened?" Ryder demanded.

"Nothing. I was fine until we left the restaurant. That was when my sense of unease shifted into high."

"*We* left the restaurant?"

Dalton sighed. Leave it to Ashe to latch onto his slip of the tongue.

"I had dinner with my mechanic. It was nice to have some company."

Dalton thought that was the end of it. He should have known better. Ashe and Ryder would have assumed the mechanic was a man. Sure, it was sexist. But even an enlightened man was allowed a slip or two. There weren't a lot of women who worked on cars. It was hard to blame his friends for their linear points of view. It took a woman—or two—to think outside that particular box.

"What's her name?" Zoe asked.

"Well, shit," Dalton muttered.

Laughing, Quinn added, "What does she look like?"

"Your mechanic is a woman?" Ashe whistled. "Maybe Midas isn't as backward as we thought."

Knowing he was stuck, Dalton took his only way out. Just the facts, ma'am.

"Her name is Colleen McNamara. She has red hair. Green eyes. The sweetest smile and fantastic legs." Dalton left out Colleen's fine ass. He considered that too much information even between best friends.

"It figures." Zoe had an expert sneer, but to her credit, the one she sent Dalton's way was toned down. "It took you less than a day to find a playmate."

"We shared one meal. No playing involved." Dalton didn't add that he hoped that would change. His friends knew him too well to assume otherwise.

"I shouldn't have to remind you what happened the last time you fooled around in Midas."

Ryder was right. Dalton didn't need reminding. However, he was older and wiser. And Colleen was neither married nor a lying, cold-hearted bitch.

"I'll be careful. Maybe too careful."

"What do you mean?"

Dalton gave a brief account of his bout of post-dinner paranoia.

"I'll give Colleen credit. She did as I asked—once I promised I would explain at a later date. If the tables were turned, I don't think I would have been as understanding."

"You trusted your instincts," Ryder said. "Keep doing that."

"I will." Dalton yawned. His early start and the day's drama had finally taken its toll. "I'll call tomorrow night."

"If you need *anything*, Dalton. Don't hesitate."

"I know."

Dalton ended the call. Stretching, he closed his eyes and relaxed his body. Even with the air conditioner at full blast, the room was unpleasantly stuffy. The sheets had the feel of a mild-grade sandpaper, and the neon sign flashed vacancy through the drawn curtain. However, he was too tired for any of that to matter.

Within minutes, Dalton drifted off to sleep with a slight smile on his lips and a final thought of the lovely Colleen. For the next six hours, he slept soundly. And blissfully dreamed of nothing.

CHAPTER SIX

EVERY MORNING, DALTON tried to run at least five miles. More if time permitted. Yesterday, he had skipped the ritual but not today. Starting at a leisurely pace, he circled behind the motel, cutting through the alley littered with a puzzlingly large amount of empty beer bottles. Was that a week's supply? A month's? Didn't the owners believe in recycling? The battered green refuse dumpster overflowed with a gag-inducing amount of malodorous black plastic bags. When the hell was garbage pick-up in this town?

Shaking off the less-than-pleasant beginning, Dalton veered onto a promising-looking path. It didn't take long for his muscles to loosen. Speeding up, he breathed with practiced ease. Running was the perfect way to explore an area. When they were on tour, Dalton never took the same route twice. It was amazing what he saw on foot. Small, interesting things that he never would have discovered riding along in a car. It was how he found his favorite boot maker. The tiny shop in the middle of an out-of-the-way neighborhood in Milan. It had been an unexpected and pleasant surprise.

Dalton didn't expect anything close to pleasant as he wound his way through the middle of Midas.

The Midas Manor—Dalton snorted at the pretentious name—was located at the point where the town began to morph from dirt poor to stinking rich. There wasn't much of a middle class in Midas, but it did exist. Somebody needed to provide essential services to the town. Food and various sundries. Dalton imagined the bulk of the clientele came from the south side of town. However, when faced with no cream for their morning coffee, the northsiders probably stooped to send a servant to pick up a pint.

Shaking his head at his fanciful thoughts, Dalton journeyed on. This wasn't something he would have done seven years ago. Today he believed a healthy body led to a healthy mind. In his early twenties, he relied upon youthful energy and stupidity. Sometimes he wondered why he hadn't landed in trouble more often. The trouble he found in Midas that fateful summer set him on a different path.

Not to salvation—Dalton had no idea what that even meant. He learned the hard way to stop coasting on his innate gifts as a drummer and a man. He began to study other musicians. He honed his craft. When he listened to the band's early recordings, he heard a wild, undisciplined boy. Now— older, more experienced, smarter—he no longer pounded the drums. He made them sing.

Of course, it was that youthful abandon that brought him to Ryder's attention. Lead singer of a fledgling band that already included Ashe, they needed a drummer. Their backgrounds were different—as were their basic personalities. But in each other they recognized something. The love of music and a burning ambition to succeed. That need brought them together. Through thick and thin—that was their motto.

Few bands lasted a year, let alone a decade. Music brought them together. Their friendship—unbreakable—kept them going strong.

Rounding a corner, Dalton's view changed considerably. Money. It made the world cleaner and greener. For the select families living in the gated community, life was beyond better. To the right, near the base of what passed for a hillside in Midas sat a mansion. It looked down on the town and the surrounding houses. Bigger, brighter, and more ornately ridiculous than the rest.

Dalton had never been inside. This was the first time he had seen it in the light of day. But he knew who lived there. Judge Manfred T. Langley.

"It's like living in the shadow of God. With all the wrath and none of the benevolence."

Surprised, Dalton shifted his gaze. A tall, slender man stood near the gate. His sun-darkened skin was shaded from the morning heat by an old, slouched hat that had seen better days. His hands were covered by well-worn work gloves and on his shoulder rested a long, metal-tined rake.

"God?" Dalton asked. He knew from experience that Judge Langley wielded a shit-load of power, but comparing him to a deity was going a bit far.

"In this town?" Dalton could hear the derision in the man's voice. "Not much difference to some folks. Those of us who think different, pray to the man above on Sunday and bow down to the judge the rest of the week."

If he lived in Midas, Dalton cringed at the thought; this was a man he would want to know. With a friendly smile, he held out his hand.

"Dalton Shaw."

"Tolliver Cline. Everyone calls me Tol." Removing his glove, Tol gave Dalton's hand a firm shake. "And I know who you are. Word spread the second you hit town, son. For various reasons."

"I can imagine."

"I'll bet," Tol chuckled. Bending, he opened a cooler that had been stashed behind a row of neatly trimmed hedges. "You look like you've been out awhile. Want some water?"

"Thanks." Dalton caught Tol's easy lob. He emptied half of the bottle in two long gulps.

"No point in rehashing the past." Tol replaced the lid after drinking from his bottle. "And no point in tiptoeing around the mammoth-sized elephant in the room. Why the hell are you back in Midas?"

At the last second, Dalton turned, spitting his mouthful of water onto the grass instead of in Tol's face. He appreciated the straightforward approach, but the question took him off guard.

"I'm visiting my sister." That was close enough to the truth and all that Tol needed to know.

"Maggie Mayhue?" Seeing Dalton's surprised expression, Tol shrugged. "Small town, son."

In Dalton's book, that excuse only cut it for so long. At some point, everybody knowing everything about everyone crossed over the line from matter of fact to disturbingly creepy. Tol had inched close but wasn't there yet.

"I don't plan on hanging around for long. A few days at the most."

"Smart. You're on the judge's radar."

"Me? What the hell did I do this time?"

"I need to get to work." Tol pulled on his glove. When Dalton started to protest, he held up his hand. "I'm not going to leave you hanging. What are you doing for dinner?"

Dalton thought of Colleen. He had hoped for a meal at her place. Some wine. A long talk, and a night in her bed. Skipping the first part was doable—if Colleen was amenable.

"I live about five miles east of town. My wife makes a mean roasted chicken and mashed potatoes. Seven o'clock work for you?" Tolliver rattled off the address.

"Sounds good."

"Bring Colleen. She'll know the way."

"How did you—"

"Small town, son. Small town."

With a shake of his head, Dalton started back toward the motel. He wasn't worried about Judge Manfred T. Langley. Seven years had placed them on an even footing. Some might say that—seven years later—the scales had tipped in Dalton's favor. His money wasn't old, but his fortune was large. And these days, a celebrity—especially one who earned his position through talent and hard work—carried more heft with more people than any political figure short of the president. As crazy as it sounded, there were times when a rock star even trumped the Commander in Chief.

However, Dalton was curious. Tolliver claimed he knew the answer— and it came with a home-cooked meal. Plus another evening spent with Colleen. Midas would never be a vacation getaway, but it turned out to be better than he could have imagined.

COLLEEN RARELY TOOK a lunch break. She got paid by the hour, but she had prodded Dole into adding a bonus clause into their employment agreement. The one she drew up when he tried to shaft her out of their agreed wage. If she finished a job ahead of schedule, Dole paid her a percentage of the final bill—a bill she looked over carefully to make certain it wasn't padded.

At 11:26 a.m., Colleen earned that bonus when she finished an engine rebuild. To celebrate, she hitched a ride to her mother's, hoping to get a meal and take care of her weekly visit all in one.

"Mom? Are you home?"

It wasn't a silly question. Sherry McNamara Higgins never locked the back door. She hadn't bothered when they lived in Kansas, and nothing changed when they moved to Arizona. For some reason, no matter how Colleen tried, she couldn't make her mother see that bolting the front door, but not the back, was like putting sunscreen on only half of your face. The thief, like the sun, would burn you one way or the other.

It seemed like a perfect simile for a beautician. And it worked. For a week or two. However, it wasn't long before Sherry forgot. Her husband had lived in the same neighborhood all his life. Rick saw nothing wrong with unlocked doors. When Colleen tried to reason with him, he simply shrugged, giving her what had to be the unofficial town motto. *It's Midas.*

The sound of laundry churning away greeted Colleen as she walked into the house. Again, nothing unusual. Between the beauty salon and the work clothes Rick shed every night when he got home from his job on the county road crew, the washing machine and dryer were in constant use. It smelled like ammonia, road tar, and Mountain Fresh Gain.

Sherry liked to joke that she married Rick for his house. It was her dream layout. All one level, each room flowed into the next. The master bedroom was located on the east side. To get to the guest room— Colleen's until she turned eighteen and moved out—it was necessary to walk from one end of the house to the other. She never worried about getting in late from a date. She simply left her bedroom window ajar and snuck in. Her mother never tried to crack down on Colleen's nocturnal activities. But looking back, she should have. Thank God for the free clinic in Phoenix that kept the kids of Midas supplied with condoms and birth control pills.

"Colleen? I'm in the kitchen, sweetheart."

Entering through the washroom door, Colleen walked to where her mother sat at the granite-covered island with a cup of coffee and her laptop. Picture perfect from the top of her frosted blond hair to the tips of her manicured nails, her mother was a walking billboard for her salon. Each morning—rain, shine, or raging flu—she refused to leave the bathroom until she put on her face. Colleen was certain there had to be a face somewhere under the face, but in all of her twenty-six years, she had never seen it.

"What is that noise?"

Puzzled, Sherry cocked her head. "It's just the overhead fan. I've gotten used to it so I don't even hear it anymore."

It sounded as though the fan was powered by a dozen mice running around a very squeaky wheel.

"Did you ask Rick to fix it?"

Sherry flicked her wrist, her expression indulgent. "The dear man tried. He emptied a can of WD-40. All it did was leave a pool of grease on my good counters."

Rick was a lousy handyman but a very good husband and stepfather. Her mother had hit the jackpot and so had Colleen. Doing odd jobs around the house didn't begin to pay him back.

Taking the proper tools from the drawer in the washroom, Colleen flipped the circuit breaker. A scant five minutes later, the squeak was gone.

"My clever girl. I don't know where you get it. I can barely change a light bulb. Your father wasn't any better. But he gave you his red hair and green eyes." Smiling, Sherry smoothed a hand across Colleen's cheek. "I

61

see him every time I look at you. Now *that* is a gift."

And that was why Colleen loved her mother. Scatterbrained, archaic in her thinking about the roles of men and women, and lost in her own world so much of the time. Out of the blue, Sherry could say something so sweet that it made Colleen forget all her faults.

Then in the next instant, her mother would turn around and make Colleen want to pull out her red hair and cross her green eyes in frustration.

"I understand you're dating a criminal."

"I'm not dating anyone. I had dinner with an interesting man. A very famous man." To illustrate her point, Colleen tapped a few keys on her mother's computer. When the YouTube video began to play, she turned the screen. "*The Ryder Hart Band*. I know you like their music."

"Infamous is more like it." Sherry had that stubborn set to her jaw that Colleen recognized only too well. Easily influenced, the fleas that a *well-meaning* friend had planted in her mother's ear would not be easily removed. "You were seen together last night *and* this morning. Did you spend the night with that—?"

"Drummer?"

"Jailbird."

Colleen had to laugh. "That term went out with Jimmy Cagney."

"Answer the question, Colleen."

"The last time you asked about my sex life I was sixteen. Do you remember my response?"

Sherry's painted red lips tightened. "You told me it was none of my business. If you'll recall, I didn't agree. That hasn't changed."

"Mom." Deciding to change her tactics, Colleen put a friendly arm around her mother's waist. "You know me. Would I associate with a dangerous criminal? I looked up the trial and read the notes."

"On the internet?" Sherry scoffed. "Nothing but secondhand information. Why didn't you ask me? I was here that summer."

Colleen was well acquainted with her mother's dicey memories. Sherry added or subtracted details to fit her idea of the truth. The gossip she heard at the salon always played a big part—the juicier, the better. To save herself a trip down that particular road, Colleen threw her sex life under the bus.

"I did not sleep with Dalton, Mom. His car broke down, and I rented him the T-Bird. I picked him up at his hotel this morning. That was what your informant witnessed."

With the enthusiasm of a brand new lottery winner, Sherry threw her arms around Colleen. Pulling back, her face wreathed in happiness, her mother nodded sagely.

"I understand that a woman has needs, Colleen."

Oh, God, Colleen tried to keep from wincing. If the earth opened up and sucked her in, she would be eternally grateful.

"Leave my needs out of it, Mom. Please."

"I simply want you to know that I understand. Dalton Shaw is a good-looking man. He's rich. Famous."

"Before you go any further." *Please don't go any further*. "Dalton won't be in town for long. A few days at the most. What could happen?"

The answer was not one that her mother would want to hear. Sex could happen. If Colleen had her way, it *would* happen. But for her mother's sake, she kept that fact to herself.

"A few days? That's all?"

"Less than a week. By Monday, probably sooner, Dalton Shaw will be back in Los Angeles where he belongs."

"That's for the best, Colleen. A man like that can only bring you heartache."

The subject closed to her satisfaction, Sherry launched into a detailed account of her last book club meeting. They were always more about gossip than literature. Tuning her mother out, Colleen took a package of sliced turkey from the refrigerator and began to assemble her lunch.

Heartache? Not likely. She wanted a little fun and excitement. Dalton was the perfect man to break the tedium of her daily life. He had nothing else to offer, and she wasn't looking for more.

Lifting the sandwich to her mouth, Colleen smiled as she took a bite. Dalton Shaw and Colleen McNamara. The perfect temporary match.

WAITING WAS NOT Dalton's strong suit. Patience—as his cellmate tried to teach him all those years ago—was called a virtue for a reason. Some of Silas Freed's lessons stuck. That one hadn't. Silas, bless his philosophical heart, hadn't let it bother him. He was a lifer. At sixty-five, prison was all he knew. More time in than out, he did his best to get Dalton to the finish line without any permanent damage.

The outside world waited for his protégé. Silas considered it his job to make certain Dalton didn't stumble along the way.

Dalton recalled a conversation he and Silas had one night after lockdown. It was a week after his arrival.

"Prison," Silas had told him, "doesn't rehabilitate. It hardens the soul."

"Your soul seems just fine."

"I struggled for a long time. Anger led to bitterness then back to anger. I got in fights. Spent a lot of time in solitary. A life devoid of hope is a useless thing. Eventually, I came to the realization that the world outside these walls was moving on without me."

Dalton's stomach had clenched at the thought. "That sounds damn hopeless to me."

"You're young. When you leave, if I've done my job, you will carry my hope with you."

"Shit, Silas. That's sounds like a lot of responsibility."

"It is." The older man's voice drifted toward sleep. "How you live your life—it's a choice. The books I've given you to read will fill your head with ideas. What you do with them is up to you."

There were times when it seemed like yesterday. Dalton visited Silas once, letting him know what he was doing—how he was living his life. The look of approval had meant the world. Silas died two months later. Heart attack. It was quick—the way he would have wanted to go.

Dalton gave back whenever possible. Tried to be kind. Didn't suffer fools easily. But most of all, he lived each day knowing it was a gift. He hoped the old man would be proud.

With a sigh, Dalton checked his phone for the tenth time, then debated his next move.

It became clear that Norris had no intention of ending this farce in a timely manner. One fucking phone call. That was all Dalton asked. They could set up a meeting and hash out what he hoped—but seriously doubted—was nothing more than a misunderstanding. It was difficult to *accidentally* give an interview. And if, as Maggie led him to believe, there were more stories to come, Norris knew exactly what he was doing. The bridge wasn't about to burn. His brother-in-law had set the explosives. One more move and boom! Obliteration.

Giving Maggie another call, Dalton growled when it went straight to voicemail.

"Fuck it."

Dalton shoved Silas' call for patience out of his head. His sister and her husband were playing a game without sharing the rules. Not only wasn't it fair, but it was also stupid. Poke the bear at your own risk. Dalton wasn't as volatile as in his youth. It took a good amount of prodding to set him off. It gave the foolish a false sense of security. Eventually, Dalton lowered the boom. And when it happened, it happened fast.

"Tell Norris he had his chance, Maggie. When he aligned himself with that gossip rag, he signed away his soul. I hope the amount was worth it. You are now officially cut off."

Tossing his phone onto the passenger seat, Dalton waited for the first wave of guilt. And waited. And waited. *Well, what do you know?* Starting the car, he adjusted the vent until a blast of cold air rushed over his face. Was it that easy to give up a habit that had plagued him most of his life? Protecting his little sister from her self-inflicted mistakes. Wasn't that what brothers did?

The problem was, Dalton had a daily reminder that was hard for anyone to live up to. Ryder and Zoe Hart. That was how the brother and sister thing should be done. Not perfect by any means. But honest. Loving. Supportive.

Dalton knew it wasn't over with Maggie. It never would be. But he was finished paying for regrets. He wished he could like his sister. He knew he was supposed to love her. He felt neither. Obligation—and that hung by a string. Whether or not the tenuous bond broke for good was up to her.

Unbidden, an old Eagles song ran through his head. *Take it Easy*. When he wrote, *don't let the sound of your own wheels drive you crazy*, the late, great Glen Frey knew what he was talking about. Too much thinking in circles got you nowhere.

There were better, and much more pleasant, ways to spend his time. With a smile of anticipation, Dalton picked up his phone. A swipe of his thumb and two quick clicks. He felt better already.

"What are you doing for dinner?"

"I think I saw this movie. *Groundhog Day*, right? Are we repeating the same conversation over and over again?"

"I'll reword that—for your benefit. It's two o'clock on a hot as hell Thursday afternoon in—excuse my French—Bumfuck, Arizona. Let's find someplace to cool off. Talk. And if you're free, we've been invited to dinner."

"We? There's a we?"

Dalton laughed. "Small town, big mouths. Our night out was observed."

"Mm. I found out the same thing. I'll tell you about it later."

Later? Dalton wanted to see Colleen soon. Now. "Can you get off work early?"

When Colleen didn't answer, Dalton resigned himself to spending the afternoon alone. But her response, when it came, was worth the wait.

"Feel like a swim?"

CHAPTER SEVEN

WHO WOULD HAVE guessed that heaven existed fifteen minutes down the road from hell? Dalton's face must have reflected his astonishment.

"Surprised?" Colleen asked as she pulled the T-Bird to a stop by a small cabin.

"A lake surrounded by shade trees? Out here? Surprised doesn't begin to cover it."

"You said you wanted to cool off. Come on."

Colleen hopped out. She had left her coveralls at work, much to Dalton's delight. The woman who met him outside the garage was another side of Colleen. Gone was the grease monkey. There was no sign of the mature, put-together woman of the night before. Standing in the glare of the summer sun, her blazing hair hanging loose, was a full-fledged teenage dream. Colleen looked about sixteen in her tight denim shorts and cropped t-shirt, her hand resting on her cocked hip. Dalton might have felt like a leering pervert. Except in that moment, he felt ten years younger.

"Nice bubble," he commented as he tossed her the keys.

Colleen leaned close before sucking her gum into her mouth with an impressive popping sound. "*Tutti fruiti*. Want a piece?"

Dalton *wanted* a taste—of Colleen. He almost gave into the impulse before he realized that eyes were everywhere. He *would* kiss her. But their first was not going to be for the entertainment of the Midas grapevine.

Taking the proffered bubble gum, Dalton slid into the passenger seat. He liked watching Colleen drive. Sure and relaxed, there was joy to her every movement. She loved being behind the wheel, and it showed. Today, he had the added bonus of the long expanse of bare legs.

Without a word about where they were headed, Colleen had cranked up the radio—classic rock—and headed east.

"Coming?" Colleen asked before closing her door.

Pulled from his thoughts, Dalton was out of the car a second later.

"What is this place?"

"Isn't it amazing?" Taking his hand, Colleen hurried to the water's edge. A wooden dock gently bobbed up and down. "My stepfather's family built it when he was in high school. As you can imagine, this time of year there is always somebody using it."

"It would be a crime not to. Yet nobody is here. How did we luck out?"

"The siblings alternate weeks—except for holidays which they spend together. This is Rick's week. He and Mom can't make it today. He was fine with us borrowing it for a few hours. I asked him not to tell my mother."

"She wouldn't approve?"

"No." Colleen tied her hair back at the base of her neck. "Mom has it in her head that you are a desperate criminal out to corrupt my virgin body."

The desperate criminal reference sailed over Dalton's head. He didn't think of himself that way. Neither did anyone he knew. Colleen's mother was the least of his worries. It was the other part that gave him pause. The way Colleen said it, Dalton was certain she was kidding. However— just to be safe—he had to ask.

"Virgin?"

Laughing, Colleen patted his arm. "Relax. I was a bit of a wild child. Not exactly indiscriminate. But I didn't wait around for a guy to put a ring on it."

Relieved, Dalton took a deep breath while he looked out at the lake. He had seen larger, grander, and more luxurious. But at this moment, he didn't think any of them could rival here and now. "What's the source?"

"I have no idea. I never asked because I don't care. I like to think of it as an Arizona miracle."

Colleen tossed her shirt onto the grass. The bra—and how she looked in it—almost made Dalton swallow his gum. Wisely, he spit it into his hand before she removed her shorts.

"There is a garbage can by the picnic table." With a flirty smile, Colleen pointed over his shoulder. "And thank you. It's been awhile since a man choked on his bubble gum because of me."

"It's been awhile for me, too." With perfect aim, Dalton tossed the gum into the barrel. "Maybe never. Do the bottoms match the top?"

"Is that akin to asking if the carpet matches the drapes?"

"No." Grinning, Dalton shook his head. "And they say men have dirty minds."

"*They* would be right." Unbuttoning her shorts, Colleen kept her eyes on his as she slowly lowered the zipper. "The bra is yellow, the panties are white, with red polka dots. As to my carpet and the drapes?"

"I already know the answer to that, Colleen."

She shimmied the shorts over her hips until they lay at her feet. In one motion, she kicked them to the side along with flip-flops.

"Do you now?"

"Yes. You're a redhead head to toe. Skin like that doesn't lie."

Playing catch up, Dalton pulled his shirt over his head. It did his ego good to see Colleen's eyes widen with appreciation. When she licked her lower lip, Dalton let out a groan. Damn. When he called Colleen, the plan hadn't been for things to go this way. He had promised her the truth, and Dalton thought it best if she had all the information before they had dinner with the Cline family. A swim had sounded like a great way to cool off.

Now, Dalton's mind traveled to thoughts of more than a quick dip and straightforward conversation.

"Last one in is a rotten egg."

"Really?" Dalton hadn't heard that one since he was a kid.

69

Sticking out her tongue, Colleen raced down the dock. At the last second, she turned.

"What are you waiting for, drummer boy?"

Not a damn thing. Removing his shoes and socks, Dalton tossed his jeans on the pile of clothing. In nothing but a pair of dark blue fitted boxers, he chased after Colleen.

"It isn't every day a woman is lucky enough to have a scantily clad rock star chase her down a dock."

Two feet away, Dalton asked, "Am I going to catch you?"

"Depends. How fast can you swim?"

Colleen dove into the water, Dalton right on her heels. He stayed underwater, marveling in the touch of the cool water sluicing over every inch of his body. As he broke the surface, pulling air into his lungs, he found Colleen just a few feet away.

"I need one of these," Dalton sighed, relaxing until he floated on his back—boneless.

Colleen mimicked him, her hand innocently brushing his. "A man-made lake outside of Midas?"

"A lake, period, smartass. I'm going to call my realtor and get her to start sorting out properties."

Hearing Colleen's less than delicate snort, Dalton frowned. "What?"

"I love how you casually talk about your realtor and sorting properties. We are from different worlds, Mr. Shaw."

Different. Dalton supposed it was true, yet he never thought of his life that way. It wasn't that he took the money and all it gave him for granted. More like it wasn't on his mind every day of every year the way it once was. When one was hungry, the feeling was different than when one was not. Did one appreciate the food any less? He didn't think so. It was simply a different kind of appreciation.

"Don't get me wrong," Colleen assured him. "I don't consider money a dirty word. One day I plan on having a nice chunk of it myself."

"Will you buy a lake?" This time, when Colleen's hand brushed his, he moved closer until the touch was no longer random.

"Perhaps. But first, I want a closet full of shoes."

Dalton grinned. "I can identify with a dream like that. Thank you for this, Colleen."

"It's a treat for me, too. This was one of those slow, catch up on paperwork afternoons. I hate paperwork. Damn."

Opening one eye, Dalton peeked Colleen's way. "Is something wrong?"

"I forgot to put on sunscreen. In another five minutes, my skin will go from light pink to lobster red."

"Do we need to go back?

"No. With a complexion like mine, I always have SPF gazillion in the glove compartment." She began swimming to shore. "Stay here. I won't be long."

Dalton gave Colleen a bit of a head start then leisurely followed. It gave him the chance to watch as she left the water. The view was spectacular. Her underwear wasn't designed for swimming, the result being an interesting see-through effect. His opinion of her ass didn't change. It was fine indeed.

"Need some help?" he asked as Colleen retrieved the sunscreen.

Lifting her arm, Colleen peered at him, her green eyes sparkling. "Rubbing lotion on me holds more appeal than the lake? I'm flattered."

"I doubt there is a straight man alive who would turn down a chance to touch you, Colleen."

"Well then." With a slow smile, Colleen handed him the bottle. "Touch away."

Dalton wasn't an untried boy, but neither was he made of stone. Was he capable of touching without taking a taste? Maybe. Now wasn't the time to test the theory.

71

"I don't have a condom with me."

Taking back the sunscreen, Colleen gave him a look of genuine regret. "As a modern, sexually active woman, I pride myself on always being prepared. But not today. Another time?"

"It feels inevitable."

That brought a big, bright, palpitation-inducing smile to Colleen's lips. When she turned away, Dalton raised a hand to his chest. He rubbed the spot just above his heart with a puzzled frown. *That was different.* He didn't have time to contemplate what it meant. If he couldn't touch Colleen, he could still enjoy the show.

"Mind if I watch?"

"Too bad that sounds kinkier than the reality." Colleen picked a patch of green grass to sit. She began at her feet and slowly worked up. "One of the ways you lured me away from work was the promise we would talk."

"Did I say that?" Dalton teased. At the moment, his interest was centered on the slope of Colleen's calf.

"Should I stop?" Colleen flipped shut the bottle's cap.

"No!" Hearing the tinge of desperation in his voice, Dalton cracked up. "You make me feel like a teenager. Can I talk you out of that bra?"

"If we were teenagers? Probably. But not today. I'll lotion up, you talk."

"Fair enough." Leaning back on his elbows, Dalton stretched out his long legs. "I wasn't a teenager, but I was just as reckless and stupid."

SEVEN YEARS EARLIER

"WHEN WE MAKE it big, our first investment will be a new van with a working air conditioner."

Sweat rolled freely down Dalton's face. The open window did nothing to ease the heat. It made it so they could breathe while they roasted.

72

"Amen, brother." Ashe drove through the Arizona afternoon wearing nothing but a pair of shorts. The old beach towel that protected him from the springs sticking out of the imitation leather seat was soaked with perspiration. His shaggy dark hair clung to the side of his sweat-drenched face. He had the seat pushed back as far as possible to accommodate his long legs.

In the back, their instruments were carefully packed beside four suitcases and some camping equipment. There were nights when the budget didn't include money for a motel room.

The Ryder Hart Band was at the end of a drive-through summer tour that had taken them through the Southwest. Their manager insisted this would be the last time. After their album hit in October, it would be first class all the way.

Dalton wasn't getting his hopes too high. The album was good—borderline great. The hard work was finally paying off. He joined Ryder and Ashe because they shared a vision. The sound they wanted to produce. The music they wanted to make. Yes, the name out front was Ryder's—something he and Ashe fully endorsed—but in every way they were equals. Writing partners, business partners. Most of all, friends.

To say it had been a struggle put it mildly. Three eighteen-year-olds with barely a pot to piss in. What they earned went toward expenses. Dalton sent as much as he could to his mother. Ryder did the same for his sister. Ashe came from money, but they cut him off when he chose music over conformity.

Slowly, they built a following—a reputation. When Ryder's sister joined the band last year, she brought an attitude and a killer lead guitar. *The Ryder Hart Band* had a unique sound that distinguished them from the pack. And Zoe was a big reason.

"Why don't you sweat?" Dalton asked the woman sitting cool, calm, and collected in the backseat.

"Heat—and the sweat that goes with it—is a state of mind," she answered with a deadpan expression. "I chose cool to be cool. It's as simple as that."

Zoe's long, blond hair sat atop her head in a messy, yet somehow put-together bun. The loose lilac-colored summer dress she wore brought out flecks of purple in her normally deep blue eyes. At eighteen, she had more poise—and snark—than a woman twice her age.

Zoe Hart was a beautiful young woman with talent to burn. Dalton loved her the same way he loved Ryder and Ashe. They were the family of his heart. However, those who didn't know the real Zoe found her intimidating as hell. Much to her delight.

"I hate you." His grin belying his words, Ryder lightly jabbed his sister in the arm. "Hand me a bottle of water before I melt away completely.

Zoe complied, tossing him a bottle from the cooler behind her seat. Ryder poured half the contents over his head. It was warm—the ice they started out with had melted about twenty miles ago. But their lead singer sighed with relief as the liquid ran down his face. He was a damn good-looking man. Dalton could admit that with no jealousy— or fear of denting his well-documented heterosexuality. Facts were facts. Ryder's face drew the ladies. And where there were pretty women, men followed. When they started out, it was a formula that put bodies in the bars where they played. They still came to see Ryder. But now, their music was as big a draw—if not bigger.

"Where are we playing tonight?" Ashe asked. In the rearview mirror, he sent Zoe a smile when she passed him a bottle of water.

"Midas," Dalton answered.

Ashe groaned. "Who is she?"

"I don't know what you're talking about." Dalton tried to look innocent, but he hadn't been able to pull that off for years.

"Shit, Dalton." Ryder kicked the back of his seat. "If you aren't bragging, there's something wrong with her."

"Even money says she's married." Zoe scoffed. She rarely cursed—it wasn't necessary. One raised eyebrow conveyed the contempt of a string of f-bombs.

Dalton could have protested, but these people knew him better than anyone. Why bother to lie?

"Bonnie and her friends were in the crowd last Saturday."

"That's where you went during our break. And after the last set."

"She had one of those older model Cadillac sedans. The backseat was huge. And, the air conditioner was in perfect working condition."

"I get it," Ashe nodded. "A bored housewife and sweat-free fuck."

"You never play a return engagement. Not with women," Ryder pointed out. "What makes Bonnie so special?"

"A big… personality?" Zoe left no doubt what she meant.

"Bonnie lives in Midas. A fact I didn't know when I mentioned the town was next on our itinerary. I know." Dalton held up a hand before anyone could comment. "It's my fault. When she asked, I didn't think."

"Men." Zoe shook her head. "There isn't enough blood in your body to power your dick and your brain at the same time."

"It isn't a big deal," Dalton shrugged.

Glancing down at his crotch, Zoe chuckled.

"*Bonnie* isn't a big deal. Get your mind off my dick."

Unfazed by the taunt, Zoe put on a pair of sunglasses, humming as she stared out the window. But the lurking smile rankled.

"Your sister is a pain in the ass."

"I know." Ryder's smile echoed Zoe's. "She's also right. The last thing we need is trouble. Groupies are one thing. Married groupies?"

"Trouble with a capital *Hell No*," Ashe chimed in.

"One more night, brothers and sister. Tomorrow we head back to civilization. What can happen in a little town like Midas?"

AFTER THREE MONTHS of endless shithole bars and music festivals,

The Thirsty Raven wasn't the worst place they had played. But as they set up their instruments, it was difficult to recall one that ranked lower.

"There is a gaping hole in the ladies' room. And no door on the stall. If I were so inclined, which I am not, I would have a scenic view of the parking lot while I peed."

"If you need to go, I'll stand guard outside the men's room. It's filthy, but the walls are solid."

"I appreciate the offer, Dalton, but I'll wait."

"Let me know if you change your mind."

It turned out to be a good crowd. A little rowdy, but the band had seen worse. During their last break, Dalton had stopped looking for Bonnie. The truth was, he was relieved. He had hoped she wouldn't show. It wasn't Ryder's warning or Zoe's ribbing. It was him. Women were fun. Sex was necessary. However, there was a reason why Dalton moved on after one night. He refused to make promises he wouldn't keep—and women expected promises.

Bonnie had a husband. That had been part of her appeal. It hadn't occurred to Dalton that she would want to see him again. And in her hometown? It would be a relief if he never saw the little brunette again.

Dalton took a deep breath of air. The crowd had thinned, making it easy to find a little peace before he had to go inside. The heat had lingered, giving the night an oppressive feel. He was ready to go home. Ready for a change. Only twenty-two, it felt like he had been on the road most of his life. It wasn't far from the truth. His mother had no interest in keeping track of her children. Where he wandered and what he did when he got there had been his choice for as long as he could remember.

Playing in pick-up bands had been easy. Nobody asked his age, so at fifteen, his weekends became devoted to music. It brought focus to his life—and a few bucks so he could help with the bills at home. A year later, he quit school. The drums became his life—and paid enough to keep him off the streets.

For the first time, Dalton's dreams had become a reality close enough to touch. When they were back in Los Angeles, they could scrap the old van and concentrate on taking the band to the next level.

"Dalton?"

Shit. Dalton recognized Bonnie's breathy voice. So much for clean and easy. He would have to man up and tell her the truth. One night was fun, two was not going to happen.

When Bonnie stepped out of the shadows, Dalton's planned friendly greeting vaporized from his brain.

"What the hell happened to your face?"

Dalton's words were harsh. When Bonnie flinched, he silently cursed himself. Taking her hand, he pulled her farther into the light. Carefully, Dalton took Bonnie's chin between his fingers, tipping her head.

"It's not as bad as it looks," Bonnie hiccupped.

"It looks like someone used your pretty face as a punching bag."

Bonnie's bottom lip had swelled to twice its size, the split crusted over with dried blood. Several bruises began to form on her face, the most prominent on her left cheek. In the morning, her right eye would be impossible to open.

"It doesn't matter. I wanted to see you before you left to let you know—" Bonnie's voice caught.

"Take it slow."

Dalton led Bonnie to an old log. Sitting next to her, he gently took her into his arms. He didn't consider himself a volatile man. It took a lot to set him off. But when it came to the abuse of women and children, Dalton's boiling point was low—minuscule. His first instinct was to protect the victim. His second—destroy the abuser.

"I needed to see you one last time." Dalton took a black bandana from his back pocket. He used it on stage to keep his hands dry, but it would do so Bonnie could wipe her tears. "That night in Winslow was very special to me. I wanted you to know that I'll never forget you."

77

"Does your husband hit you often?" It was a stupid question. One time was too many.

"Collier isn't a bad man. I know it's my fault. When he drinks, I say stupid things."

"Honey, there isn't anything you could say that would give that bastard the right to lay a finger on you."

"He's always sorry. Tomorrow he'll bring me flowers."

"That isn't going to happen."

"Why not?" Bonnie asked in a small, pitiful voice.

"Because tonight, I'm going to put him in the hospital."

"No!" When Dalton tried to stand, Bonnie clutched at his arm. "He'll hurt you. Collier was captain of his college boxing team."

Now instead of beating up on other over-privileged idiots, Collier pounded on his wife. And nobody stopped him. What about her family? Or his? They had to know.

"I can take care of myself."

"I—"

"Jesus, Bonnie. I look the other way when you go slumming out of town. But this is unacceptable. A musician? What the fuck?"

"Collier!" Bonnie cringed. "It isn't how it looks."

Collier. The name suited him, Dalton thought. Tall, blond, and arrogant. He looked trim, but he must have outweighed his wife by at least seventy pounds. Standing, Dalton planted his feet in front of Bonnie's cowering figure.

"Make a move toward her and I will crush you."

Crossing his arms, Collier smirked. "Nice, Bonnie. You found yourself a tough guy. But is he tough enough to take down me *and* my friends?"

Out of the shadows stepped two men. As they flanked Collier, Dalton thought that if those thugs were his friends, Dalton was next in line to the

British throne. There was no doubt who they were. Hired muscle. It was their job to make certain Collier didn't muss a single strand of his perfectly styled hair.

"Typical," Dalton spat. "You beat your wife. Why not? She can't fight back. I bet your daddy fixed all those fancy boxing matches of yours. He knew you couldn't win a fair fight. And so does everyone else."

Taunting Collier into losing his cool turned out to be easier than Dalton expected. Apparently, that daddy dig hit close to home.

"You think you can take me down? Give it your best shot."

"Mr. Langley," one of the bruisers put a hand on Collier's arm. "I don't think this is a good idea."

Shaking him off, Collier snarled, "You aren't paid to think, Wilcox. I'm warning you, if you want to keep your job, do not interfere. Understood?"

Wilcox and the other man exchanged looks. With identical shrugs, they stepped back.

His entire life, if he wanted something, Dalton had to fight for it. Sometimes with his fists. Sometimes with his brains. Either way, his skills were honed by years of hard living—something Collier would never understand. Where Dalton came from, he didn't survive unless he learned to fight dirty. With one or two blows, he could have ended the fight before it began. However, that would have been too easy. Collier thought he would win because he was socially, intellectually, and physically the better man. Dalton didn't give a shit about society. When it came to brains and brawn, he was about to teach Collier a lesson he would never forget.

Collier put up his fists as though waiting for the opening bell. Mistake number one. The Marquis of Queensbury had no place in this fight. Dalton easily dodged the first punch, countering with one of his own to Collier's mid-section. He followed with a quick jab to his chin, and Collier hit the ground like a ton of bricks.

"Fucking glass jaw," Wilcox muttered.

Disappointed that it was over so quickly, Dalton turned away in disgust. He wanted to do some damage, but he didn't hit a man who was down for the count.

"Do you want me to take you someplace?" Dalton asked a weeping Bonnie. He didn't know who her tears were for, and he didn't care. All Dalton wanted was to get out of this crazy town as quickly as possible.

"Where would I go?" Bonnie asked, genuinely puzzled. "Collier is my husband. I live with him."

Dalton wasn't surprised by Bonnie's answer. She hadn't left Collier before. Why would tonight be any different? He gave her an option. She turned him down. It was no longer any of his business.

"Watch out!"

Instinct and quick reflexes were all that saved Dalton from a smashed skull. He dove to his right, before rolling to his feet. As it was, Collier managed to clip Dalton's shoulder with the fist-sized rock.

"You got lucky, asshole. You won't take me down again."

"This won't end well." Slightly crouched, Dalton waited for Collier to make his move. "Walk away while you still can."

"Hey, punk. Are you feeling lucky? Because that's the only way you're getting past me again."

Dalton didn't know if Collier had purposely paraphrased Clint Eastwood. Time wasn't on his side, or he would have called the idiot out. But Collier chose that moment to swing. Dalton went low, swung his foot around, and took the other man's legs out from under him. The air knocked out of him, he lay on his back gasping for air.

Dalton was pissed off by the entire situation—especially Bonnie who was enjoying the fight way too much for a woman who just minutes earlier had been a weeping, cowering, traumatized mess. Her eyes seemed to glow with a sick kind of excitement. He didn't know what the hell was going on there.

Dusting off his jeans, Dalton winced. Damn, his shoulder had taken a

80

harder hit than he realized. All he could think was that it better not fuck up his drumming. He had already put Collier and Bonnie in his rearview mirror. As far as Dalton was concerned, it was over. Case closed.

Unfortunately, Collier had other ideas. Humiliated. Taken down by a man he viewed as inferior in every way. He needed to vent his frustration and rise from his humiliation. Reaching for the only weapon he had, Collier slung the rock at Dalton.

Dalton wheeled around seconds after the rock sailed past his head. "Are you fucking kidding me?"

Seeing red, Dalton lost every ounce of cool he possessed. It was the moment that changed his young life forever.

PRESENT DAY

"I BEAT THE shit out of him. I like to think I would have stopped at that, but I'll never know for sure. Collier's muscle men pulled me off before I could do permanent damage."

"Do you honestly think you would have killed him?" Colleen asked. She sat with her arms wrapped around her pulled-in knees, her cheek resting on top.

"Maybe."

"That is total bullshit." Colleen didn't move, but her eyes narrowed. "You had your chance to take him out. Twice. You barely did more than dirty his rich-boy clothes. The third time you vented. It's understandable. But murder? Please."

"My fists punching the smug expression off Collier's face felt damn good."

"I'll bet." Colleen shook her head. "I know Collier. I'm afraid the smug came back. Tenfold."

"He came to court. Everyday. Smirking."

"You were railroaded."

"I was guilty."

Colleen turned her head until she looked out on the lake.

"Money can do so much good—in the right hands. Collier's father used his to make certain you paid for his son's crime." She frowned. "It's like a slight of hand trick. The magician draws the attention of his audience one way, distracting from what is really happening. That is what Judge Langley did."

"I was the distraction?"

"Exactly. Collier beat his wife. He started the fight. When you tried to walk away, he found a way to keep it going. In a world not ruled by Langley power and money, you wouldn't have been charged, let alone convicted. I read the newspaper stories. They played up the fact that you didn't have a scratch on you while Collier looked like he had been hit by a large, fast-moving truck."

Dalton remembered. His lawyer had tried his best to counter the accusations, but the three witnesses backed up Collier's side of the story. It was his word against theirs. When Bonnie took the stand, she claimed Dalton had beaten her because she refused to sleep with him.

"By the end of that trial, Collier and Bonnie came off as the perfect couple. You were the evil outsider trying to destroy their love." Colleen made a gagging sound. "When I read that, I almost lost my dinner."

"How do you know it wasn't the truth?"

"Living in Midas all these years, I know Collier's and Bonnie's reputations."

"Ah." Dalton was deciding how to take that when Colleen laughed.

"Did you expect me to proclaim my absolute faith in you? We've known each other for less than forty-eight hours, Dalton. I think you are a good guy. But I don't *know* it."

The good guy label was tough for Dalton. He wanted to do the right thing. He lived his life in a way he hoped would have made his mentor—Silas Freed—proud. However, *good* equated boring. He pictured a rocking chair and Saturday nights watching PBS and drinking hot cocoa. Someday. Maybe. Not now. He certainly didn't want Colleen to think of him that way.

As if reading his mind, Colleen met his gaze. What he saw took his breath away. That was not the look a woman gave a man she found boring.

"You are sexy as hell, Dalton Shaw. I don't have to know you to sleep with you. Or trust you. However…"

"Yes?" As far as Dalton was concerned, Colleen could have stopped with *sexy as hell*.

"When we sleep together—"

"When, not if?"

"When we sleep together," Colleen continued as though he hadn't interrupted. "I want to trust you enough to let go completely."

"How do we get there?"

"Tell me something nobody else knows."

There wasn't much to tell. Ryder, Ashe, and Zoe knew him inside and out. Long hours together on the road with nothing to do but talk. They shared so much of themselves. Nobody knew him better. But everyone had their secrets. Little things they kept to themselves. Dalton had a few. There was one—exactly the kind of thing Colleen meant. It wasn't an earthshaking revelation. It wouldn't destroy him if it hit the press. Only one other person knew, and he was dead. If he told Colleen.

"I would never tell another soul."

Dalton had no reason to believe Colleen. Yet, for some reason, he did. Meeting her emerald gaze, he felt something indefinable pass between them. It was a moment, so brief it might not have happened. Dalton felt it and so did Colleen. He kept his eyes locked with hers.

"My first night in the state penitentiary. After the lights were out. When I knew without a doubt, this was my new reality. I cried myself to sleep."

Silently, Colleen closed the distance between them, taking him in her arms. Dalton saw the sheen of tears in her eyes.

"I survived."

"Yes, you did." Colleen brushed her lips across his cheek. "But it's wrong that you had to."

CHAPTER EIGHT

COLLEEN SOMETIMES WONDERED if her feelings about Midas and the people who lived there were unjustly skewed in a negative manner. When her mother remarried—for the first time—moving them from Kansas, Colleen had not been happy. Kansas hadn't been perfect, but leaving meant breaking with friends she had known all her life. Starting over. Her mindset hadn't been the best.

Arizona wasn't a bad place. It boasted the Grand Canyon, for Christ's sake. But they didn't settle in Phoenix. Or Albuquerque. Or any place resembling civilization. For a girl just entering her teens, it felt like a barren desert. Socially, Colleen found her niche. Academically, she did fine. But she never shook the idea that there was something not quite right about Midas.

After listening to Dalton's story, Colleen would never again question that feeling. Judge Manfred T. Langley had used his fortune, his undue influence, and his oppressive power to cover up for his worthless son. In the process, he blithely did his best to ruin a life. It was never about Dalton. He could have been anyone. The goal was to maintain the family's lustrous public image. Collier was proof positive that it was all a money-fortified veneer.

Colleen couldn't help but wonder how Judge Langley continued to clean up his son's messes. It had to be a full-time job—for more than one person. Their world was small, but social media made it difficult to keep anything secret. Perhaps Collier had settled down. Colleen doubted it. More likely, he made his mistakes close to home, where Daddy continued to sweep them away.

After taking another quick swim, Colleen and Dalton had headed back to Midas. On the drive back, he mentioned the dinner invitation from Tolliver Cline.

"Do you know the family?"

"I knew Tolliver's daughter—a little. Rita was a year ahead of me in school. I have a nodding acquaintance with the rest of the family."

"I thought everybody hung out in small towns."

"This is Midas, not Mayberry, Dalton. The divides are deep and rarely crossed. Tolliver runs a very successful landscaping business. The northsiders keep him busy. And from what I understand, well compensated. In fact, I didn't think he did any of the physical labor anymore. He has a big crew that takes care of that."

"Tol seemed like a nice guy. Friendly."

"I suppose it depends on who you are. My mother does his wife's hair. I work on the family's transportation. But we do not socialize."

"It's that bad?"

Dalton looked surprised. Colleen had to remind herself that he was an outsider. It was hard to grasp the way things worked when he hadn't lived here as long as she had.

"Most residents wouldn't call it good or bad. It just is."

"What do you call it?"

"Massively screwed up." Colleen turned the T-Bird onto her street. "My mother likes Midas. As she puts it, every town has its little quirks."

"Your mother has an interesting way of looking at things."

"Tell me about it." Like Midas, her mother was hard to explain. "I love her, but I will never understand her. Naturally, that goes both ways. We've learned to live with our differences. Mostly."

"Families are tricky."

"You still haven't heard from your brother-in-law?"

While they swam, Dalton had given Colleen an overview of why he was in Midas. She had always wished for a sibling. Now, she wondered if she had been the lucky one. The life of an only child could be lonely, but there was nobody to surprise her with a knife in the back. Tricky. And terrifyingly treacherous.

Dalton glanced at his phone, then sighed. "It doesn't make any sense. If I didn't know any better, I would think Maggie hadn't passed on my message."

Colleen didn't want to open a bigger rift between brother and sister, but she had to ask. "Is that a possibility?"

"Not long ago, I would have said no. Maggie is too fond of the money I send her every month. But now—after speaking to her—I don't know."

Pulling to a stop outside her apartment building, Colleen grabbed her bag from the backseat.

"I say screw the two of them. But I don't have the history or the blood ties."

Dalton ran a hand through his short, dark hair. "That whole blood is thicker than water thing? In my case, it's pretty much bullshit."

"It's sad, I know. But you're lucky. You found your real family."

If she were ever lucky enough to meet the members of Dalton's band, Colleen would have her little fangirl moment. Then, she would thank them. They had been there at the critical times in Dalton's life. When he was young and needed something solid to anchor himself. Through the lean years when they could have let ego and petty arguments tear them apart.

When it all could have fallen apart, they stood by him. The trial. His time in prison. According to Dalton, they visited every week. Sometimes together, sometimes individually. *Every week.* Without fail. When he was paroled, his place with the band was there just as promised. Colleen had always admired their music. Now, *The Ryder Hart Band* was more than four people standing on a stage. Because of Dalton, they were real people. Good and admirable.

"I'll pick you up about quarter to seven."

With a nod, Colleen handed Dalton the car keys, then laughed.

"You've rented my car, but you're rarely behind the wheel."

"I like watching you drive."

"The lotion, now the driving. Is this watching thing a fetish you want to tell me about?"

"If it's a fetish, it just started." Smiling, Dalton ran a hand up her arm. "Blame yourself."

"That *should* be creepy."

"But?"

"I guess I like to be watched—by you."

Colleen knew the kiss was coming. It had seemed inevitable from the moment they met. Often, that much anticipation was not a good thing. It turned out to be one of those rare instances when reality actually exceeded anticipation.

Dalton's strong arms pulled her close, his eyes on her lips. Colleen sighed as he brushed his mouth across hers.

"Harder," she demanded.

Instead, Dalton smiled, kissing her lightly. Colleen wound her arms around his neck. Her fingers burrowed into the soft strands of his hair, trying her best to tug him closer.

"Patience. I want to take my time." Dalton tasted her, his tongue tracing the outline of her mouth.

"Tease," she said accusingly, but Colleen had to admit, there was something to be said for Dalton's version of slow and sweet.

Again and again, until Colleen lost track. Dalton's feathered kisses left her wanting more while heightening her senses. She became aware of his hands on her back. On tiptoe, her bare thighs brushed against his, the denim of his jeans impossibly soft. Convinced that Dalton wouldn't alter the pace, she decided to stop worrying and enjoy. That was the moment his arms tightened, and everything changed.

Dalton's mouth opened over hers, voraciously taking. Happy to oblige, Colleen twined her legs around his hips and held on for a wild ride. Before she knew what had happened, her back was pressed against the car, Dalton's body rubbing deliciously against her front.

"You taste so damn good," Dalton murmured.

"No," Colleen sighed when he licked her neck. "It's you."

In truth, it was the combination. Dalton and Colleen. Fine on their own. Together? Spectacular. Colleen couldn't get enough of him. Dalton seemed to feel the same. She had no idea how long the kiss lasted. Or how they refrained from ripping off their clothes. It wasn't modesty—not on her part. If it weren't for Dalton coming to his senses, who knew how it would have ended.

"I didn't expect that kiss to get so out of hand," Dalton said, his breath ragged.

Feeling almost tipsy, Colleen leaned against him for support. She knew her legs worked, remembering how was going to take a little while. Colleen knew if she didn't move soon, she was going to kiss him again. If she did that, the only place they would end up was the bed in her apartment.

"Dinner. Remember?"

"Vaguely." Dalton rested his forehead against hers. "I'll leave. Unless you need me to wash your back."

"I need you to..." There were so many choices. Colleen decided to pick responsible adult. "Go to your motel room. Get cleaned up."

Colleen pushed Dalton into the driver's seat. Before she could close the door, he took her hand. The heat in his gaze had cooled to a warmth that made her stomach do a slow roll.

"Thank you for today."

"Thank you for trusting me."

When Dalton brushed his lips against her hand, Colleen felt her heart take a funny leap. *First her stomach, now her heart?* Either there was an odd strain of the flu going around or she was on the brink of something dangerous.

Standing back, Colleen waved as Dalton pulled the T-Bird away from the curb. She had to remind herself—and continue to do so—that Dalton was fun and games. The second she forgot? The instant she let him become more? Colleen refused to answer those tricky questions.

The solution was simply. Don't let it happen.

FOR A SMALL town, Midas had more twists and turns than Stephen King at his finest. It wasn't the roads—they were pretty straightforward. It was the people. The ins and outs of a social and financial hierarchy that needed a program to keep track of the players and their roles.

When he accepted Tolliver Cline's dinner invitation, Dalton thought he would be eating with a gardener. While he appreciated a man who was self-made, finding out Tolliver was the head of a multi-million-dollar business changed the dynamics of the evening. It made him question the man's motives. What did he want? And what the hell did it have to do with Dalton?

"Something odd is going on in Midas."

"That isn't news to me," Colleen smoothed the skirt of her dress. A very pretty pastel green dress that showed off her spectacular legs. "Midas is weird. Last summer they organized a Peach Festival."

Dalton waited for more information. It didn't come. "Is there a punch line I'm missing?"

"Nobody grows peaches in Midas. Not enough to warrant a festival." Colleen shook her head. "I know that Area 51 is in New Mexico. *I* think the aliens landed here."

"It's a theory. What do you say we put it aside for now?" Teasingly, Dalton poked Colleen on the arm. "Unless there's something you want to tell me?"

"Red-blooded human being all the way." Colleen took his hand, placing it in the interesting vicinity of her heart. An inch higher and he would be sliding into second base.

It took a dose of willpower, but Dalton manned up, returning his hand to the steering wheel.

"No argument here," he said, clearing his throat.

Colleen gave a delighted chuckle. "What were you saying?"

Dalton thought about it. He knew there was a stream of thought in there somewhere. Then it clicked. "Why is anybody in this town interested in me?"

"Well..."

Dalton shot Colleen a grin. "Besides you. If I were going to cause trouble, I would have done it long ago. A year after I was released, we had the number one album in the country. My name suddenly meant something. I could have sued for a myriad of reasons. Judge Langley would have topped a long, illustrious list of defendants."

"Why didn't you?"

"Besides the fact that I wanted to forget it ever happened?"

"That's reason enough," Colleen agreed.

She placed a comforting hand on his leg. It was crazy. A minute ago, their exchange was filled with teasing innuendo. When Dalton touched Colleen, his thoughts had been filled with how the weight of her breast would feel in his hand. There was nothing sexual about Colleen rubbing his thigh. It warmed his heart, not his libido. The dichotomy intrigued him. As did the woman.

"I had my friends to consider. The publicity involved in a messy legal battle was not what we were looking for. We made a pact. *The Ryder Hart Band* was about the music. Period. We kept our interviews to a minimum and then, we only spoke about the band. Our private lives remained exactly that."

"In this day and age. With so many gossip sites and twenty-four-hour news cycles to fill, I don't know how you've done it."

"It's simple. Unity. If none of us talks—no matter the provocation—the story dies. Fire needs oxygen, Colleen."

"The gossip dies from suffocation? Kind of a grisly image." Colleen rubbed her hands together, a diabolically gleeful smile on her lips. "I like

90

it."

That made Dalton beam like a proud brother. "Zoe would love you."

"Take the next left," Colleen instructed.

They traveled east, as Tolliver instructed him that morning. Colleen hadn't hesitated when Dalton asked if she knew the way. She told him that she might not know where everyone in Midas lived, but she knew where the Cline family lived. About ten years ago, they built their house from the ground up. The construction had taken almost two years, dominating coffee klatch conversations. Which naturally filtered to Colleen via her mother. No matter how hard she tried, there was no avoiding town gossip. Unless she cut her mother out of her life. Tempting at times, that was not going to happen.

"Tolliver dangled a big, juicy carrot when he asked us to dinner. Why has my return put the judge's panties in a twist? However, he didn't mention his agenda. A man with money who made it clear he was not a fan of the Langley family does not casually host a stranger for the evening."

"Unless he wants something." Colleen guided him through the next turn. "I agree. The machinations between factions in Midas would make Richard III look like a piker."

Putting on the brakes, Dalton pulled the car to a stop on the side of the road.

"What?" Colleen asked.

"Exactly." He shifted into park. "What are we doing? This isn't my home turf, but why should I play by their rules? Langley. Cline. Am I their pawn? Is it about them or me? And why the hell should I care?"

"Curiosity?"

Frustrated, Dalton let out a puff of air. "Isn't there a cliché about that?"

"I know. The cat dies every time. Then makes a miraculous recovery."

"He does?" Dalton didn't remember that part but was willing to take Colleen's word for it.

"Knowledge is power, my friend—even if it's a one-sided version."

"Fair enough." Dalton set the car in motion. "Just in case, I let Ryder know where we'll be."

"Good idea. A little paranoia never hurts."

As they rounded the next curve, Tolliver Cline's house came into view. Dalton let out a whistle. He hadn't known what to expect, but this was a surprise. It rivaled Judge Langley's home for size and scope. The ostentatious design didn't seem to fit the man he met that morning. Dalton didn't envy the person who had the job of washing the windows. Glass lined every one of the three levels. The view wasn't much. A few trees and a thirsty-looking field. To the side, a backhoe sat in front of a rickety old shed.

"Soon to be a swimming pool. Covered, if the grapevine has it right— which it usually does."

Dalton turned off the engine. Wooden stakes and long lengths of string stretched out, encompassing most of the field. From the look of the outline, the pool would be huge. "I guess if you want to put down roots in the middle of nowhere, you might as well be comfortable."

"Is this comfort?" Colleen asked as he helped her from the car. "Not for me. I couldn't relax inside that gilded airplane hangar."

"That's it," Dalton laughed. "I knew it reminded me of something."

Before he could use the gold gargoyle knocker, the door swung open.

"Welcome."

As he had that morning, Tolliver held out his hand to Dalton. That was the only similarity. He wouldn't have recognized their smartly dressed host. Precisely creased trousers had replaced the worn jeans. His shirt was silk instead of cotton. And he smelled like French cologne, not dirt and grass clippings. This man wasn't Tol, the gardener. He was a Tolliver, head to toe.

Dalton understood his feelings weren't logical. He wasn't exactly dressed like a bum. His custom-made shoes, tailored slacks, and linen shirt cost more than his first car. Judging a man on what he wore—expensive or bargain basement—wasn't normally how Dalton rolled. Something felt off. Until he knew what was on Tolliver's mind, it would be impossible for him to view his host with an unjaundiced eye.

As though sensing his reticence, Colleen drew Tolliver's attention her way. She took the man's hand, shaking it, her smile warm.

"Hello, Mr. Cline. Thank you for inviting me."

"It is something we should have done long ago. Come," Tolliver smiled back. "My daughter and her husband are joining us tonight. She's looking forward to catching up with you."

Dalton saw the flash of surprise in Colleen's eyes. After what she had told him, he didn't blame her. Rita hadn't been her friend. They went to the same school, different years, and according to Colleen, did not socialize.

"I can hardly wait," Colleen said, recovering quickly.

Over Tolliver's shoulder, Colleen sent Dalton a, *I have no idea what is going on*, look. The one he sent back echoed hers. The evening had turned from odd to strange. Could bizarre be far behind?

They followed Tolliver through the foyer. Dalton didn't know much about such things, but he supposed the area would be termed *grand*. The ceilings were high, the floors marble and highly polished. Colleen's high heels clicked with each step. It was the only sound in the eerily quiet room.

"We are having drinks in the salon. It's a small gathering. Family and a few friends. I hope that's all right with you."

"If we said it wasn't?"

It was all Dalton could do not to laugh. Loudly. Between Colleen's unexpectedly frank question and the expression on Tolliver's face, the moment had a farcical quality that made him sputter, then cough. He didn't try to hide his grin.

Not that it mattered. Tolliver's attention was focused on Colleen. To the man's credit, he managed to smile politely, though it didn't quite reach his dark eyes. Instead, they narrowed, as though reassessing Colleen. He had found out something Dalton already knew. She wasn't simply the town mechanic—albeit an attractive one. Brains first, beauty second.

"I suppose my question was a trifle redundant."

"No," Colleen laid a conciliatory hand on Tolliver's arm. "I have the habit of blurting out the first thing that pops into my head—no matter how rude. I apologize."

"Not at all." Placated, Tolliver's smile warmed. He took Colleen's hand, placing it in the crook of his elbow, motioning for Dalton to follow.

Tolliver hadn't lied. The number of people waiting in the salon was not large. He introduced Dalton and Colleen to his wife. Mandy Cline was a striking woman. Tall, her posture almost regal, she wore her dark hair in a perfectly coifed French twist. Her light blue dress—in a lightweight summer silk—was simple but elegant.

"I was so pleased when Tolliver told me he had invited you." She offered them a choice of drinks. Colleen took the white wine, Dalton an iced tea, since he was driving. The truth was, he wanted to keep his faculties sharp. Normally, he had no problem handling a drink or two. But tonight, he wasn't taking any chances.

Mandy took over as hostess, introducing them to the rest of the guests. Rita and her husband, Brock Bentley. State Senator Rand Charles and his wife, Pearl. And finally, two friends who lived and had businesses in Phoenix. Delbert Trent and Sarah Lloyd.

Dalton didn't know what to make of the group. If they were simply a group of old friends getting together, why invite him? Or Colleen? If there were something else going on—if they had gathered for his benefit—Dalton was at a complete loss. He made it through cocktails, though small talk was not his strong suit. When they were seated at the long, formal dining room table, laid out with expensive china and silver, Dalton's patience began to fray. This was crazy. He preferred to put his cards on the table. Colleen hadn't been afraid to say what was on her mind. Neither was he. Seated to Mandy's right, Dalton turned to his hostess.

"Why are we here?"

"I'm sorry," In the middle of taking a bite of perfectly rare beef tenderloin, Mandy looked taken aback. "What do you mean?"

"I mean, when your husband invited me to dinner, I expected something more low key. A family dinner. Roast chicken and mashed potatoes?" Dalton looked down the table at Tolliver. "Don't get me wrong, the food is delicious. It's the trappings that have me confused."

"You're right, Dalton," Tolliver dabbed the corner of his mouth with his linen napkin. "My motive was not completely innocent."

Dalton felt a chill run down his spine. For good measure, it turned around, retracing its path.

"Our meeting wasn't accidental." Dalton made it a statement, not a question. "You were waiting for me."

"I had heard you were in town."

"There was no way you could know I would go for a run. Or the direction I would take." This time, the chill jumped from Dalton's spine, invading his entire body. "You had me watched?"

"Don't take it the wrong way," Tolliver soothed. "You make it sound nefarious when it was anything but. If you let me explain, it will all make sense."

"Maybe. In your world. Not mine." Across the table, Dalton met Colleen's gaze. Silently, they exchanged understanding looks. She calmly set her napkin on the table. Together they started to get to their feet.

"Please." Mandy placed a hand on Colleen's, wisely directing her appeal away from Dalton. "Listen to what Tolliver has to say. If you still want to leave, we won't detain you."

Detain? Dalton was certain it sounded more *film noir* than intended. This wasn't a Hollywood flick. Still, if Colleen had given him the signal, he would have kept moving. With a shrug, she sat down. He followed suit

"Are you sure?" Dalton asked her.

"You deserve some answers." Deliberately, Colleen took her napkin, placing it on her lap. "And I'm nosy."

The whole time, she held Dalton's gaze. He saw the twinkle and relaxed—slightly. *Okay*, he told her with his eyes. *You asked for it.* Inexplicably, Colleen's lips twitched. She found humor in the situation. Dalton wasn't quite there. However, realizing how she felt—that Colleen wasn't concerned—helped the tension seep from his shoulders. When she winked, Dalton almost smiled.

Waiting a beat, he turned to Tolliver. "You're on."

"I had hoped to wait until we had finished this excellent meal before broaching this very serious subject."

"I can eat and listen." That said, Dalton kept his hands in his lap. Unconsciously, his fingers drummed a beat on the side of his leg.

"Will you indulge me for a few minutes? There is a bit of a backstory."

"There always is." This bit of snarky irony came from Colleen.

Finally, Dalton smiled. The woman was amazing. If this were a painting, she would look right at home with the hand-painted porcelain and antique silver. To the manor born. However, she wasn't one of them. There wasn't a pretentious bone in Colleen McNamara's body. She was smart. Sassy. Sexy. And would look a person in the eye, telling it like it was. No, she didn't belong here. Thank God.

"If you're going to tell your tale, Tolliver, you might as well tell it all."

Around them, the rest of the guests continued with their meal, though it was clear their attention was focused on their host, not the creamed peas and tiny onions. Taking a sip of wine, Tolliver began.

"Midas has always been my home. Manfred Langley Senior gave me my first job. Junior attended a Boston boarding school, acquiring the polish his father never had but always coveted."

Dalton wanted answers, not an HBO docudrama. But, in spite of himself, he was interested.

"The Langley money came from railroads?"

"Among other things," snorted the senator.

"No one has ever proved those rumors, Rand," his wife reminded him.

"Drugs. Prostitution. Lord knows what else," Tolliver nodded. "But as Pearl pointed out, that is only speculation. Tonight, we are dealing in facts. I made my money working for men—and women—like Langley. My dream was to be one of them. And I was. We bought a house behind that brick wall. We socialized with our neighbors. Though the Langleys always held themselves apart, we were friendly."

"What changed?" Dalton asked.

"It wasn't one thing. I," Tolliver smiled at his wife, the love he felt right there for all to see. "We began to realize that we didn't belong. Part of it was political—a big part. I'm ashamed that it took us so long. But when it became clear that Manfred Junior believed his family was above the law, it was the last straw."

"I wish we could have helped you," Mandy said to Dalton. "Like many in this town, we believed the lies. Judge Langley paid off a lot of people to make those lies stick. Some people still believe you were guilty."

"You don't?" Before, Dalton had been mildly interested. Now, they had his full attention.

"The bastard bragged about it," Tolliver shook his head. "Not right away. It was a few years after you were convicted. He was damn proud of himself. *Saved the family name*, was how he put it. You were nobody. Why shouldn't you take the fall?"

"I could give him a few reasons," Dalton ground out. This wasn't news, but it rankled to hear it. Not proof, but as close as he would get.

"That was when we decided to sell that house and build a home."

"You were born here, I understand that. Why did you stay in Midas?" Colleen didn't look puzzled, she looked mystified. "You could live anywhere."

"I want to make my town better, Colleen." Seeing the doubt on her face, he nodded. "I know it doesn't seem that way. But change takes time. My money is new. That was easy. Power takes longer. With the help of some good friends, we're making progress."

"Not that I can see."

"I understand your frustration. This fall, we finally have some important initiatives on the ballot. They have a good chance of passing. But to make a big move, we need the right people representing us." Tolliver's gaze shifted from Colleen to Dalton. "That's where you come in."

"Me?" Dalton was certain he misheard.

"Don't try to suck Dalton into your convoluted push for power." Colleen dropped her good guest persona. In its place, the protective friend came out swinging. "I have lived in Midas for close to half my life. Do we know each other? Do we?" she asked Tolliver's daughter, Rita. The woman, startled that Colleen had suddenly dragged her into the fray, opened her mouth, but nothing came out. Colleen sent Tolliver a satisfied nod. "There's your answer. No. Because we live in the same town, but our worlds never meet. You can pontificate all you want about working for the good of Midas. It's a load of crap."

As Colleen spoke, Tolliver's mouth tightened. Dalton waited for his response, ready to shoot him down if he dared to unload on Colleen for telling nothing but the truth. Breathing deeply, Tolliver laid his hands on the table as though steadying his emotions. When he spoke, his voice was steady and relatively calm.

"You are welcome to your opinion, Colleen. You're wrong, but I refuse to defend myself in my own home."

"We won't stay for dessert," Dalton said, stating the obvious. "Finish what you have to say; you won't get another chance."

"Very well. Here is the bottom line. Next year, Collier Langley will announce his candidacy for the U.S. Senate. The incumbent is set to retire. With his father's money and power behind him, we believe his chances are good."

"You think I can stop him?" Dalton kept his expression neutral.

"Yes." Tolliver nodded. The others at the table, mostly silent until now, murmured their agreement. "Use your celebrity, and your story, to stop this idiocy in its tracks."

"No." Calmly, Dalton rose to his feet. Walking around the table, he ignored the expressions that ranged from startled, to amazed and appalled. He helped Colleen from her chair. "Ready to go?"

"Yes. Please."

"Wait." Tolliver rushed after them. "At least let me tell you our plan."

Dalton turned—slowly. Proving he wasn't stupid, Tolliver took a step back. Then took two more.

"I know what it's like to be screwed over by a rich man from Midas. Never again."

Taking Colleen's hand, Dalton exited the house. He took a deep, cleansing breath.

"It smells different out here."

"True," Colleen didn't let him linger on the porch. "But the scent of bullshit lingers. Let's open the windows, drive fast, and air ourselves out."

Getting behind the wheel, Dalton waited until Colleen buckled her seatbelt. Snaking his arm around her waist, he kissed her. Long and deep, he savored her taste. Like no one else. Sweet and spicy and irresistible.

"Let's get out of here."

They rode in silence, the wind whipping around them—warm yet refreshing. Reaching for Colleen, he threaded his fingers through hers. What would she say if he kept driving? Out of Midas. All the way to Los Angeles. Dalton was tempted to find out.

"You aren't going to let Collier Langley get elected."

"Not in this lifetime or any other."

"Good."

Raising Colleen's hand to his lips, Dalton took his eyes off the road long enough to meet her emerald gaze. The connection was brief, but he saw all he needed. In only a few days, Colleen knew him well enough to understand what Tolliver and his crew never would. Dalton would have his revenge. But on his own terms.

CHAPTER NINE

Dalton drove blind, his brain trying to process a load of new information while he decided what to do about it. Because he was going to do something. The important thing was not to jump without looking up, down, sideways, and back again. He relied on Colleen to tell him when to turn right, left or not at all.

"Stop."

Surprised, Dalton looked around. They were at the lake. Smiling, he let the air out of his lungs, wondering how long he had gone without breathing properly.

"You approve?" Colleen asked.

"Completely."

"Good." She opened her door. "There is a blanket in the trunk. And while you're at it, grab the cooler."

"Cooler?" Intrigued, Dalton inserted the car key into the lock, raising the trunk to peer inside. He didn't know when Colleen had slipped it in, but next to a thick, light blue blanket, sat a cooler. "You are full of surprises."

"This way." Removing her shoes, Colleen crooked her finger. "That surprise is only the beginning.

Dalton was happy to follow. The cooler wasn't large, but it had quite a heft. He couldn't wait to find out what treasures Colleen had packed inside.

The lake looked different in the day's waning light. In the glow of the setting sun, the oasis had turned from magical to mysterious. Shadows crept toward its shores. The water sparkled as though stars had embedded themselves in the depths. It calmed Dalton's mind. At the same time, the woman next to him heated his blood.

"I was afraid Mom and Rick might be here."

"What if they were?"

"I would have told you to turn the car around. Immediately."

Dalton didn't understand the dynamics between a mother and daughter. His situation—his mother and sister—was so far from the norm he wouldn't begin to judge. Or compare it to Colleen's. However, he couldn't help but wonder. Obviously, she loved her mother. Yet they seemed to be at odds about... everything.

"Your mother," he said, handing her the blanket.

"Where?" Colleen's head whipped around.

Her reaction was so comically over the top, Dalton had to laugh.

"I was going to say, your mother sounds like a complicated woman."

Colleen spread the blanket on the same grassy patch where they lay that afternoon.

"That's putting it mildly. Mom means well. And we muddle through. I think we'll be happier when I'm in a different zip code."

Setting down the cooler, Dalton followed Colleen's lead, taking off his shoes and socks. Without thinking, he automatically put them, and Colleen's sandals, in a neat row on the picnic table, smiling when he heard her laugh.

"I love my shoes," he admitted. Dalton took Colleen's hand. Kissing the back, he lowered her to the blanket. "I will toss my clothes in every direction, but what I wear on my feet gets special attention."

"Any particular reason?" she asked as he joined her. She opened the cooler and removed beers, the bottles glistening with condensation. Skillfully, she removed the caps, handed one to Dalton, and then took a sip.

Dalton did more than take a sip. He drained half the bottle, more for the quenching liquid than the alcohol. Whatever else Colleen had in the cooler could wait. This was nice. Very nice. With a sigh, Dalton leaned back, closing his eyes. The night sounds became more pronounced. Playing lead, a cricket sent his music across the lake. A frog chimed in

101

now and then. Other animals and insects followed. Nature's band, he thought. In perfect harmony.

"My cellmate had a theory about shoes," he began. Before Dalton knew it, he told Colleen about Silas Freed and all the things the wise man taught him. Not enough people remembered his old friend. It felt good to pass Silas' wisdom on.

"I wish I could meet him." Colleen lay next to him on her side, her head pillowed on her arm. "I would thank Silas for imparting his wisdom and for taking care of you."

"He did that," Dalton nodded with a sigh. "I thought I was prepared for prison. Ryder hired a coach."

"A coach?" Colleen's eyebrows shot up. "That's a thing?"

"It is. And, for me, it was a waste of money. Without Silas, I would have survived. But it would have been a much bumpier ride. He's the reason I was out in just under a year. Good behavior." Dalton laughed at the thought. That was the first time anyone used those words in association with him—and the last.

"He would be proud of you, Dalton."

"I hope so."

Dalton squeezed Colleen's hand, the one she had placed on his arm while he spoke. Turning to face her, his eyes level with hers, Dalton wondered at the people in his life. Ones who stood beside him and kept him close through the bad times as well as the good. What had he done to deserve Ryder, Ashe, and Zoe? Getting Silas as a cellmate had been sheer luck—the good kind.

Now Colleen? What if his car hadn't broken down? Or it was her day off. Life was filled with small moments that changed things forever. Change one, and he might be a different person. The idea made Dalton shudder. He liked who he was. *Where* he was. Personally and professionally. If he hadn't met Colleen, would he have cared? Of course not. However, they *had* met—thank God. In a short time, she had become important. Perhaps vital. He would have to think about that.

"About tonight and the aborted dinner party. I've suspected for some time that there is something in the water." Colleen moved closer until the sides of their arms brushed. "The residents of Midas are strange. Not just the rich ones."

"You aren't strange."

"Put in context, that might be the nicest thing anyone has ever said to me."

Picking up a lock of Colleen's long, red hair, Dalton wound the end around his finger. It felt like silk. Breathing deeply, he smiled. And smelled like a field of wildflowers. If he didn't know better, he would never guess that she spent her days elbow deep in motor oil.

"Dangling revenge as a reward, Tolliver and his cronies believed I would jump through their carefully placed hoops. They believe they're better than Judge Langley."

"It's relative." Colleen stared at the star-filled sky. "Pick your poison. They'll both kill you, but one is a little less painful."

"Which one?" Dalton speculated.

"Luckily, you won't have to find out. What are you going to do about Collier?"

Dalton wished he knew. "I could throw my support and money behind his opponent. But who's to say he—or she—would be any better?"

"Whatever you decide, it doesn't have to be tonight."

"There's always Tolliver's solution."

"No," Colleen said calmly—matter of factly. "Times have changed. It takes a lot to ruin a politician. I have no doubt your fans would believe you, but the court records tell a different story. You were convicted. Good luck getting the witnesses to admit they lied. Unfortunately, I'm afraid Judge Langley's money—and influence—bought a lifetime of silence."

"It *is* my word against theirs." Turning on his side, Dalton leaned over Colleen, their faces inches apart. He needed to look into her expressive

103

green eyes. "Why do *you* believe me?"

Colleen touched his cheek, her expression serene. Yet something fierce and intense lay in the green depths of her gaze.

"Sometimes you just know, Dalton. My trust isn't blind. But until you show me I'm wrong, it *is* absolute."

Colleen's words acted like a spark touched to a pile of kindling. Dalton couldn't wait a second longer. Pulling her close, he pressed his mouth to hers. This was not a tentative kiss. There was no easing in or gentle exploration. He had wanted Colleen from the moment he saw her. Less than forty-eight hours. It felt like forever.

"I came prepared." Tasting the patch of skin just below Colleen's ear, Dalton ran his tongue along her neck. *Mm. Like the sweetest candy.*

"So did I." The sound Colleen made was half laugh, half moan. "There is a box of condoms in my purse."

"Too far away." From his pocket, Dalton produced a strip of foil packets. "Between us, we should have enough." His lips curved against hers. "At least for tonight."

Smiling, Colleen tugged playfully at his hair. "Stop bragging and get to work, drummer boy."

"No work involved. This is pure pleasure."

Clothing first. Dalton craved the touch of Colleen's soft skin. There was something about the easy slide of a zipper on a woman's dress. He felt as though he was opening a present. In this case, the wrapping covered a warm, willing, sexy gift. A practically naked Colleen.

Peeling the material away, he followed with his mouth. Following the slope of Colleen's shoulder, he used his teeth to slide her bra strap down her arm. When his fingers found the front clasp, he didn't know whose sigh was louder, his or Colleen's. Lord, she was lovely. Her breasts were perfect, as though they were made to fit in his hand.

"You've done this before," Colleen said as he tossed her bra away. Her teasing laugh became a low moan the second his mouth closed over the

104

hard, straining tip.

"Once or twice," Dalton admitted, biting lightly.

While Dalton made a feast of Colleen's breasts, he slid the dress down her hips, pushing it all the way off. Straddling her hips, Dalton made quick work of his shirt, all the while taking in the view. Colleen stretched her arms over her head, a knowing smile on her lips.

"My, you're pretty," she purred, her gaze taking in Dalton's bare chest and flat stomach.

"Glad you like what you see." In a few efficient moves, the rest of Dalton's clothes joined the growing pile at the bottom of the blanket.

"Like doesn't cover it."

Colleen reached for him, her fingers closing over his erection. Dalton breathed deeply, using all his willpower. A few strokes of her talented hand and this might end before they got to the good part. Reluctantly, he peeled her fingers away. He wasn't moved by her murmur of displeasure.

"You want to play?" Dalton asked as he rolled on a condom.

"I want to taste."

"Jesus, Colleen." Her words, plus the way she licked her lips, made his heated flesh jump in his hand. He grabbed her panties, ripping the scrap of lace in two. "I can't wait another second."

"Good." Colleen twined her legs around his, her hands sliding up his chest. "Neither can I."

With a sigh of relief, Dalton sank into Colleen. Slow. Steady. He wanted her to feel every inch of him. He wanted to savor her tight, slick heat. Colleen's green eyes glowed emerald. It was a heady moment. Her body opened for him—welcomed him. When he could seemingly edge no further, Dalton surged forward, taking one more inch. Colleen gasped with pleasure, her fingers digging into his back.

"Sweet spot?" Dalton asked. Before Colleen could answer, he hit it again. This time, she didn't gasp. She purred.

"Where has that been all my life?" Colleen panted, licking her bottom lip.

"Hold on. The ride has just begun."

Unable to resist, Dalton took Colleen's mouth with his, sucking on her bottom lip, savoring her taste. When had kissing become so vital? For him, it had always been nice. A pathway to warming up his partner. A kiss, or ten, led to sex—always his endgame. But it was different with Colleen. He wanted—needed—all of her. The touch of her skin. The brush of her lips. Her tongue against his. Her breasts pressing into his chest. Her legs wrapped around his and the tantalizing massage of her foot as it moved up and down his calf. Dalton was aware of everything. His senses heightened.

For the first time in Dalton's life, sex wasn't about rushing toward the conclusion. He opened his mind—and his body—to all the little moments. Suddenly, being with a woman—with Colleen—became more than it had ever been.

"Dalton," Colleen breathed, her teeth sinking into his shoulder. "Please. I need—"

"I know what you need," Dalton kissed her again. Hard. Desperate. "I'm with you, Colleen. All the way."

Dalton always set the rhythm. It was his job, and nobody did it better. However, the best drummers fed those around him. It was Colleen who showed him when to slow things down. He set the beat, but she set the tone. It was a gradual blending of styles until they hit that moment. The peak. A perfect blending of bodies. They reached the pinnacle and toppled over into oblivion—together.

"I CAN'T BELIEVE you packed all this food." Dalton took a bite of chicken leg, sighing with contentment.

"About six months ago, a deli opened on the main drag. I wouldn't say that civilization has come to Midas. But *The Hungry Traveler* improved the takeout options by leaps and bounds."

"I approve wholeheartedly."

"I dated one of the Midas elite," Colleen continued. Seeing Dalton's raised eyebrows, she shrugged. "Briefly. In my defense, it was one long, cold winter. It seemed like a good idea at the time. Something to break the monotony."

"It didn't work out?" Setting aside the chicken, Dalton dug into a pile of creamy potato salad.

"Next to Hector Plank, monotony seemed exciting."

"Ouch. Poor Hector."

Colleen chuckled, taking a sip from her bottle of water. Dalton nursed his second beer. "I won't lie. The disappointment went both ways. I thought he would add some fun to my life. He thought some wrong-side-of-the-tracks sex would give him bragging rights with his friends."

"And?" Dalton asked, fascinated to know the answer.

"Again. Poor Hector. One limp-lipped kiss and I knew it wouldn't work."

"I can't feel a whole lot of sympathy for Hector." Dalton passed Colleen a napkin. "What does any of that have to do with our current feast?"

"For our third—and last date—Hector took me to dinner at his parents' house. His too, since he lived at home. Still does."

"Naturally," Dalton sneered.

"It's fairly common in Hector's world. Collier and Bonnie are firmly ensconced with Judge Langley. But I digress." Colleen popped an olive into her mouth. "Dinner consisted of tiny portions swimming in oddly seasoned sauces. That was bad enough for my digestion. Add an icy glare from Hector's mother and his father's ill-concealed leers. I dumped my date at my front door then chowed down on peanut butter and saltines. The chances of that happening again were slim. However…"

"Mm. Forearmed, so to speak." Dalton smiled as he raised his bottle. An hour ago, he couldn't imagine finding humor in the Tolliver situation, but here he was. Sexually satiated—for the time being. A full stomach. The world looked infinitely brighter.

"Exactly. If we hadn't needed the food, I would have put it in my refrigerator and feasted for the next few days."

Dalton sat on his side of the picnic table, watching Colleen clean her plate with unapologetic ease. He had dated women who picked at a salad while managing to take a bite or two—maybe. Then there were the ones, like Colleen, who enjoyed their food. They didn't agonize over every calorie. Dalton—and every man he knew—preferred the latter. He understood the pressure society put on women. The unrealistic body images projected on the cover of over-photoshopped fashion magazines. It wasn't fair. But it was the reality.

"I hope you left room for dessert," Colleen said, pushing away her empty plate. "Because waiting in that cooler is the most decadently delicious batch of brownies ever created."

Dalton wanted dessert. But not the kind baked in an oven. Leaning across the table, he slipped a hand behind Colleen's neck. His fingers tightened around the strands of her soft, moonlight-caressed hair. Once, twice, three times he brushed his lips across hers.

"The brownies sound good. But my sweet tooth is craving something sweeter. Can you guess what I want?"

"Me?" Colleen sighed, coyly batting her eyelashes.

Vaulting over the table, he lifted Colleen into his arms. In two strides, he had her laid out on the blanket. His eyes locked with hers, he slid his hand slowly up her smooth leg.

Dalton covered Colleen's body with his and whispered, "You got it right in one."

CHAPTER TEN

ANOTHER MORNING, ANOTHER run through the deserted streets of Midas. There were differences. This time, Dalton paid attention to more than the feel of the ground beneath his feet and the sad, dusty buildings that populated this part of town. Keeping his eyes peeled, he watched for someone who might be following him. Hardly an expert on surveillance, Dalton wasn't sure what he was looking for. It seemed unlikely that he would spot a man in a trench coat pointing a huge pair of binoculars his way.

However, as Dalton stepped out of his motel room, he went to one knee. Ostensibly, he was there to check the lace on his right shoe. Instead, his eyes searched the parking lot, the scraggly patch of trees to his right, and for good measure, the panes of dirty glass that separated him from the other rooms. If somebody really wanted to keep an eye on Dalton's activities, what better way than to park his butt on a crappy chair behind the crappier curtains.

By the end of his first mile, he had to laugh at himself. Apparently, Tolliver Cline and his machinations had freaked Dalton out more than he realized. He knew what it was like to be the center of attention. Paparazzi went out of their way to track him down in the oddest places. If he couldn't handle a little small-town craziness, he might as well pack up his drumsticks and retire. Still, for his own peace of mind, Dalton took a different route than yesterday. If he unexpectedly ran into one of Tolliver's cronies, he would know the game was afoot.

Dalton snorted. One had to love Sherlock Holmes.

The sun was clear of the eastern horizon when Dalton let himself back into his room. The bed was empty, but he could hear the distinct sound of water running. Pulling his sweat-drenched t-shirt over his head, Dalton toed off his shoes. Next came his shorts until the only thing he wore was an anticipatory smile.

Steam rose to the bathroom ceiling. To Dalton's surprise, behind the plastic shower curtain, Colleen belted out a polished rendition of *I Will Survive*. One that would have done Gloria Gaynor proud.

109

Pulling back the curtain, Dalton joined Colleen, sliding his arms around her waist. Impressed that his sudden appearance didn't make her miss a beat, he began harmonizing, his deep voice crooning near her ear. She leaned back, finishing the last line before turning her head and taking his mouth with a long, lusty kiss.

With a growl of pleasure, Dalton took Colleen's hands, pressing them flat against the side of the shower. Reaching around the curtain, his fumbled around the counter until his hand made contact with the familiar feel of a foil-enclosed condom. Quickly efficient, Dalton rolled on the protection then sheathed himself inside Colleen.

"That must have been some run," Colleen gasped, her head falling back.

"Invigorating," Dalton whispered against the side of her neck, his tongue lapping at the Colleen-flavored water.

"Mm. Invigorating." Reaching back, Colleen threaded her fingers through Dalton's hair, tightening her grasp when, without warning, he thrust his hips forward. "The run? Or me?"

"Both."

Dalton cupped Colleen's breast with his hand, the other sliding between her legs. One more push, one stroke of his finger, sent her over the edge. With the feel of her orgasm rippling over his erection and the sound of her pleasure-filled moans, Dalton followed close behind.

Lightly kissing Colleen's back, Dalton grinned. *Best post-run shower ever.*

"HAVE YOU EVER considered doing that for a living?"

The question earned Dalton a wet towel in the face.

"Watch it, fella. The last man who offered me money to shower with him didn't walk straight for a week."

"I was talking about your singing, not your aquatic sexual prowess." Dalton tossed the towel on the floor. One of the few good things about the motel was the maid service. The quality of the linen sucked, but it was freshly laundered and replaced daily.

"My voice is average—at best. But thank you for the compliment."

110

Colleen's smile turned into a frown as she attempted to finish drying herself. To say the ratty piece of cloth lacked absorbency put it mildly. Mostly, she ended up pushing the water from one part of her arm to another. "Tell me again why we ended up here instead of my place?"

"Because you were half-asleep and this place was closer. When I asked if you had a preference, you mumbled something unintelligible. I didn't hear any complaints when I carried you in."

To be fair, Colleen admitted silently, that sounded like her. Her brain wasn't at full speed when she needed sleep. However, as crappy as this place was, she liked the idea of Dalton carrying her to bed. She wished her memory wasn't quite so fuzzy. Holding a shoe in one hand, Colleen looked around the room. She hoped the other one wasn't under the bed because there was no way in hell she was putting her face within three feet of that carpet. Avoiding the cringe-worthy stains was hard enough while standing.

"Do you want to get some breakfast?" Dalton inquired, handing her the missing sandal.

Using Dalton's arm for balance, she had both shoes on in a flash. She knew it was a little too late, but she felt better with the barrier between her feet and the worn carpet that had seen better days.

"I can't. There is a leaky oil pan waiting for me. Can you run me by my apartment before dropping me at the garage?"

"No problem," Dalton said as he checked the messages on his phone. "Shit."

"Did your sister call? Or Tolliver?"

"Ryder. And Ashe." Dalton scrolled further down. "Ryder again. Zoe left a voicemail."

"What the hell, you idiot? If Quinn hadn't talked him down, Ryder would have left for *Wherever the Hell*, Arizona hours ago. Call. Now!"

"That seems a bit over the top," Colleen laughed. Then, her eyes widening, she had a sudden thought. "Are you and Zoe Hart—?"

"Don't say it," Dalton quickly interjected. "Jesus, Colleen. I think of Zoe as a sister."

"Okay."

Colleen slowly combed her hair. It wasn't any of her business, but she couldn't help feeling...? Relieved? It was as good a word as any. She avoided other women's men like the plague. She was fine with acting as Dalton's small-town fling, as long as he was free and clear. She would have been bitterly disappointed if he had turned her into something she abhorred. A cheat.

"I know how it must sound, but I promised Ryder and the rest of them that I would keep in touch. When I didn't call last night—"

"They are worried that you're in Midas. Alone."

Dalton took the comb from Colleen, gently running it through her hair.

"I'm not alone," he said, then kissed the end of her nose. "But they don't know that. I better call them back."

Taking the comb from Dalton's outstretched hand, Colleen felt as though something monumental had occurred. *I'm not alone*. It was obvious from his casual kiss—*on her nose, no less*—that he had no idea what he had said. The import of those words. Or how they had affected her.

Colleen put a hand on her stomach. The fluttering wasn't butterflies. This feeling wasn't nerves. It was different—and more. Then there was her heart. What was going on there? A slight tightening followed by some crazy, wild pounding. The last time she had felt anything close was when she put the final touch on her restored T-Bird. That had been pride and accomplishment. And hope for the future. Colleen's hand drifted up to where her heart tried to beat its way out of her chest. Whatever was going on, she wanted it to stop. Immediately. Before it was too late.

"Are you okay?" Dalton frowned. "You're awfully pale."

"How can you tell the difference?" Colleen quipped. *Go for a laugh, she thought. Do not let Dalton know where your thoughts are wandering.*

Dalton laughed, as Colleen hoped he would. His reaction calmed her stomach and settled her heart into a reasonable rhythm. She would work on figuring everything out later when she was alone. Or perhaps she would pretend it never happened. Treat it as an anomaly. *Brilliant!* Colleen had never been a *stick her head in the sand* type, but right now seemed like the perfect time to temporarily leave her self-awareness in the rearview mirror.

"Your complexion is creamy, not ghostlike." Eyes narrowed, Dalton lightly ran a finger over Colleen's cheek. "I didn't let you get a lot of sleep last night."

"You make it sound like I had no choice." The merest suggestion that Colleen wasn't making her own decisions was the fastest way to bring color to her face. She could feel the blood rushing upward accompanied by a fair amount of heat. "It could be argued that *I'm* the one who kept *you* up. In more ways than one."

"Neither of us has time for sexual innuendo, Red."

"There was no innuendo. And never call me Red."

With a grin, Dalton tapped her cheek, then tugged playfully on her hair. "If the shoe fits."

So much for the *warm and fuzzy*. Colleen's eyes narrowed as Dalton lifted his phone. Red. Admittedly, when Dalton called her the dreaded nickname, she didn't feel the usual amount of animosity. However, it was annoying. An infinitely safer emotion than… Colleen put on the breaks. She wasn't willing to acknowledge the problem. Naming it would be a huge mistake.

"I need to get going." Colleen slid the comb into her purse. "Do you mind making your call while I drive?"

"It's ringing." Dalton grabbed the keys, tossing them to Colleen. "Let's go. I can walk and talk. Then sit and talk."

The conversation was one-sided—on Colleen's end. However, it was obvious to anyone listening that Dalton's friends were on the other end. Mostly, he listened. His expression ranging from amused to annoyed. Occasionally, antagonistic. Now and then he would throw in a comment. Colleen had just pulled into the garage at her apartment building when Dalton took over.

"I said I was sorry. Time got away from me. Yes, Ryder, I understand how to check my messages. If you shut up for five seconds, I will tell you what happened."

For one panicked minute, Colleen thought Dalton meant what happened at the lake. When he started recounting his initial meeting with Tolliver, she rolled her eyes. Talk about self-centered. *It isn't all about you, Colleen.* Leaving Dalton to finish his call in private, she jogged up the stairs, unlocking the door that led directly into her kitchen.

The attached garage had been the apartment's chief selling point. In a pinch, she could have left the T-Bird at her mother's. Sherry and Rick had plenty of room. However, her car was meant to be driven. Though it was a classic, she believed in enjoying the fruits of her labors. She hadn't put in all those hours bringing it back to life only to keep it locked away untouched. The Ford Motor Company produced the Thunderbird to be taken out on the road. As far as Colleen was concerned, sixty years later, the car's raison d'être hadn't changed.

As she rushed around, changing from last night's dress to her daily uniform of shorts, a t-shirt, followed by coveralls, heavy socks and work boots, Colleen made a mental list of what she needed to get done. There were three jobs pending at the garage. Nothing major. Things—that if pushed—she could do with her eyes closed and one hand tied behind her back. Not exactly busy work, since they were the bread and butter of any mechanic. They paid the bills. However, it would be nice if something came in that was more of a challenge.

Dalton's car would have qualified. But as she told him, no matter what she did, the Porsche was bound to break down again. It would be the equivalent of tossing his money—and her labor—down a garbage disposal.

Braiding her hair, Colleen twisted the end into a loop, clipping at the base of her neck where it would stay out of her way. Challenges at work were hard to come by. She needed to find another project. Something along the lines of the Thunderbird. It would be nice to have a project in the hopper—one that made the tips of her fingers tingle with anticipation. She looked around. Something was bound to catch her interest. When she found it, Colleen would jump in. But not now. Today, she had to pay the bills.

Colleen found Dalton in the kitchen. The cooler sat empty as he transferred the last of its contents into the refrigerator.

114

"Everything looks like it survived the night. I tossed the potato salad—just in case. You can never be too careful when mayonnaise is involved. What?" Dalton asked when he saw her amused expression.

"World-class drummer and food safety expert? That's quite a resume."

"Food poisoning is no laughing matter."

But there was a smile on Dalton's face as he carried the cooler to the garage. Stowing it where Colleen indicated, he took the keys from her hand.

"Did you get things smoothed over with your friends?" Colleen asked as they climbed into the car.

"They have my back." Dalton skillfully backed out of the garage, heading out of the parking lot. "Once I explained, and promised not to miss another call, things were cool."

"It must be nice. That kind of support system is rare."

Dalton nodded, his gaze thoughtful. "We work. On stage and off. We are as tight a group as you'll find. When I met Ryder and Ashe, I was content to drift from gig to gig. I wasn't interested in anything permanent. Or so I thought."

"A wandering troubadour." Colleen could picture it. Have drumsticks, will travel. She felt a touch of envy.

"We all were. Ryder was the one who wanted something stable."

"Because of Zoe?"

Dalton's fingers tightened on the steering wheel—enough to turn his knuckles white. The look he shot her sent a chill down Colleen's spine. She didn't know what she had said, but it was enough to drop the temperature in the car to a frosty level.

"What makes you think that?" Dalton demanded.

"Their story is common knowledge." It felt odd defending herself when she had no idea why. Colleen was sorry that Dalton was upset, but unless he explained, she wasn't going to offer up a blind apology.

"Well, shit." Pulling next to the curb outside *Dole's Auto Repair*, Dalton killed the engine. With a sigh, he ran a hand through his hair, removing his sunglasses. Colleen saw wariness in his gaze. But it was the regret,

115

the contriteness, which melted her growing anger. "My friends and I have a pact. We don't talk about each other to anyone outside the group. What I know about Ashe, or Ryder and Zoe, I keep to myself. And vice versa. It's a touchy subject."

"You don't say," Colleen sniped, but it was done gently. When Dalton smiled, she felt the knot in her shoulders loosen.

"Over the years, reporters have pumped us for information. Sometimes with flattery. Sometimes trickery. A few have attempted the old Mata Hari routine."

"You'll have to explain that one."

"They have tried to sex the information out of us."

"Ah," Colleen nodded. She would have to keep on her toes. She wasn't used to hanging out with a man who made World War I spy references. Discovering that about him made Colleen like Dalton all the more.

"The point is, I might have overreacted. Just a tad. I'm sorry, Colleen."

"Raise that tad to a trifle, and we're good."

"Consider it done." Dalton slid his hand behind Colleen's neck, pulling her in for a kiss. "I'm off to track down my sister and her wayward husband."

"Good luck."

"Dinner?"

"Absolutely, I—" Suddenly, Colleen remembered something she had conveniently put out of her mind. "I'll have to pass—reluctantly. Today is my mother's birthday. My stepfather likes to make a fuss. Mom likes to be fussed over. It's one of the reasons their marriage works. There will be a big family meal. Friends. Cake. Presents. The whole shebang."

"Sounds like fun. Is there someplace in town where I can buy your mother a gift?"

Colleen's eyes widened. "Are you crazy?" Reaching over, she pressed the back of her hand to Dalton's forehead. "You don't seem to be feverish."

"Fit as a fiddle." Taking Colleen's hand, Dalton brushed her fingers with his lips. "What time do you get off work?"

"You honestly want to do this?" When Dalton nodded, Colleen abandoned the myriad of arguments swirling from one side of her brain to the other. In Midas, Sherry's birthday parties were as close as a person could get to a zoo—with the touch of a carnival fun house tossed in for good measure. An invitation was a hot ticket. Why shouldn't Dalton get a taste of what her mother's brand of crazy looked like?

"Give me a ring around four o'clock. I'll let you know if I'm going to be delayed."

"Will do." When Colleen hesitated, Dalton gave her a gentle push out the door. "Relax. I can't wait to meet your mother. And about that gift?"

"Try *Weaver's* down on Birch. Mom loves earrings. Think big and bold."

Colleen watched as the T-Bird turned at the intersection. Dalton and her mother? In the same room? It had disaster written all over it—in big neon lights. There was one consolation. Sherry was easily distracted by shiny things. And in Colleen's opinion, Dalton Shaw was the shiniest object she had ever met.

BUSY DIDN'T BEGIN to describe Colleen's morning. What had promised to be routine and uneventful, quickly turned into an unprecedented barrage of flat tires, blown gaskets, and one savagely ripped out carburetor.

Gary Newcomb was practically in tears when the tow truck dropped him and his brand new Ford Explorer off at the garage. Gary wanted Colleen's sympathy. All she could give him was her expertise and a bit of advice. Never cheat on a woman who knows what's what under the hood of his car. Especially when that woman is his wife.

"I didn't do anything I haven't done before," Gary whined, clutching the carburetor in his hand. "Why now? Why not the old Chevy I traded in last week? Hell, Colleen. How can I forgive a woman who could do such a thing?"

"You should be down on your knees begging Stacey's forgiveness. And

117

be grateful this is all the damage she did."

Since Colleen had taught Stacey everything she knew about cars, if Gary's wife had been so inclined, she could have taken the Explorer's engine apart, holding each part for ransom. That's what Colleen suggested when Stacey called her around eight thirty. Now, two hours later, Colleen figured that Gary—and his new SUV—got off easy.

"But—" Gary sputtered.

Colleen had heard enough. Work was piling up. If Gary wanted a kick in the ass, she would be happy to oblige. If he wanted his truck fixed, he would have to get in line. "It will be a couple of hours. Maybe more. Leave the carburetor. Dole will call you when I'm done."

Five minutes later, an irate Dole waddled into the work area. His face was red—redder than usual.

"Gary Newcomb says you were rude to him. He's one of our best customers, Mac. I want you to apologize."

"And I want a villa in the south of France. Neither is likely. But I'll bet I get my wish first."

"You're too clever for your own good, Mac." Dole wiped at the sweat that poured down his face. More followed, making the effort a losing battle.

Colleen sighed. Lifting the newly patched tire, she leveraged it onto her old English teacher's Chrysler. Since Mrs. Black was one of the few people in Midas that Colleen looked on with affection, she wanted to send the retired teacher on her way as quickly as possible. Dole was not helping.

"If I were as clever as you claim, I wouldn't be working for you. But since I am," Colleen ratcheted the last lug nut into place. "Thank your goddamned lucky stars and leave me to it."

"One of these days—"

"What?" Colleen rounded on Dole, pointing the hydraulic wrench like a gun. "Go on," she urged when he took a step back. "One of these days...?"

Dole held up his hands. Perhaps Colleen couldn't shoot him, but he wasn't taking any chances. "Don't get your panties in a twist. And get back to work. The bodies in the waiting room are piling up."

"Here." Colleen tossed the wrench to Dole. He fumbled, but managed to hold on.

"Jesus, that fucker is hot," he muttered, fumbling, but awkwardly managing to maintain his grip.

No kidding, Colleen thought. She had the tiny burn scars to prove it. "See those?" She pointed at the four tires lined up in a neat row.

Leery, Dole nodded.

"I know your father taught you the basics. I patched the flats. Make yourself useful and put them on the cars."

Colleen didn't wait around to see if Dole followed her orders. Taking a deep breath, she checked the board. Not bad. If she worked straight through lunch, she might get out of here by five. All things considered, she would take that.

For the first time since she walked into the garage, Colleen had a second to take a breath. With a sigh, she started the next job. Some joker had clipped a stop sign turning onto Main Street. How it happened, he wouldn't say, though Colleen suspected alcohol was involved. But nobody had been hurt, the only casualty his side-view mirror. Shaking her head, she picked up a screwdriver and got back to work.

Colleen hoped Dalton's day was going better than hers.

CHAPTER ELEVEN

AFTER LEAVING COLLEEN, Dalton made the obligatory phone call to his sister. Voicemail. Again.

"I will call you one more time, Maggie. Three o'clock this afternoon. Answer or don't. It's up to you."

The truth was, it didn't matter. Dalton had no intention of paying her or her husband another dime. It was time to leave his past behind him. Sad as it was, that past included Maggie. They were never close, but she was the only blood relative he knew. Keeping that tie had always seemed important. Now? He didn't feel the emotions he would have expected. Not a bit of guilt. Not a tinge of sadness.

The only thing Dalton felt was relief.

Dalton stopped the car in front of an old rundown building. In the parking lot, amidst some scraggly weeds, sat two pickup trucks. One red. One black. Both were old models but looked to be in fairly good condition. He exited the T-Bird, his boots stirring up a swirl of dust.

The Thirsty Raven. Dalton's memories had little to do with the front parking lot. Ask him about the back area—the place of his arrest—and he could still describe the way it looked that night in vivid, Technicolor detail. What he did remember from seven years ago was commenting to his bandmates that *The Thirsty Raven* looked as though it was held together by a few nails and a prayer. Not much had changed.

Dalton tried the front door. What would it hurt? To his surprise, the knob turned in his hand. His plan had been to take a look around, make his final peace, and be on his way. However, since he was here, and the place was open, he might as well go all the way.

The door squeaked—loud and long. Funny, Dalton could recall the sound clearly. The bar and seating area were small. Smaller than the pictures in his mind. He supposed most of the places the band had played in those early days would be the same. Like returning to a childhood home where everything seemed miniature compared to his recollections. After years

120

of playing sold-out arenas and massive concert halls, Dalton's perspective was different.

As Dalton made his way across the room, he breathed in the scent of stale beer and industrial-strength cleaner. Now there was a smell he would never forget. Every small-town bar he had ever played carried the same unpleasant odor. Though the way his boots stuck to the floor, Dalton wondered why the fragrance left from the cleaner was so prevalent. From his estimation, the layer of spilled booze had been there for a long, long time. If anyone had mopped up in the last seven years, Dalton would be surprised.

"We don't start serving until eleven," a man behind the bar called out in a raspy, smoke-roughened voice. He wasn't a young man. Or particularly old—at least in Dalton's estimation. "If you need a drink that bad, pick up a bottle at the grocery store."

"I don't want a drink."

"Then what do you want at—" There was a pause while he looked at his watch. "Jesus. Is that the time? Andy? You in the office?"

"Yes!" Someone yelled through the open door to Dalton's left. "What do you want now?"

"What the hell am I doing here at this time of the morning?"

"We planned on going over the books for last month. Jesus, Willard. Your brain is like a goddamned sieve."

"Fuck you, Andy." Eyeing Dalton with an air of suspicion, Willard slapped his hand down on the top of the bar. "State your business."

"No business." Though he *was* enjoying the show unwittingly put on by Willard and Andy. "I'm just passing through."

"Through Midas, I get. Through *The Thirsty Raven*? Son, this ain't no tourist attraction. You won't find one of those until you hit Phoenix."

Dalton was stuck for a comeback. What could he say? *Seven years ago, I was arrested behind your bar. Mind if I take a look for old time's sake?*

"Are you talking to yourself again, Willard?" The man who wandered

121

out of the office looked to be around fifty. Short and thin, his dark hair had receded so far back it wasn't fair to call what he had left a hairline.

"No," Willard sneered, jabbing a thumb in Dalton's direction. "I'm talking to him. And don't ask me who he is. I haven't the slightest idea."

"I do." Andy took a few steps closer. "I'll be damned. It is. I heard you were in town, but I figured it was wild gossip. We get a lot of that. This is the last place I figured to ever see you again."

Willard peered over the bar. "Who the hell are you?"

Dalton was about to answer, but Andy beat him to it.

"This is Dalton Shaw, you old fool."

Willard didn't look impressed. "And who the hell is he when the lights come on?"

"You'll have to forgive my partner. There was a time when his mind was sharp as a tack. Time has dulled it considerably." Andy held out his hand. "I would say welcome back, but..."

"I'm as surprised as you are." Dalton looked around. "It hasn't changed much."

"Nope. Not much reason. Our customers don't come for the ambiance."

"Or the music?" Dalton asked.

"It's the truth." Andy shook his head. "Imagine, *The Ryder Hart Band* played here. It does give us a bit of distinction."

"One night," Willard said under his breath.

Andy rolled his eyes. "What's that, you old coot? If you have something to say, speak up."

"I said," Willard's grumble became something resembling a shout. "*The Ryder Hart Band* played here for one night. They were booked two. Left us high and dry. Not very professional if you ask me."

"Of all the—" Andy sent Dalton an apologetic look. "Willard, do us all a favor and read that newspaper clipping hanging behind the bar. The one

122

that's been there for the past seven years."

Famous or infamous? Dalton supposed the two went hand in hand. He was grateful that the rest of the world had long ago moved past his jailbird days. All they cared about were his music skills. The way he played the drum or the quality of his latest composition. In Midas—specifically at *The Thirsty Raven*—Dalton's notoriety was frozen in time. From the look of the framed item Willard perused, not only frozen but well documented.

"That was you?" Scratching his head, Willard looked Dalton up and down. "I remember somebody scrawnier. And shorter. You have a growth spurt?"

"No, sir," Dalton laughed. "Just older and filled out."

Suddenly, Dalton was glad for his impromptu visit. There was nothing malicious in Willard's words. The man was genuinely perplexed. He couldn't remember the last time his appearance elicited anything but frenzied excitement. If nothing else, his visit to Midas had reminded him that not everyone was impressed by fame—no matter how hard earned.

"Can I get you something to drink?" Looking at ease, Andy clapped him on the back. "You'll forgive me if I don't remember your poison of choice."

"Honestly? I would be a little creeped out if you did."

Andy chuckled. Willard seemed to find the poor attempt at a joke over-the-top hilarious.

"As I was saying," Andy said, drawing Dalton away from the bar and a braying Willard. "What would you like? On the house."

"Nothing. Thank you, Andy." Dalton felt awkward asking, but it *was* why he stopped. "Would you mind if I take a look out back?"

"You mean where…?" To Dalton's relief, Andy left it at that. "Sure. Take your time. But before you go, could I get your autograph?"

Andy scampered to his office, returning with a CD—the band's first. One signature and a few pictures later, Dalton hoped one of the shots of himself, Andy and Willard would replace the old newspaper clipping behind the bar. He was philosophical enough to understand that wasn't likely. *The Thirsty Raven* had one claim to fame. It wasn't much, but it was all they had. Plus a couple of freshly minted selfies of the owners and the infamous man himself.

Walking from the darkened bar to the glaringly bright parking lot was a shock—not just to Dalton's eyesight. Pulling out his sunglasses, he waited for his senses to adjust. Whatever he had expected. Anxiety. Anger. Regret. None of it appeared.

Though Dalton could see the farce play out, it was as though it happened to someone else. He wasn't that person anymore. He always said that given the chance to do it again, nothing would change. Yes, he would always defend himself if he believed himself in physical danger. But the rest? The blasé attitude about sleeping with a married woman? The hothead bristling with ambition and immaturity? The belief that he was invincible? That man no longer existed.

Something else Dalton realized as he relived the brief, but monumental chapter of his old life. He wouldn't be the man he was today if he hadn't lived through the mistakes. Unlike many of the inmates he had met, Dalton hadn't just survived. He flourished.

It was a good life. Better than good. And the past—important as it was— no longer held any power over him. Maybe he owed Maggie and her husband thanks for getting him back to Midas. Unwittingly, they had forced him to take stock. Of the past *and* present. The future was wide open. The possibilities bright and endless. How many people could say that with any conviction?

Conviction. Dalton laughed at his own unintentional joke. Prison humor wasn't part of his usual repertoire. It had to be a good sign.

Hoping to stay on a roll, Dalton rounded the bar, unlocking the T-Bird. Climbing in, he took out his phone. He hadn't expected to find a message from his sister, but it would have been nice. With a resigned sigh, he scrolled down his list of contacts and tapped her number.

Perhaps Maggie had come to the realization that the time for games was over. More likely, she believed she could manipulate him the way she had when they were kids. Either way, after ignoring him for two days, she had finally answered. The first words out of her mouth told him that nothing had changed. His sister was incapable of taking responsibility for her actions. When in doubt, put the blame on anyone—or anything—else.

"I've been trying to get in touch with you, Dalton. Why haven't you returned my calls?"

Dalton's head fell back, his eyes closing as he counted to ten. *Here we go.*

"That crap isn't going to fly, Maggie. I called you. Repeatedly. Not the other way around."

"Really? Honestly, Dalton. I called and called. You know me, I'm helpless when it comes to technology."

Dalton could almost see Maggie's wide-eyed innocent look. Over the years, she perfected it. However, his sister had used it too often on him. Overexposure had rendered him immune.

"It doesn't matter."

"Good," she breathed with a giggle. "I knew you would understand."

"No, Maggie. It doesn't matter because we've hit the end of a very long, frustrating road. I felt guilty for a long time, and you played on it. More power to you. The money I paid you was to make me feel better. But no more. I hope Norris finds a good job because starting today, you're on your own."

"You don't mean that."

From the lilting tone of her voice, it was obvious Maggie didn't believe him. Not that Dalton blamed her. He always caved. Why should she think he would change? Little sister was about to learn a necessary lesson—the hard way. Dalton had his breaking point. And she had shattered it. Humpty Dumpty had a better shot of getting put back together again.

"Consider the cash machine closed. Permanently. However, if you need me, I'll be there. But don't push your luck, Maggie."

"Dalton..." That whine. The exact replica of their mother's. It was Dalton's fingernails on a chalkboard.

"Look on the bright side. It costs a lot less to live in Midas than Buffalo. You're already ahead of the game."

"But—"

"Take care, Maggie."

Dalton's only regret was that he couldn't say, *I love you, Maggie*. It would have been a lie. However, he did want his sister to have a good life. To find peace with herself. If he could do it, there was hope for anyone.

Starting the car, Dalton's thoughts turned to something—someone—more pleasant. Colleen. He got a kick out of her reaction when he invited himself to her mother's birthday party. He gave her props. She could have protested. Or insisted he not attend. Instead, she rolled with the situation. It was an admirable quality. Just one of many. Whatever Colleen's faults—and Dalton was certain she had them—*she* wasn't a whiner. Just the thought lifted his spirits again.

Now, he thought as he pulled onto the street, he needed to buy a gift. What had Colleen told him? *Earrings*. That was it. Big and bold.

STRETCHING, COLLEEN WINCED when she felt her back pop. At the moment, all she wanted was a blissfully cool shower, a juicy hamburger, and Dalton. Preferably naked. The bath she could manage. If luck were on her side, Rich would have the charcoals on the barbecue blazing and the beef sizzling. As for Dalton? He was on his way to pick her up. The naked would have to wait until after her mother's birthday party.

Looking at her watch, Colleen figured Dalton's ETA to be about fifteen minutes. When she called him almost an hour ago, there had been a jauntiness in Dalton's voice. Feeling anything but, Colleen asked what had happened to brighten his day.

"I'll tell you when I see you," he said.

In spite of her crappy day, Colleen ended the call with a smile on her face. Dalton seemed to have that effect on her. As she set her phone out of harm's way, she caught sight of Dole—obviously eavesdropping. Realizing that Colleen had caught him, he turned, knocking into a tool cart and sending most of them to the floor. Without pausing, he shuffled back to his office.

Before calling it a day, she cleaned up the mess Dole had left her.

"That's it," Colleen said, sticking her head into his office. The smell of sweaty man, Royal Crown Cola, and tuna fish filled the room, making her nose wrinkle. The tiny electric fan did nothing to alleviate the problem. It simply continually redistributed the offending odors. "I finished aligning the Cadillac's steering column. Anything else can wait until tomorrow."

"Wait." Dole didn't move fast very often. His body—and his disposition—weren't in the proper condition. But now and then he could be surprisingly agile.

"I don't have time, Dole."

"Collier Langley is on his way. There's a knock under his hood. I told him you would look at it."

As much as Colleen wanted to make a nasty comment, she made a herculean effort, keeping her opinion of Collier's knock to herself.

"Call him back. I won't be here."

"Too late. He's here."

Dole sounded strangely gleeful. It was no secret that her boss coveted a friendship with Collier. He made no secret of it. Just as Collier made no attempt to hide his contempt for Dole. Collier's sudden car emergency had a bad smell to it. Worse than Dole's office.

Collier Langley was an attractive man. Not tall or short, he kept his body

127

trim. Though, by the look of his forearms, Colleen suspected that under his perfectly pressed Chinos and oddly eighties-style Ralph Lauren polo shirt, he had the muscle tone of a twelve-year-old boy. His light brown hair was beginning to thin at the top, a fact that he overcompensated for by fluffing what was left into a modified pompadour. White-toothed smile had future politician written all over it. In other words, bland and obviously insincere.

"Hello, Colleen. You're looking as beautiful as ever."

Collier hit on every woman he met. Like a dog salivating at the tinkling of a bell, he would have done Pavlov proud. For years, he had been after Colleen. She knew it was her utter lack of interest that kept him coming back. Periodically, he made the same pass. Periodically, she turned him down.

However, Collier tended to avoid her while she was at work. He might not be picky about his sexual partners, but he had his own warped standards. He preferred them clean, perfumed and ready for action. At the moment, Colleen was a sweaty, grungy mess. Beautiful? Hardly.

Why had Collier chosen now to turn on his oily version of charm? The bad smell radiating from this meeting was getting more and more rank by the second.

When Dole snickered—actually it was more of a laugh/snort hybrid—the light bulb went off in Colleen's weary, hard day's work diminished brain. Why hadn't she thought of it sooner? This wasn't about a knocking engine. Or how sexy she looked with limp hair and motor oil smudged across her chin. It was about Dalton. *And* Dole's pathetic attempt to score brownie points with Collier.

"You should leave," Colleen stated calmly.

Colleen was proud of her cool demeanor. Inside, the temperature of her blood had spiked. Already flushed from the heat, it was hard to read her mood. Her bright red cheeks were usually a dead giveaway that trouble was brewing. However, if Collier had bothered to look, he would have noticed another warning sign. Her blazing green eyes. A smart man would have backed away. Instead, the fool moved closer, putting his arm

128

around Colleen's shoulders.

It proved what she had always suspected. Mensa would never come knocking at Collier's door.

"You look like you could use a little fun, Colleen. With a real man."

To emphasize his point, Collier settled his groin against Colleen's hip. The bulge in his pants wasn't huge, but she got his point. It was time for Collier to get *hers*.

"Do you think I'm a fool?" Colleen smiled, but there was no welcoming light in her eyes. In one smooth movement, she slipped free of Collier's arm, grabbing a pair of pliers. "What did you think was going to happen? Was the plan to use me to create a replay of seven years ago? Is there a police officer waiting to arrive just in time to play witness as you goad Dalton into throwing a punch?"

Colleen's rapid fire questions seemed to throw Collier off his game. As she advanced, he retreated. He wasn't used to a woman turning him down—or standing up to him. Looking over his shoulder for Dole's support did him no good. The other man had retreated to the safety of his office where he could watch how things played through a crack in the barely open door.

Collier didn't possess much backbone, but he managed to scrounge up enough to attempt to push back. Halting before Colleen pushed him out of the garage, he straightened to his full height.

"Why would I give a damn about Dalton Shaw? He's nothing but a meaningless musician. A speck under my shoe."

"I'm certain Judge Langley has pointed out that Dalton could be a huge thorn in your political future." Colleen looked Collier up and down with every ounce of contempt she felt. "Does Daddy Dearest know what you're up to?"

The flash of concern that passed over Collier's face told Colleen everything she needed to know. The clunky attempt to take Dalton down didn't seem like Judge Langley's style. It was too in your face. Too poorly thought out. There were too many things that could go wrong. Not the least of which was Colleen. She had a pair of pliers, and she wasn't afraid to use them.

Knowing that Dalton could arrive at any second, Colleen decided it was time to end this farce. She chose a way that would make Collier think twice before trying anything like this again. As a bonus, it felt damn good.

"Think about this." Colleen clamped the pliers around the now flaccid bulge in Collier's pants. Not too hard. Just enough to have his eyes bulging with pain—but mostly concern. "If you ever come near me or Dalton Shaw again, I will make certain you live the rest of your life sans balls."

"You wouldn't dare." Collier yelped when Colleen tightened her grip. "You'll go to prison. For a lot longer than your boyfriend."

"I'll have a jury of my peers. In a town this size, there's bound to be at least one woman you've screwed. Or her husband." Colleen smiled as though she relished the thought. "I'll walk, Collier. Hell, they'll throw me a parade."

The sweat rolling down Collier's face had nothing to do with the Arizona heat. It took all of twenty seconds and a slight twist of Colleen's wrist before he caved like a termite-infested floorboard.

"Fine," Collier ground out. "I'll stay away."

"It's good to know you have a few brains under that overly styled hairdo. Now, be a good boy and join Dole in his office. Stay there until Dalton and I are well out of sight. Understood?"

Colleen wasn't a fool. She knew that the chances of Collier letting the indignity she had served him today pass without recourse were slim to none. She could see the murder in his eyes as he closed the office door behind him. But for now, she had diverted a potentially disastrous situation the only way she knew how. And just in the nick of time.

Dalton honked as he pulled the T-Bird to a stop outside the garage door.

"Ready to go," he asked, leaning out the open window, a carefree grin on his handsome face.

"Perfect timing." Colleen shucked her coveralls, placing them in the trunk of the car before sliding into the passenger seat. Out of the corner of her eye, she caught sight of a police car parked down the street. One of Collier's cronies, no doubt. Her jaw tightened. So she had been right about everything.

"You look beat." Concern in his blue eyes, Dalton lightly touched her flushed cheek.

"It was one of those days." *And then some*. It took some effort, but Colleen mustered up a smile. "It's looking up."

Brushing his lips across hers, Dalton eased out of the parking lot. "I hope that has something to do with me."

"You. The promise of a cool shower. And food. I need food."

Settling back, Colleen closed her eyes, breathing freely for the first time since Collier's arrival at the garage. She doubted Dalton would appreciate her efforts on his behalf. He struck her as the kind of man who liked to take care of his problems on his own. *Well, too damn bad, buddy*. There was no need for Dalton to find out what she had done. And with any luck, he would be out of Midas and safely back in Los Angeles before Collier mustered the courage to retaliate.

Colleen would miss Dalton. More than she liked to admit. She had hoped he might stick around longer than originally planned so they could enjoy each other's company. However, after today, Colleen realized that for Dalton's sake, the sooner he left Midas, the better.

Opening her eyes, Colleen turned her head. Dalton Shaw. So handsome. So funny. Infinitely kind. Outrageously sexy. As though sensing her attention, he glanced her way. And oh, those killer blue eyes. Feeling a little tug at her heart, Colleen reached for Dalton's hand, not the least bit surprised when he didn't hesitate to lace his fingers through hers. This might be her last night with him. She wasn't going to spend it worrying about Collier *or* the future.

One last night? Colleen was going to make certain it was one neither of them forgot.

CHAPTER TWELVE

THERE WERE MANY modern conveniences Colleen believed she could live without. Indoor plumbing was not one of them. The thought of trudging out to do her business—winter, spring, summer, or fall—over a hole in the ground was a big *hell no*. Given no choice, she supposed could get used to it—maybe. However, the ability to enjoy a shower with hot and cold running water after a long day at work, was a pleasure she would fight to the death before giving up.

The world was a brighter place as Colleen turned off the taps than fifteen minutes earlier when she had wearily turned them on. Full blast and goosebumps-inducing cold. Toward the end, she amped up the heat to rinse the shampoo from her hair. Colleen smiled as she reached for a towel. Never underestimate the power of excellent water pressure.

Walking from the bathroom, Colleen headed down the hall. It was the only one in the apartment, but her place was small and didn't lend itself to guests—another plus. Going out to socialize meant she could leave whenever she wanted. Bad date? *Adios*. Obnoxious friends? *See ya*. Her home wasn't luxurious. But it—and her bathroom—were hers and hers alone.

However, there was something to be said for finding six feet plus of sexy man lying on her bed. Dalton was propped up against her headboard. Right where she left him. Shoes neatly placed on the floor at the end of the bed. His white cotton shirt unbuttoned halfway down his chest, his long legs stretched out, Dalton looked up as Colleen walked into the room. She could get used to a sight like that.

Nope, she chided herself. She wouldn't go down that dead end road. She would take a snapshot in her head, pulling it out now and then when her spirits needed a boost.

"Look at you. Better than an expensive bedspread any day."

Colleen sat next to Dalton. Because she could, she traced his upper lip with her index finger, marveling at how soft it felt in contrast to the

132

bristly texture of his close-cropped mustache. Playfully, he nipped at her finger, taking it between his teeth, his tongue lapping at the tip. His gaze moved from Colleen's face to the towel wrapped around her body.

"Was that necessary?" Straight-faced, but blue eyes twinkling, Dalton tugged at the cloth. "I've seen you without clothing. A sight to behold, by the way. Walk around naked. I won't complain."

"I'm all wet, Dalton." Hearing how that sounded—combined with Dalton's waggling eyebrows—Colleen burst out laughing. "Get your mind out of the gutter."

"Ladies first."

"Fair enough," Colleen nodded, slapping Dalton's hand away before it slid from her outer to inner thigh.

"What is this?"

In an instant, Dalton's expression morphed from playful to concerned, his gaze centering on her chest. Looking down, Colleen sighed with relief.

"It's called a rash, Dalton. The way you were staring I expected something serious."

Dalton carefully touched the reddened skin, his frown deepening. "I don't remember seeing it there last night."

Unconcerned, Colleen shrugged. "It's the curse of having this pale, Irish complexion."

"What caused it?"

"You did. Or rather your beard."

Dalton's hand flew to his face. "Well, shit."

"Relax. I put some cream on it after my shower. In an hour or so, you won't know it was there."

Hiding her smile, Colleen couldn't resist kissing Dalton's earnest frown away. It didn't take long. Soon her towel was on the floor, followed by his shirt and jeans. As he nuzzled her breast, his tongue caressing the hard tip, Colleen decided that an itty bitty rash was a small price to pay for this much toe-curling pleasure.

"I'm going to be sorry later," Dalton told her as his lips trailed over her creamy skin.

"No, you won't," Colleen assured him, her fingers digging into his scalp, holding him close. "No regrets—for either of us."

IN DALTON'S EXPERIENCE, few things lived up to their hype. Claiming to be the biggest. The best. The greatest. More often than not it led to disappointment all around. However, he had to give it to Colleen. She promised that her mother's birthday party would be an over-the-top extravaganza. If anything, Dalton would say for once, reality exceeded expectations. And he enjoyed every second. By the whooping and hollering around him, it seemed the crowd of party goers felt the same.

As he watched Colleen weave her way toward him, a drink in each hand, Dalton had to wonder. Would he feel the same if he were related to the woman dancing on top of the picnic table to the strains of *Do You Think I'm Sexy?* The one dressed head to toe in a bright orange leopard-print bodysuit?

"My role model." Colleen handed Dalton a glass of iced tea. "It would be perfect if my dream had been to become a stripper."

"Your mom has moves. And a damn fine tush."

"Words every woman wants to hear from her date."

There was no heat behind Colleen's words. Looking closer, Dalton found a definite twinkle that made her emerald eyes shine with an inviting warmth. It was good, he thought. Better than good. Colleen told him she loved her mother. But those were only words. For a man who grew up without a solid maternal presence in his life, it was encouraging to witness affection first hand.

The party was already in full swing by the time Dalton and Colleen arrived at the lake. They were a bit later than planned, thanks to what Colleen laughingly called a romp. She used the word as she pulled her hair out of the way, allowing Dalton to zip up her dress. Fire-engine red with a splash of white flowers decorating the skirt, it flattered her red hair and pale skin perfectly. He wondered if she realized how beautiful she was. He doubted it. Colleen didn't fuss with her hair or makeup. She didn't spend hours worrying about what she wore. He noticed when she opened her closet that it was less than half full.

Dalton knew women who worked endlessly, their goal a look of casual, effortless elegance. With little thought, Colleen achieved what they couldn't by simply being herself. A flick of the comb through her thick, glossy red hair. A touch of color applied to her full lips and she was ready to go.

"You're staring." Colleen frowned, raising her hand to her chin. Do you see some motor oil? That stuff can be brutal to remove. Every now and then I miss a bit."

Shaking his head, Dalton took Colleen's hand. "Your face is perfect. Gorgeous."

"You think so?" Colleen sounded pleased—and a little surprised. "I was about to say the same to you."

"I prefer devastatingly handsome. Irresistibly sexy. Irrefutably talented. Undeniably—"

"Full of shit?" Colleen finished for him, batting her big, green, mockingly innocent eyes at him.

"Indubitably," he said with a wink.

If Dalton hadn't learned to laugh at himself—never taking the highs or the lows too seriously—he would have washed out of the music industry years ago. He and his bandmates kept each other grounded. After everything they had been through, they knew which soft spots to jab and which were off limits. Or at the very least, needed to be handled with kid gloves. Colleen could take as good as she gave. In Dalton's book, that quality wasn't just admirable. It was essential.

As the song ended, Colleen's mother swiveled her hips one last time before waving her arms in the air. The whoop she let out set off an

135

echoing response throughout the crowd.

"Where's my man?" Sherry demanded as someone handed her a bottle of beer. Tipping her head back, she took several long pulls.

"Here I am, baby," a deep voice called out.

Without warning—her laugh carefree—Sherry jumped. With ease, her husband caught her. Grabbing his ears, Sherry pulled him in for a long, lusty kiss, bringing a cheer from the crowd.

Rick Higgins was a big man. At least six five and closer to three hundred pounds than two. When Colleen introduced them, he sized Dalton up with a firm handshake and a keen eye. Though he appeared easy going, Dalton wondered how far that jovial manner would go if someone messed with him or his family. In only a few seemingly innocuous words, Rick made it clear that Colleen might not be blood, but in every way that counted, she was his daughter. Only a fool would miss the less than subtle warning.

"They look happy." Dalton watched as Rick set Sherry down as though she were a porcelain doll.

"Mom hit pay dirt with Rick."

"And vice versa?"

"He thinks so." Colleen shook her head, as though puzzled. Then she shrugged. "I guess that's all that matters."

"You love your mother. So does Rick." As the music changed to a slower, hold your woman close, ballad, Dalton took Colleen into his arms. "You don't understand how she works. It seems he does."

"You're right." Colleen relaxed, letting her head rest on Dalton's shoulder. "What makes you so wise?"

"Wisdom is easy from a distance. When it comes to my sister, I haven't a clue."

"I don't agree. You know exactly who Maggie is."

"Mm." Colleen's body gently brushed against his, mimicking the song's subtle backbeat. "She's our mother all over again. Absolutely self-absorbed. Manipulative. I haven't seen signs of alcohol or drug abuse, but I wouldn't be surprised. As for the men?" Dalton shrugged. "Her husband seems devoted."

"Do you think—?"

"Go on. I'm curious to get your input."

"You told me that your sister's husband was behind the tabloid's story. That *he* was the one who wanted money to keep quiet. *He* kept Maggie from not visiting you more often. What if..."

"You think Maggie controls Norris, not the other way around?"

Colleen met his gaze. "You've always known, haven't you?"

"Yes."

"I'm sorry."

It wasn't just her words. Dalton felt Colleen's concern—her empathy. She wrapped her arms around him, drawing him closer. *A healing touch?* That might have been overstating it just a bit. However, Dalton felt better having Colleen near. A thought flitted through his mind. Impractical. Unrealistic. Something he could never say aloud. But there it was. In that instant, as his lips brushed Colleen's temple and he breathed in the heady fragrance that was uniquely her, Dalton wished he never had to let her go.

They didn't speak, their movements minimal. More of a sway than a dance. It was easy to block out everyone else, imagining the two of them were alone under the stars. Then, the mellow notes faded. The next selection? Dalton wasn't surprised to hear a guitar blast from none other than Jimi Hendrix. Dalton had to applaud the eclectic selection.

"Mom loves this music," Colleen explained "Hungry?"

"Starving. The smell of barbecue is driving me crazy."

Taking Dalton's hand, Colleen led him toward the layout of food.

"Janis Joplin. The Doors. Mom considers herself an honorary child of the sixties. Without the free love and drugs."

"I don't think your mother gets the point of the sixties."

"My mother lives in blissful ignorance of many things."

Colleen handed him a paper plate, filling her own from the endless choices crowded onto the table. Citronella candles burned bright, placed strategically in an attempt to keep bugs at bay. From what Dalton could see, they were doing a fine job. Not a mosquito in sight.

"You like to face things head on." Dalton felt confident in his assessment. "Maybe you were switched at birth."

As they were meant to, Dalton's words made Colleen laugh. "You've guessed my guilty secret. I used to wish that were true. I used to fantasize that my real parents were fabulously wealthy.

"And?"

"And that was it." Colleen held a cherry tomato to Dalton's mouth. Obligingly, he opened, letting her pop it in. "I was extremely shallow. Instead of appreciating what I had. A loving mother. Plenty to eat. A warm, clean bed to sleep in. I dreamed of endless pocket money to spend however I desired."

"You were a kid."

"I had that dream last week."

Mouth still filled with tomato, it was all Dalton could do not to spew the juice onto the array of casseroles and salads. At the last second, he covered his mouth with a napkin, diverting disaster.

"Jesus, Colleen. Never make a person laugh when their mouth is full."

"I was serious," Colleen said with a straight face. Her eyes, on the other hand, brimmed with mirth. "Sort of."

"I know." Dalton tapped her chin. "*Sort of* is why it's funny."

"A man who gets my sense of humor? I never thought I would see the day."

"Never say never, Colleen. The world is filled with endless wonders."

This time, it was Colleen's turn to laugh. Such a lovely sound, Dalton thought, scooping up a serving of potato salad. Natural and wonderfully contagious. An intriguing idea formed in his brain. It needed some tinkering. Putting it aside for now, he followed Colleen to the edge of the lake and a couple of empty folding chairs.

138

"What can I get you to drink?" Dalton asked, setting his plate on the nearby folding table.

"Something soft. I think there's lemonade." Colleen gave him a grateful smile. Frowning, her attention shifted to a point over his shoulder. "I don't believe what I'm seeing. That ballsy bitch."

"What?" Dalton looked but saw nothing out of the ordinary.

"Bonnie Langley at twelve o'clock."

Certain there must be some kind of mistake, Dalton shifted his gaze. *Well, damn.* Colleen was right. Standing near the steps of the cabin was none other than the woman who literally changed his life. Not exactly a blast from the past. But close enough—if that blast included nothing but bad memories.

"What do you think she wants?"

"We both know the answer to that," Colleen scoffed. "Look at the way she's dressed. Short shorts. A barely there halter top. Hooker heels. She might as well be sporting an open for business sign. Of course, you're the only customer she's targeting."

"Does she think I'm an idiot?" Amazed at the woman's gall, Dalton snickered. When Colleen didn't join in, he checked her face. He didn't like what he saw. "Do *you* think I'm an idiot?"

"I think you should talk to her. In regards to your idiocy? Doubtful. But she turned your head before. And I'll say one thing about Bonnie. She has a spectacular set of tatas."

"Colleen—"

Finally, Colleen laughed, though it wasn't as carefree as before. "You want to put a period on the past, Dalton. Whatever her motives, Bonnie has presented you with a chance to close another door for good."

Dalton knew Colleen was right. It made sense. Yet, he hesitated. "She's crashing the party. Your stepfather could throw her out."

"Half these people weren't invited. That's the way it goes at these get-togethers, Dalton. Go," Colleen urged when he didn't move. "I'll be here when you've finished."

139

"Promise?"

"Where would I go?"

Up until now, Dalton had drawn little attention beyond mild curiosity. His celebrity caused some buzz, but nothing more than a few whispers and couple of shout outs from a fan or two. Understandably, as he approached Bonnie, that changed. With each step he took. As more and more partygoers became aware of him, Bonnie, and their history, the interest shifted his way. Dalton was used to having thousands of eyes on him. Sometimes hundreds of thousands. However, this was different. On stage, he knew his part. He could improvise a drum riff in his sleep. What he felt didn't qualify as nerves. Or anger. It was closer to staring into the unknown, certain nothing good was on the other side. There was nothing wrong with a little trepidation, Dalton decided. It would keep him on his toes.

Out of nowhere, a nonsensical thought hit Dalton. He had been inside this woman. In more than one orifice. Yet he knew almost nothing about her besides her name, that she wasn't a natural blonde, and her duplicitous nature. Come to think of it, that was all he needed—or wanted to know.

"Bonnie." Dalton didn't add a hello, a how have you been, or a kiss my ass. He simply looked her straight in the eyes and waited.

If Dalton felt hesitant over this meeting, Bonnie seemed to have no such reservations. Placing a hand on her curvy hip, she cocked it in Dalton's direction. She was a little rounder than he remembered. But he had to admit, the extra pounds looked good on her. Seeing what she interpreted as male interest, Bonnie's smile widened as though she greeted an old lover instead of the man who she helped send to prison.

It must be nice to have a short memory. And a convenient one. Dalton had neither. Memories—good and bad—were etched in painfully potent acid. Then there was his tendency to hold a grudge. Dalton had never been one to turn the other cheek.

"I don't have to ask how you are." Bonnie giggled. That was bad enough, but when she batted her eyes, he rolled his. "Mr. Famous Rock Star. My friends don't believe when I tell them I knew you when. In the biblical

140

sense."

Bonnie leaned close, placing a hand in the middle of Dalton's chest. To those watching, it probably seemed like an intimate gesture. Dalton stepped back, breaking contact. The woman had to be out of her mind.

"Did you mention to your friends that you perjured yourself in court? Lied about me and what happened the night I was arrested?"

Suddenly, Bonnie seemed uncomfortable as the center of attention. Lowering her voice, she tried the big, sad eyes routine. "You have to understand. I didn't have a choice. Collier forced me."

"I understand."

Brightening, Bonnie regained some of her female confidence. "I knew you would."

"I understand that I don't give a damn."

"Excuse me?" Not what she expected, Dalton's response put a confused frown between Bonnie's eyebrows.

"I used to lie in my cell at night imagining what you would say if we were to meet again. I fantasized about your remorse. Your tears. Your apologies. I wanted you to beg so that I could throw it back in your face."

"Of course, I want to apologize."

To Dalton's amazement, he swore he saw a drop of moisture in the corner of Bonnie's eyes. She had missed her calling as an actress. The problem was, acting took drive and ambition. Blowjobs and free fucks would have gotten her only so far—outside of the porn industry.

"Save your breath. I've realized I don't want or need anything from you."

"Are you sure about that?" Bonnie purred.

Though the thought of touching her made his skin crawl, Dalton had to give the woman points for perseverance.

"I don't know if your husband sent you or if it was your idea. Either way, I want you to think about this, Bonnie. This time, when I leave Midas, it will be for good. On the other hand, you are stuck in this town—with Collier—for life."

"You're wrong. Collier is going to be a United States senator."

Dalton would have laughed, but several people in the crowd beat him to it.

"In your dreams, Bonnie," a woman called out.

"Senator Collier Langley? Hell, no," added someone else.

"There's your answer, Bonnie," Dalton said.

The look of panic in Bonnie's eyes. The dawning horrified realization that the dream of getting out of Midas might be just that—a dream—was all the revenge Dalton needed.

Not sparing Bonnie another glance, Dalton turned, seeking out Colleen. As promised, she was right there. Waiting.

"Your food is waiting. And, Mom is almost ready to cut her birthday cake."

"What kind?" Dalton asked.

Colleen searched his eyes. With a satisfied nod at what she saw, she looped her arm through his. Casually, as though Bonnie wasn't staring daggers at their backs, she strolled with him, the crowd parting.

"We are talking about my mother, Dalton. Ten layers, ten flavors."

"Can't go wrong with that." Dalton brought Colleen's hand to his lips for a lingering kiss. "I can't wait to see if she likes the gift I got for her."

"Big and bold?"

"As big and bold as I could find. Not to mention shiny as hell."

Colleen grinned. "Mom will be over the moon."

CHAPTER THIRTEEN

COLLEEN WOKE FROM a deep, dreamless sleep with a smile on her face. The same smile she wore as she dozed—happy and sated. Why did she have to open her eyes? Last night had been magical. There was no way today could possibly live up to such lofty standards. Determined to make perfection last a few moments longer, she snuggled down under the covers.

"Good morning."

"It is." Colleen reached for Dalton but found the mattress beside her empty and the sheets disturbingly cold. "I've changed my mind. How can it be good when I'm here, and you aren't?"

The bed sagged. *That* was promising.

"Why don't you come out from under there? I want to ask you a question."

"Ask away." Colleen lifted one corner of the covers. "Under here. With me."

"Okay."

"Why did you get dressed?" She wanted bare skin. Blue jeans and a t-shirt didn't cut it. "I'm not."

"I had to go out for a few minutes. The world tends to frown on a naked man walking down a public street."

"The world would change its collective mind once it got a load of you."

To her chagrin, Dalton stopped her from pushing his shirt up his chest. Instead, he rolled them over until she was on her back, firmly pinned down. Colleen tugged, but Dalton firmly held her wrists over her head.

"I like this feisty mood," Dalton grinned. "Normally, you're already up and on your way to work."

Colleen wasn't in the mood to think about work. Not after what happened yesterday. She wasn't going to let anything interfere with her morning happy. Stretching, she blinked the last of the sleep from her eyes, bringing Dalton into focus for the first time.

"What did you do?"

"I was wondering when you were going to notice."

"You shaved!" Colleen pulled her wrists free, reversing their positions. Fascinated, she carefully touched his smooth cheek, as though uncertain it wasn't an illusion. "Why?"

Watching her closely, Dalton shrugged. "I felt like a change. What do you think?"

"Did you do this because of me?" Colleen couldn't help but ask. If the answer was yes, it had to mean Dalton meant to stick around a little longer. Otherwise, why bother?

Dalton nodded, causing Colleen's heartbeat to flutter. Shrugging, he met her gaze. "I don't like hurting you. I know you said the rash was no big deal... Besides, I can always grow it back."

It was obvious how uncomfortable Dalton was with delving into the implications of his impulsive actions. Colleen was more than satisfied with his answer, so she dropped it, circling back to his initial inquiry.

"I think you're prettier than I am."

"Jesus, Colleen. That wasn't exactly the reaction I was hoping for."

"Just stating the facts," she stated with a teasing smile.

So smooth, Colleen thought, brushing his chin with her lips. The beard had given Dalton a rakish air. She may have overstated the pretty part. Beautiful. And younger. Almost vulnerable. *That* she wouldn't tell him. But it made her want to protect him from the evil she knew lurked around the corners of Midas.

Bonnie's appearance last night reinforced what Colleen had learned from Collier's visit to the garage. Greasing the path to his election was paramount. Irrationally, the Langley family seemed to view Dalton as a major obstacle to that goal. They were loose cannons. Unpredictable.

How desperate were they? Was Dalton in danger? Were they capable of setting something in motion that would cause him bodily harm? The thought sent a shiver up Colleen's spine.

"Earth to Colleen." Grinning, Dalton gently tapped the side of her head. "Where did you go?"

144

"Deep thoughts about transmissions and fuel injectors." *And how to get you out of town as fast as possible.* Selfishly, Colleen wanted Dalton to stay. However, a few more days of fun weren't worth keeping him in the Langley's crosshairs. "Dalton—"

"Put on some clothes." Dalton jumped from the bed, opening the top drawer of her dresser. "Panties. T-shirt. Shorts. That's all you need for now."

Dalton tossed the bundle onto the bed. Then crossed his arms and waited. Laughing, Colleen shimmied into the underwear.

"How about a bra?"

His lips quirked, a small smile forming. Considering, he stared at her chest. "Nope."

Not the least bit offended, Colleen donned the shirt. The shorts quickly followed. "I'll admit, my assets are less than overflowing, but..."

"Your assets are perfect." Dalton handed her a pair of flip flops. "But we aren't going far. Indulge my perverse need to know I could slip my hand under your shirt and find nothing but skin."

"If that's as perverse as you get—"

Colleen gasped as Dalton unexpectedly wrapped his arms around her waist, lifting her until they were eye to eye, feet dangling inches from the floor.

"This?" his palm cupped her breast—under the t-shirt. "Perverse-lite. There are other things—needs—in my head that would put a red hot blush all over your soft, pretty skin."

Colleen's eyes widened. She wasn't sure what to say.

"Surprised?" Dalton asked, his hot breath bathing the curve of her ear.

"Yes."

"Scared?"

That made her pause. Colleen thought about it, rolled it around, then thought some more. She didn't know exactly what Dalton meant. Couldn't know unless he decided to elaborate. But scared?

"No. I'm not."

"Maybe I'll tell you about it someday." With a brush of his lips against hers, Dalton set Colleen down. "If you're interested."

"Maybe I am."

"Maybe?" Dalton's eyes had darkened from bright to midnight blue.

Colleen had to admit, she was intrigued. Licking her lips, she let out a breath she hadn't realized she was holding.

"Probably."

"Another time," Dalton nodded.

As fast as that, he dropped intense for playful. Dalton didn't seem the least bit fazed by the quick change. However, Colleen was a little disoriented. It emphasized what was so easy to forget. She didn't know this man. Deep down, Colleen felt they were connected. She was certain she could trust Dalton. Sharing her body had been a no-brainer. More difficult was remembering how long she had known him. A few days. That was all. There were parts of him she didn't know or understand. The same was true for her. Yet...

"I've told you things no one else knows."

Dalton nodded. "Me, too."

"I shouldn't feel this comfortable with a relative stranger." Colleen shook her head, her gaze puzzled. "Should I?"

"I clicked with Ryder and Ashe the instant we met." Dalton paused, trying to find the right words. "Musically. Emotionally. The bond formed, then and there. Time and our shared experiences have strengthened it, but we were brothers from the very beginning."

Colleen understood what Dalton was saying. Hours. Days. Years. That unexplainable connection couldn't be measured by time. She had it with Dalton. When he was back in Los Angeles—hundreds of miles away—it would still exist. Colleen found the thought comforting. And distressing.

"Come on." Dalton took her hand, pulling her toward the door.

Laughing at his impatience, Colleen pulled back. "Give me a couple of minutes to wash my face. And take a pee."

"Fine. But hurry."

Colleen sped through her usual morning routine. A shower could wait. Brushing her teeth couldn't. While she was at it, she ran a comb through her hair, clipping it back into a modified ponytail, finishing with a dab of lip gloss.

Waiting by the front door—pacing was more like it—Dalton sent Colleen a quizzical look as she entered the living room.

"You look the same—but different."

"I combed my hair."

"It's more than that." Taking her mouth with his in a long, slow kiss, Dalton pulled away, running his tongue over his bottom lip. "Watermelon?"

"Nice taster." Colleen motioned for Dalton to follow her outside. "Now, what's the big deal? I—"

"It was delivered this morning. Our band manager, Alden Christopher pulled a few strings with the dealership in Los Angeles."

A brand new Porsche. The car must have come in from Phoenix. Not a big deal for a big name rock star, but that kind of preferential treatment wasn't an everyday occurrence in Colleen's world. Or every week. Or year.

Reverentially, Colleen ran her hand over the gleaming finish. Not a speck of dust in sight. The person who delivered the car must have washed and polished it before handing the keys to Dalton. She doubted that he noticed. He would be used to little touches like that. It emphasized in flashing neon how different his world was from hers.

"You didn't get the same color."

Placing his hand on the car's surface—almost touching Colleen's—Dalton said casually, "I've grown partial to red."

There was nothing casual about the butterflies his words caused in Colleen's stomach. They stood next to the vehicle that would carry him out of her life, and he chose this moment to slather on another layer of charm? *Jerk*.

"Did you say something?"

Colleen was certain she hadn't. Has Dalton read her mind? Connected

147

was one thing. Telepathy was a level of togetherness she wasn't certain she was ready to explore. Ever.

"It's gorgeous."

Dalton dangled the keys in front of Colleen. "Want to take her for a drive?"

"Does a bear do his business in the woods?" Practically giddy, Colleen grabbed the keys, then looked at her feet. "It's a stick shift. I need different shoes. And a bra. This t-shirt is practically see-through. If we meet up with someone, I don't feel like giving them a free show."

"While you're changing, pack a bag."

That stopped Colleen in her tracks. "Where are we going?"

"Los Angeles."

Slowly, Colleen walked back toward Dalton. She must have misheard.

"Los Angeles, California?"

"Is there another?" Dalton's lips twitched before morphing into a full-on grin. "You should see your face. Wait." Lickety-split, he pulled out his phone, taking Colleen's picture. "Look. I'd title this one *flabbergasted*."

Colleen pushed the phone away. Yes, she looked surprised. Who wouldn't? Dalton Shaw—casual as you please—had just asked her to accompany him to Los Angeles. With no warning. No lead-up. Out of the freaking blue. How else was she supposed to react?

"It's a little far to go for a test drive."

"It's September."

"But it feels like the middle of July. So?" Colleen needed more than a reminder of the changing calendar. She needed details.

"Let's go inside. Pretty soon, your nose will be as red as the car."

"A few minutes ago you were all charm. Now you're comparing me to one of Santa's reindeer?"

"Santa's *heroic* reindeer." Dalton reminded Colleen, guiding her into the apartment.

"Never mind." Colleen wasn't in the mood to debate fictional North Pole dwellers. "What do Los Angeles, September, and most importantly, me, have to do with each other?"

Seating her first, Dalton flopped onto the sofa. "I've done the, *remember the bad times tour.* For the most part, I would say it was a hit. Not that there weren't a few sour notes. I learned a few things about myself and my sister. I may have changed your mother's opinion of me from bad to good."

Colleen couldn't argue with that. "She's a sucker for a good present. The earrings you gave her have leapfrogged to the top of her favorites."

"*And* I met you. Which, in order of importance, should have been mentioned first."

"There's that charm again."

"It isn't deliberate."

"That's what makes it so lethal."

Dalton's arm swung around Colleen's shoulders. "Here's the low down. The last thing I said to my friends was, *see you in September.* We are headlining a benefit concert on Wednesday—which I can't miss. Come with me. Watch the concert. You've never seen us live."

"My job."

To be honest, *Dole's Auto Repair* could sink into the dusty ground for all she cared. Chances were, she had ratcheted her last lug nut at that place. Other than some back salary, Colleen never wanted to see the greasy walls again. She wanted desperately to tell Dalton yes. Just as desperately—illogical as it may be—she grasped at a reason to say no.

"If you want, you can come back on Thursday. Private jet. Train. Hell, I'll send you by taxi."

Colleen didn't care about her mode of transportation. If was the first part of Dalton's statement that stuck in her head.

"*If* I want to come back?" Did she have a choice?

"You can stay as long as you want. I wouldn't argue if you never left."

"Dalton—"

Pressing his hand to Colleen's lips, Dalton met her gaze. It was hard to read what was going on behind those brilliant blue eyes. "For now, all I'm asking is that you come with me. Think of it as a vacation. When was the last time you took one of those?"

"I don't know. Maybe never."

"To say you're overdue puts it mildly."

"I want to say yes." More than anything.

"Then it's settled." Dalton gave her a gentle kiss. "We can talk about the rest later."

It didn't take Colleen long to change her clothes. Or pack the few things she deemed appropriate to wear in Los Angeles. Before heading out, she called her mother, expecting all kinds of arguments on why going away with Dalton was a colossally bad idea. After all, a pair of big, bold, shiny earrings only bought so much goodwill. Leave it to Sherry to surprise her daughter once again. Instead of a lecture, Colleen received a blessing and a bon voyage. Mothers, Colleen shook her head. She would never figure hers out.

"Ready?" Dalton asked, securing his seatbelt.

"Let's hit the road."

Life was filled with unforgettable moments. Colleen had a feeling, when she looked back, this one would rank near the top. She sat behind the wheel of a brand new, fire-engine red Porsche. On her way to Los Angeles. And riding shotgun, Dalton Shaw. *Was this actually happening?*

As the sign Colleen had seen so often in her dreams whizzed by, she had her answer. *Leaving Midas.* Damn straight this was happening. And best of all, she was wide awake, savoring every second.

CHAPTER FOURTEEN

THE TRIP FROM Midas to Los Angeles flew by. On the day Dalton left for Arizona, all he could think about was coming home. However, from the second they left Midas in their rearview mirror, he wished for time to slow down. All because of Colleen.

First, watching the enjoyment she received from driving the Porsche was a sight to see. Dalton had never met anyone—man or woman—who appreciated a car's every nuance the way Colleen did. She sighed over the powerful engine. Chuckled as she shifted into high gear, breathing in the smell of expensive leather as the air from the open window blew her hair in every direction.

Observing her, Dalton was reminded of a drawing he saw in a Paris museum. The subject lay in a pool of water, her long, dark hair swirling in the water. This was similar. With a major difference. The woman in the painting wept. There were no tears for Colleen. Her smile was brighter than the Arizona sun and twice as warm.

"It's going to take an hour to comb the tangles from my hair," Colleen said, raising her voice over the sound of the wind and the tunes blasting from the radio.

"Want to close the windows?" Dalton only asked to play along. They both knew the answer.

"Hell, no." Turning toward Dalton, Colleen tipped her sunglasses down. Her green eyes glowed emerald bright. "Do you know what this feels like?"

"Tell me."

"Freedom."

Dalton didn't know how long they drove in silence. Colleen bopped to some classic rock, he watched Colleen. At some point, with no warning, she rolled up the windows, adjusted the air conditioning, and turned off the radio. That was when time really began to fly. When they started talking. There was no set topic. It wasn't about gleaning deep insights.

151

Though, in a way, that's exactly what happened.

"I had sex for the first time on my sixteenth birthday."

Colleen's hands were busy pulling her hair into a semblance of a ponytail while Dalton steered from the passenger seat. He didn't think anything of it when she told him to grab the wheel. The stretch of road was long, curve-free and there wasn't another vehicle in sight.

"I beat you by a year."

"I concede defeat," Colleen laughed, taking back control of the car. "I didn't sleep around, though my reputation says otherwise. And it wasn't about rebellion. Or boredom. I liked sex. The boys I dated made up for lack of skill with youthful vigor. I contributed enthusiasm."

"Sounds fair." Dalton wasn't jealous. Though he couldn't help envying any boy lucky enough to have known the teenage Colleen.

"I thought so. Gossip runs rampant in a small town. I wasn't oblivious. My skin wasn't as tough as it is now. But looking back, I wouldn't change a thing."

"You scared them."

"How do you mean?" Colleen asked, her expression puzzled.

"It doesn't matter what century we live in. Girls are expected to act a certain way. You were a confident young woman who unapologetically embraced her sexuality. For those small-minded Midas assholes, you must have been a fucking nightmare."

"You think so?"

"I do." Dalton patted her knee. Another plus to Colleen driving. Because she wore shorts, he was able to admire the long expanse of her creamy legs.

"I like your way of thinking." Colleen's hand covered his, squeezing. "Why the drums?"

It was a startling turn in the conversation, but Dalton didn't hesitate to answer.

"It started out as a way to take out my aggression."

"Were you an angry boy?"

"I was…" Dalton tried to find the right word. "Frustrated. I never knew my father. My mother lived in her own drug and alcohol-filled world. Maggie was always a handful. I needed an outlet and finding someone to fight was never a problem. We were boys."

"If you say so." Colleen shook her head with a perplexed smile.

"Girls are different," Dalton agreed.

"Don't get me started on how girls deal with each other. That would take hours and boxes of Kleenex. I'm interested in you and your childhood need to pound things."

"I got lucky."

A teacher stepped into one of Dalton's fights. Mr. Dedham could have done the expected thing and sent the boys to the principal. Instead, he had them meet him after school in the auditorium.

"Pound on these instead of each other. Try it for one afternoon."

These turned out to be a set of drums. The other boy, Dalton had long ago forgotten his name, did what he was told then left. Dalton came back the next day. Then the next. He had no idea he had found his calling. But from the first instant, he loved the feel of the sticks in his hands. He was hooked.

"And magically, you never got into another fight."

"Fair point, smartass," Dalton chuckled. "I've had my share since then. None since prison. I stopped blaming myself for that one long before my latest visit to Midas."

"Glad to hear it." Colleen took her foot off the gas. "I need to stretch my legs. While I check out the bathroom, why don't you get us something cold?"

The rest stop was full-service. Gasoline. Restrooms. The store had a big sign boasting fresh-picked local produce.

153

"Water or juice," Dalton asked, stepping out of the car. Colleen was right. He needed to move around.

"Anything without bubbles. I know you think I'm irresistible, but you might change your mind if you have to listen to me belch from here to Los Angeles."

Dalton was still smiling when the bell over the convenience store door signaled his entrance. The place wasn't crowded, but the young man behind the counter seemed to be doing a steady business. He estimated seven or eight patrons of varying ages. Walking toward the refrigerated coolers that lined the back wall, he was about to reach for a carton of orange juice when he heard the first whisper.

"Is that...?" a female voice whispered.

"OMG!" said someone else with a definite squeal. "I think you're right."

Amused, Dalton waited. He could have hurried down the far aisle—in the opposite direction. The exit wasn't that far away. Avoiding the inevitable would have been a piece of cake. Instead, he let them make their move. Or not. Fans were part of the price he paid for his success. A small, and more often than not, enjoyable price.

"Excuse me."

Turning, Dalton removed his sunglasses and smiled. The response made him grin. Unadulterated adoration. It was something he never got used to. Or tired of. After all, he was only human.

Two women, he guessed they were in their late thirties, stared at him with wide eyes surrounded by sunburned faces. They were dressed for the weather in baggy shorts and t-shirts. The brunette's shirt proclaimed her love for *The Ryder Hart Band* in bold red letters. He recognized it as the logo from their last tour.

"Did you make it to a concert?" Dalton asked, taking the pen from the woman's numb fingers. Unable to speak, she nodded, turning so he could autograph the back part of her shoulder.

"I was there, too." The other woman spoke up, pushing her mute friend

154

aside.

"I hope you had a good time."

"Oh," she gulped, blinked, and then swallowed again. "It was the best show ever. Ever! Can I get a picture?"

"Absolutely."

That opened the floodgates. Every person in the store wanted an autograph, a picture, and a few moments of Dalton's time. He didn't know how, but their numbers seemed to multiply. Taking it in stride, he posed, keeping an eye out for Colleen.

"My granddaughter is going to have a fit when I post this on Facebook." Grinning, the woman who didn't look like anybody's grandmother, smooshed her face next to his before snapping the selfie. "Ella was supposed to be with me today but opted to sleep away the morning rather than take a boring road trip. Boring, my ass. By the way, you look even sexier without the beard." She planted her lips on Dalton's cheek, catching the moment on her phone.

Amused, Dalton shook his head. Out of the corner of his eye, he noticed Colleen next to a display of *Hostess Twinkies*, hands in her pockets, grinning as she observed him and his fans. She opened her mouth, about to hit with a cheeky observation, no doubt, but was interrupted by Ella's grandmother.

"Don't be shy, honey." The woman grabbed Colleen's hand, depositing her next to Dalton. "You may never get another chance to meet a bona fide rock star."

Wide eyed, Colleen gave Dalton what he assumed was supposed to be a shy smile. Colleen may have fooled the people observing their exchange, but not him. She was many things—most of them good—but shy was not on the list.

"I didn't want to be a bother."

"No bother," Dalton assured her, wondering how far she was going to take this.

155

"I don't have anything for you to autograph," Colleen said, rooting around in her purse. All she came out with was a felt-tipped pen. With a twinkle in her green eyes, she kept her back to the interested crowd. "Will this do?"

When Colleen whipped up her shirt, showing him her lace-covered breasts, Dalton had to bite the inside of his cheek. It was either that or burst out laughing. The expressions on everyone's faces were priceless. Shocked. Amazed. Intrigued. Dalton caught Colleen's gaze. *I dare you*, she seemed to say. Taking the pen, perfectly aware that cameras were catching every moment, Dalton leaned close to her chest, until his lips were within kissing distance.

"Wait until I get you alone," he breathed. Instead of signing his name, Dalton left a tiny bullseye.

"I can't wait." Replacing her shirt, Colleen held up her camera before putting her arm around Dalton. "Smile."

A few minutes later, they were pulling out of the parking lot, Dalton behind the wheel. Colleen had slipped the keys into his pocket while she took their picture. When she followed him to his car, sliding into the passenger seat, it appeared he was giving a ride to a beautiful, redheaded stranger.

"One of them might have seen us arrive together," Dalton pointed out as Colleen had a good laugh.

"Maybe. But so what? We gave them a show they won't soon forget. Good, relatively clean, PG-rated fun. When Grandma recounts her meeting with Dalton Shaw—and me—the granddaughter will be kicking herself in her sleepy ass for years to come."

Colleen sipped her juice. When Dalton didn't respond, she looked at him, her eyes concerned.

"Did I mess up?"

"No."

"Then tell me what you're thinking."

Dalton raised Colleen's hands to his lips, his eyes brimming with warmth.

"Best road trip ever."

"WE'RE ABOUT FIVE minutes from my house." Dalton slowed, cautiously maneuvering the hairpin curve. He had Ryder on speaker phone.

"We figured that's where you would head. Are you going to introduce me?"

"Colleen McNamara. Ryder Hart. He's bossy, but the rest of us have learned to live with it."

"Hello, Colleen."

"Hello, Ryder." Colleen seemed to find the exchange highly amusing.

"We'll see you soon. Both of you."

"Shit." Dalton ended the connection.

"What?"

"He's waiting for us. At my house. They all are."

"Ah." Colleen nodded in complete understanding. "Your friends want to check me out."

"No." When he saw her lips curve upward, Dalton sighed. "Maybe. Ashe dated a woman for a short time. She considered herself an amateur psychiatrist. In her opinion, the members of *The Ryder Hart Band* are codependent and emotionally stunted. On her way out the door—helped with a figurative kick by Ashe—she suggested we should seek professional help. Immediately."

"I'll reserve judgment. However, Ashe's lady friend sounds like she wanted him to herself."

"We've been a tight unit for a long time. For the most part, Quinn slid right in."

157

"You don't think they'll like me?" Colleen frowned.

That wasn't the problem. Only somebody with a screw loose wouldn't like Colleen. Dalton felt the same about his friends—his brothers and sister. He couldn't imagine anyone not embracing them immediately. However, the way he felt wasn't at issue.

"I want you to like them."

That perked her up. "*I* like you. *They* like you. That puts the odds in our favor."

"You like me, huh?" Dalton shot her a provocative smile. "How much?"

"What are you, twelve?" Laughing, Colleen swatted his hand away as his fingers tiptoed up her thigh.

"How much?" Dalton persisted, his hand continuing to roam.

"Remember that thing I did for you last night? The one that left you unable to move for a good five minutes?"

"Mm." Special did not begin to define it.

"You are the only person I've ever *satisfied* in that way."

"Really?" Dalton was thrilled—and surprised. "You did it with such confidence."

"I was inspired." Colleen placed her hand over his where it rested on her upper thigh.

"I'm flattered. And grateful." Dalton knew he should stop while he was way ahead, but he couldn't resist. "Where did you learn to do that with your tongue?"

Colleen shrugged. "I read it in a book. And no, not the Karma Sutra. Which, by the way, is overrated."

"You've read the Karma Sutra?" With a sly smile, Colleen nodded. "You're killing me, Red."

"*Overrated*, Dalton."

"The book has been around for almost a thousand years. Don't you think

158

we owe it a chance—or two—before writing it off completely?"

Considering, Colleen tapped her chin. "Fine. Find a copy and we'll give one position a whirl. Your choice. Honestly, Dalton. It's a lot of kerfuffles."

"As a reasonable, intelligent adult, I would like to find that out for myself."

"Fine," she sighed. "I hope this puts to rest your question about how much I like you."

It did. However, Dalton's belief in Colleen's feelings had nothing to do with wild, sexual positions. It was something else. Something he doubted Colleen was aware had happened. He had called her Red—more than once. It was a nickname she claimed to hate, yet she hadn't complained. Or batted an eye.

Shifting into low, Dalton smiled. There was no doubt that Colleen liked him. More than she realized.

"I OWE QUINN five bucks," Ryder said, resting his arm across the back of the sofa. His fingers played with a few strands of Quinn's dark hair.

Dalton took a sip of his beer. "Then pay the woman. You can afford it."

They were seated in Dalton's living room. Ashe and Zoe opposite him, Ryder and Quinn to his right. After the usual warm greetings, Dalton had introduced Colleen. It went well—not that he was surprised. Hello and nice to meet you rarely unearthed any hidden landmines. His friends were open and welcoming. Colleen the same. The initial meeting went well.

Dalton showed Colleen to the master bedroom. Where, after a few minutes, she shooed him out. Ostensibly, she claimed she wanted to unpack and freshen up. In reality, she was giving him some time alone with his friends. His first instinct was to assure Colleen that it wasn't necessary. He hadn't been gone that long. How much catching up did they need to do? They spoke on the phone every day he was away.

It was the expression on Colleen's face that stopped him. She didn't look overwhelmed—exactly. Hesitant. This wasn't her territory. It made sense that she would need a few minutes to acclimate before jumping into a fully formed group of friends.

"The question isn't Ryder's ability to pay. It's why he needs to."

"Okay," Dalton could tell Ashe was bursting to share. "I'll jump. Why does Ryder owe Quinn five dollars?"

"Quinn believed there was more to you and Colleen than a little lust in the dust of Arizona. Ryder wasn't convinced. I thought it was a sure bet." Ashe took a five from his wallet, passing it to Quinn. Ryder did the same. "Zoe played Sphinx—as always."

"My money is still my own," Zoe said with a satisfied smirk. She wasn't one to laugh at her friend's misfortune—no matter how minor. However, she couldn't hide the laughter that sparkled in her blue eyes.

"What made you think so?" Dalton inquired of Quinn. She was fairly new to their circle. What had she noticed that his old friends hadn't?

"You told us that Colleen had the sweetest smile," Quinn reminded him.

"That's it?" Dalton kept an eye on the stairs. He was curious, but he didn't want Colleen walking in on this conversation.

"My words exactly." Ryder tugged on Quinn's hair, earning him a slap that was more playful than angry. The couple looked at each other with such a mixture of love and desire, Dalton started to get a contact high.

"Before I suggest you two get a room," Ashe said, apparently feeling the same as Dalton, "I'm certain Dalton would like to know why we conceded the bet to Quinn."

"Well?" Genuinely perplexed, Dalton looked around the room.

"You shaved," Ashe grinned as if those two words said it all.

Automatically, Dalton's hand went to his face. It felt strange to find a small bit of stubble instead of the beard he had cultivated for the past five years.

160

"I felt like a change."

"Right. And Ryder has developed a sudden scissors phobia." Zoe rolled her eyes, making her opinion obvious. "Men are so easy."

"I wouldn't object if Ryder wanted to go shorter." Smiling, Quinn touched the dark wavy hair that brushed Ryder's shoulders. "Yes, I think longer is sexy. But it's only an opinion."

"I'll get it cut." Ryder returned Quinn's smile, his eyes locked with hers. "Eventually."

"See what I mean?" Zoe had to laugh. She loved her brother. He loved Quinn. He was happy. That was all that mattered. "What did Colleen say to get you to shave?"

"Nothing." Dalton knew he sounded defensive. When Zoe gave him one of her patented stares, he stared back. Truth was on his side. "Colleen didn't say a damn thing."

"Right." Zoe wasn't convinced.

Colleen chose that moment to appear, saving Dalton the embarrassment of explaining. He knew it was only a matter of time. Eventually, he would cave under the intense blue of Zoe's stare. It was good to be home. Good to have his friends around him. It felt right. Normal. However, it changed the dynamics between him and Colleen.

In Midas, there had been a feeling of him against the world. Colleen had quickly become his ally. This thing between them grew rapidly. Faster than if they had met here in Los Angeles. It hadn't taken Dalton long to realize what was happening. As crazy as it sounded, he was falling in love with Colleen. Hell, he was so close to being all in it wasn't funny. It was too soon to expect her to be there with him. *Wasn't it?*

The chemistry was undeniable. That zing that zipped through Dalton the second he laid eyes on Colleen had been mutual. They had established that she liked him. Plus, she cared. She proved that more than once by defending him during that farce of a dinner party. Tolliver Cline soon discovered that Colleen outmatched and outclassed him in every way.

But love? Colleen walked down the staircase, smiling as she met Dalton's gaze. She had tamed her long red hair, securing it into a sassy ponytail. A natural beauty, she looked like a dream—one he wanted desperately to turn into a reality. The question was, how?

Dalton was afraid he had outdistanced Colleen on the emotional front. He didn't have long to help her play catch up. Already she had mentioned leaving the day after the concert. A home-field advantage played in his favor. Getting her to Los Angeles had been easier than he expected. *Keeping* her here would be the challenge.

CHAPTER FIFTEEN

COLLEEN FELT LIKE she had come home. She wasn't a big believer in love at first sight, but it happened to her. One look at Los Angeles was all it took to have a *where have you been all my life* moment. The energy. The hustle and bustle. The bright lights and endless opportunities. If she had ever questioned her desire to live in a big city, all doubts had been dispelled. This was where Colleen McNamara belonged.

It helped that she wasn't on her own. During the day, Dalton showed her around. She wouldn't classify what they did as touristy sight-seeing expeditions. More along the lines of getting in the car and driving. Breakfast in Beverly Hills. Lunch downtown. Dinner in the Valley. In between, they would stop if the mood hit. Park and walk. Colleen couldn't think of the last time her days were so unstructured. There were no timetables. No deadlines. No rules.

Tonight was the first time since their arrival that they had a fixed place to be. Dalton was meeting the rest of the band to rehearse for tomorrow night's benefit concert. After, they were all going out to eat at a downtown hot spot.

"You bought this place for the view." Colleen made it a statement, not a question.

Standing in front of the bank of windows, she could see the city laid out before her. Casting a late afternoon glow, the sun was starting to set. It felt as though nature was putting on a show for her alone.

"Spectacular, isn't it?" From behind, Dalton slid his arms around her waist. "Growing up, I had dreams. The first time I walked into this room, I wondered at how far I had come. My first thought was, *I'm a fraud. I don't belong here.* Certain the realtor was going to realize her mistake and call the cops, do you know what I did?"

"What?" Colleen snuggled close. She loved when Dalton shared such intimate moments. It made all of this—her time with him—seem real.

163

"I found a corner where I knew I wouldn't be overheard. Calling Ryder, I made him promise it wasn't all going to disappear. The fame. The success. The money. I asked if it was real. Had we really made it? Was it going to last?"

"He talked you down?"

"That's one of the things Ryder does best. A minor panic attack is what he called it. At the time, it felt anything but minor. Calmly, he reminded me we had a three-album deal. A sold-out concert tour. Three songs in the top ten—two of which I coauthored. The royalties from those alone would keep me in the black for a long, long, time."

It was funny. From the outside looking in, Colleen never would have guessed that Dalton possessed any insecurities. He came across—on stage and off—as a man totally in control. He exuded confidence. Success had a lot to do with that. Riding the top of the charts, screaming fans telling you with ticket sales and record-breaking albums that you were at the top of your game.

Colleen always assumed that if her bank account grew hefty enough, all her doubts would disappear. Money made the world safe. Stable. Secure. What she had learned since meeting Dalton was that, yes, money greased many paths. However, look at the wealthy residents of Midas. She had only a short glimpse at their underbellies, and it wasn't a pretty sight. The push to grasp more never ended. There was always somebody else standing in the spot one coveted. Satisfaction was fleeting for men like Tolliver Cline and Manfred T. Langley. Always wanting more might be keeping them on their toes. But happiness. How was that possible when neither had learned how to appreciate the here and now?

Had Dalton? Colleen felt compelled to ask.

"What about now? Do you feel like you've made it?"

"Artistically? Hell no. We push each other to be better—every day. As musicians. We want our sound to evolve. Stagnation is a death knell for any group. As for the money? I would be lying if I said it wasn't important. My lifestyle is comfortable."

Looking around, Colleen snickered. The view. The house. The gleaming hardwood floors and luxurious furnishings. She had peeked inside Dalton's closet. It was massive. With all those shoes, it had to be.

"I can hear that fascinating mind of yours turning." Dalton tugged at a lock of her hair. "Comfort is relative. I turned my nose up at Tolliver Cline and his McMansion. That wasn't fair."

"Sure it was. Tolliver built his house to impress. To lord it over Judge Langley and the rest of the Midas elite. He called it a home, but it was a show place. Did anybody at that dinner party look happy? No."

"We might have had something to do with their discomfort. Tolliver is a man used to getting what he wants. His friends are the same. I'm sure it's been awhile since they heard the word no."

"But you said it in such a colorful manner. Personally, I enjoyed the show—if not the meal."

"I preferred our picnic by the lake."

Colleen smiled at the shared memory. "You can still appreciate the simpler things in life."

"I meant the sex."

Turning in his arms, Colleen wound her arms around Dalton's neck. "What about the fried chicken?"

"A distant second." Dalton lifted her into his arms, taking the stairs two at a time. "I love the money, Red. The fame and adulation are great." Pausing by the bed, his took her mouth with his. Sweet and hot. "You aren't for sale."

From someone else, Colleen might have taken that as a question, not a statement. A hint that maybe—for the right price—she *could* be bought. Dalton knew the truth. She was with him because of him, not his net worth.

"I could change my mind—for the right price. What are you offering?" she teased.

"Hm." Dalton lowered her to the bed. Thoughtfully, he pulled his shirt

165

over his head. "You were impressed by my Porsche."

Lying back to enjoy the show, Colleen pretended to think about it. Then shook her head. "Nope. What else have you got?"

"Cash?"

"Tempting. But no."

"Name your price."

Tossing his last piece of clothing onto a chair, Dalton stood before her, gloriously naked and so naturally unselfconscious, it made Colleen's mouth water. Taking her time, she looked him up and down. Head to toe. Pausing in all the interesting places. Of which there were many.

"I want your most precious possession."

His grin crooked, Dalton reached for the hem of her dress, disposing of the garment in one smooth movement.

"And what would that be?" Dalton asked, covering her body with his.

An image flashed through Colleen's brain. She was a contestant on a game show, excitedly jumping up and down, certain she had the correct answer. *Dalton Shaw's most precious possession for all the marbles, Alex.* Easy. She didn't have to think twice. What did she want? What would mean the most? What was the one thing he could give her that she would treasure, now and always? It was the one thing she couldn't bring herself to ask for. The only thing she wanted was Dalton's heart. *His love.*

Unaware of the serious turn of Colleen's thoughts, Dalton hovered over her, his blue eyes filled with laughter.

"Have you made up your mind?"

"You. All I want is you."

Colleen touched the smooth, freshly shaved skin of Dalton's cheek. If all she could have was his body, she would take it. Placing her hand on his chest, she smiled at the feel of its increased rhythm—the beat. Dalton's heart came with the package. For now, it was hers.

166

FIRST THING THE next day, Zoe and Quinn dropped by Dalton's house. He was out for an early morning run when the women arrived. Colleen didn't think anything of it until Quinn casually asked her what she was wearing to the concert.

"Clothes?" Colleen answered, finding the question a bit perplexing.

Did Quinn think they were in danger of showing up in the same outfit? Not likely. Colleen shopped bargain basement. Neither Quinn nor Zoe looked as though they could say the same. Casually elegant. That was how she would describe the women. Quinn in jeans and a silk blouse. Zoe in form-fitting teal-colored pants and a dove gray jacket made out of the softest-looking leather Colleen had ever seen.

"The thing is—" Quinn began only to be interrupted by Zoe.

"Dalton asked us to suss out if you needed a little boost to your wardrobe."

Quinn rolled her eyes. "Oh, good Lord."

Zoe simply shrugged, unconcerned by Quinn's displeasure.

Colleen frowned. "Why didn't he simply ask me himself?" Since when had Dalton needed help digging for information? His straightforward approach was one of his best qualities.

"I suppose he didn't want to embarrass you. Dalton mentioned that you pay your own way. Offering to buy you a dress might come under the heading of—"

"Mooching off your rich boyfriend."

"That's it." Quinn rounded on Zoe. "You promised to behave. Not every woman is out to take your men's money."

"My men?" Zoe's blue eyes narrowed. "Perhaps you would like to rephrase that."

Colleen didn't know what was going on, but she felt as though she had been set down in the middle of a long-standing argument. Fascinated, she

167

waited for Quinn's return volley.

"Ryder, Ashe, and Dalton? I know the four of you are family. Tight-knit. But families grow, Zoe. You've accepted me."

Zoe simply raised her eyebrows.

"Admit it," Quinn laughed.

"Ryder loves you." There was a small smile on Zoe's lips. "I don't think he's made the worst choice in the world."

"Practically a declaration of sisterhood." Hugging Zoe, one that was reluctantly returned, Quinn turned her attention back to Colleen. "Now there is Colleen and Dalton."

"Don't add me to your growing mix." The thought was too tempting and the last thing she wanted to talk about. "More coffee?"

"You and Dalton? Too soon? I get it." Quinn held up her hands. "We strayed from the point."

"We?" Zoe sipped at her freshly filled cup of coffee. For the first time, she spoke directly to Colleen. "Do you need a dress or not?"

"Not."

"Tonight will be fairly swanky, Colleen. If you're holding back because of my snarky remarks, don't. I was kidding." This time, it was Colleen who raised her eyebrows. Zoe's smile widened. "It is possible that Quinn is right about one thing."

"Wait." Quinn rummaged through her purse, triumphantly pulling out her phone. "Say that again, I want to set it as your ringtone."

"The woman likes to push her luck." Zoe chuckled. It was a nice sound, Colleen decided. "Dalton *is* family. My brother in every way but blood. If I get a bit protective—"

Quinn snorted. "A bit?"

Zoe continued as though Quinn hadn't spoken. "It's because we watch out for each other. Are you going to hurt Dalton?"

"I hope not." Colleen couldn't imagine a scenario where it would happen. However, she wasn't going to make a sweeping declaration. Shit happened. Sometimes life had a way of tossing out unforeseen curveballs. "I would never deliberately hurt Dalton. That's all I can promise."

Zoe held Colleen's gaze for several beats, as though assessing her words. Then, she shrugged. "It's Dalton's money. Let him spend it."

Hardly an overwhelming endorsement, but from the satisfied expression on Quinn's face, Colleen guessed it was Zoe's version.

"I honestly don't need a new dress. I do wish Dalton had asked me himself. It would have saved the two of you a trip." Colleen hesitated. "Is tonight really that big of a deal? Dalton said it was a benefit concert."

"*The* benefit concert," Quinn stated. Zoe nodded. "This is one of those crossover events. Musicians, actors, authors, directors. And so on. A ton of press. I assume from your expression Dalton didn't tell you any of that."

"He did not."

"In his defense, he *did* think about your dress."

Quinn had her there. Colleen felt her rising hackles ease back down. It would have been nice if Dalton had been more specific. On the other hand, she hadn't asked. She knew better than to make assumptions. Blaming the whirlwind nature of her trip to California was no excuse. Whatever his intent, Dalton had given her time enough to acclimate— something Colleen was very good at doing.

"I've seen events like this online and in magazines. I know what women wear." Colleen felt a bit of doubt seep in. "Just to be certain, will you give me your opinions?"

"I'm certain your dress is fine." Zoe exchanged nods with Quinn. "We would be happy to look if it would make you feel better."

Colleen started up the stairs, Zoe and Quinn at her heels. "I know the answer is to say I wouldn't want to embarrass Dalton. The truth is, I don't want to embarrass myself."

"As it should be." Quinn took a seat on the edge of the bed. "Most men could care less what we wear. As long as it comes off at the end of the night."

Flopping down next to Quinn, a move that seemed incongruous to her elegant appearance, Zoe expertly flipped her hair. "If that is a reference to your sex life, I would rather not know."

"Poor Zoe. She prefers to think of Ryder as a cloistered monk."

"He's my brother. I prefer not to think about that aspect of his life at all."

Leaving them to their slightly heated but easy banter, Colleen moved across the room where a gorgeous antique dresser sat. Dalton had offered her as much space in it as she wanted. Plus, more closet space than she would have known what to do with. In the end, she claimed three roomy drawers.

Seeing the dress that she had put away only a few days before, Colleen smiled. A present from her mother last Christmas, it wasn't something she ever would have bought for herself. Not that the flowing red jersey knit didn't suit her. It did. The problem wasn't the dress. It was the price. And the fact that Colleen couldn't imagine having a reason to wear it. Sherry's response of, *you never know,* had become prophetic.

For once, her mother chose a gift with Colleen's taste in mind—not her own. That old adage that redheads should never wear clothing in the same color spectrum was shot to pieces the second Colleen tried on the crimson dress. Instead of clashing, the bold shade made her hair almost glow and her green eyes pop. The confidence she would feel on Dalton's arm would be worth her mother's inevitable *I told you so.*

"It's perfect." Quinn hopped from the bed.

"It is, isn't it?" Colleen held it under her chin.

"And soft as butter. Is it cut to your navel? Dalton's tongue will hit the floor when he sees you in this."

"You have the perfect breasts." Zoe rolled her eyes when Quinn sent her

170

a questioning grin. "God."

"Did I miss something?" Colleen asked.

"Go on," Quinn chuckled. "Tell Colleen."

With a resigned sigh, Zoe crossed her long legs. "There is a story making the rounds questioning my sexuality."

"So?"

"Thank you, Colleen. That was my response. I don't care what people think. Gay. Straight. Bi. Does it really matter?"

"Not to me." Colleen laid the dress on the bed.

"Quinn doesn't give a flying leap." Zoe stuck her tongue out at her brother's girlfriend. It didn't come off as a childish or silly gesture. Instead, it humanized the other woman, giving Colleen another glimpse past her cool, polished exterior. "She loves that *I* have become the focus of media attention."

"And *why* is that, Zoe?" Quinn crossed her arms, waiting.

"If I tell Colleen everything, will you and I finally be even?"

Quinn pondered the question as though it was of extreme importance. Finally, she nodded. "Yes. Clean slate all the way."

"There was a story a few weeks back," Zoe said, jumping right in.

"The one planted by Dalton's brother-in-law?"

"That's the one. I mistakenly blamed Quinn. A fact that she hasn't let me forget. Though I apologized. Profusely."

"Let's not get carried away." Joining her on the bed, Quinn gave Zoe a friendly bump with her hip. "The only thing Zoe does profusely is play the guitar. *Badass* is the term used by the guys in the band."

Zoe shrugged off Quinn's words, but the pleasure in her blue eyes was obvious. Colleen didn't blame her. *Badass guitar player*? Who wouldn't be happy with such an assessment?

"You were with Dalton in Midas." Zoe's gaze turned serious. "He downplayed his trip. Was it as innocuous as he led us to believe?"

The question made Colleen pause. There was something Dalton didn't know. Something he couldn't have shared with his friends. She wanted to tell Zoe and Quinn about Collier's visit to the garage. It would have felt good to get it off her chest. The problem was, she couldn't expect them to keep her secret. It wouldn't be fair to ask. Dalton wasn't going back. Judge Langley couldn't hurt him. He was out of Tolliver Cline's reach.

Dalton shared what he wanted to share. It wasn't up to her to elaborate. In the end, Colleen decided to adopt the theory that what happened in Midas should stay in Midas.

"Dalton gave it to you straight. Midas no longer has a hold on him."

That seemed to satisfy Quinn. Zoe was harder to read, but she let it go. That left Colleen to think about the evening ahead. Dress, shoes, makeup, hair. She wasn't worried about any of that. Landing on her face in front of all those people? That would be difficult to live down.

With a sigh, Colleen decided to stop thinking about what could go wrong and relax. All she had to do was smile and hold onto Dalton. She knew he wouldn't let her fall.

HOW MANY PEOPLE had the opportunity to walk an honest to goodness Hollywood red carpet? The flashing lights. The screaming fans. The glitz and glamor. Colleen had seen the highlights. Hundreds. Thousands of times. It wasn't something she thought of after the fact or dreamed of attending. Moments like these were otherworldly. She couldn't relate. Why would it occur to her that someday, she would be the one strutting her stuff in front of members of the press from all over the world? Yet, here she was. Colleen McNamara. Humble mechanic.

"So much for stage fright." Dalton tightened his grip on her hand. "You look like you were born posing for the camera."

"It's easy. I've decided to embrace the moment." Colleen paused when a photographer shouted Dalton's name. "You're the talent. I'm the eye candy. When these pictures hit the internet, my mother is going to have bragging rights at the beauty salon for the next six months."

"Never mind the internet. Try magazines and newspapers."

"People? Entertainment Weekly?"

"At the very least," Dalton nodded.

"Did I say six months?" Colleen flashed her best, *I'm with the band*, smile. "My mother will work this for at least a year."

Though Colleen enjoyed herself immensely, it wasn't what she had expected when Dalton mentioned a benefit. *The Ryder Hart Band* equaled rock and roll. In her mind, that meant t-shirts, jeans, and suspicious-smelling puffs of smoke. Woodstock. Monterey. What she found was more upscale.

That morning, Quinn and Zoe had given her a bit of a heads-up. They tried to prepare her. Colleen quickly discovered the red carpet and all the glitz were things one had to experience to truly understand. This was a moment she wanted to savor. She wanted to see everything. Take little snapshots in her mind. Tonight was once in a lifetime. Colleen was determined to enjoy every second. Especially the man next to her.

"Have I told you how gorgeous you look tonight?"

Dalton shook his head when the usher holding the door for them snorted, trying unsuccessfully to contain a laugh.

"That is supposed to be my line, Red."

"You told me. Four times."

"And you mentioned that I looked mighty fine in my tuxedo. Handsome was the word you used in the car." Dalton lightly flicked a finger under her chin. "Remember it the next time anybody is in earshot."

"Handsome. Gorgeous. Both apply." Colleen needlessly fussed with Dalton's tie. It gave her an excuse to stare into his deep blue eyes. When he rested his hands on her hips, she smiled. "You look as good in clothes as out of them. Not all men can say that."

"Right back at you." Dalton's gaze dipped to the plunging neckline of her dress. "How am I supposed to keep my eyes off you? Long, bare legs and all that creamy skin?" His roaming finger stopped between the base of Colleen's neck and the swell of her breasts.

Colleen had watched video after video of Dalton playing the drums. His skill and concentration had left her breathless.

"Once you're on stage, you won't know I'm around."

"Not likely, Red."

Dalton kissed her ever so lightly. It was a moment. The kind she would never forget. By the way he looked at her, Colleen was certain he felt the same. Together, they inhaled. Deeply.

"Time to get changed, lover boy." Ryder slapped Dalton on the back. "We open and close this shindig. You can canoodle with Colleen at the after party."

"What about you and me?" Quinn, stunning in a form-fitting yellow sheath, tugged on Ryder's hand.

"Canoodle. Snuggle. Smooch. Name it. I'm there."

"Oh, for crying out loud." Zoe exchanged looks with Ashe. "Would you give these two a move-it-along kick in the ass? I would do it, but this dress won't let me lift my foot that high."

Zoe wasn't exaggerating. The long column of her shimmering skirt was fabulously flattering. However, it made certain the soles of her strappy silver sandals stayed firmly on the ground.

Amused, Dalton winked at Colleen, following behind Ryder. "I'll see you after the concert."

"Want to watch the fun from the audience or join me backstage?" Quinn slung a canvas bag over her shoulder. "I can't resist a chance to take pictures of the band."

"Backstage," Colleen said with enthusiasm. Falling in step, she nodded toward the bag. "Is that how you and Ryder met? Taking his picture?"

"Dalton didn't tell you?" Before Colleen could answer, Quinn laughed.

"Why am I asking? I have never met a more close-mouthed bunch in my entire life."

"Dalton told me that they don't talk about each other's business."

"Did he mention why?" Quinn showed her badge to a burly security guard. With a nod, he let them pass. It was a different entrance than the one the band had taken. Colleen assumed the other door led to the dressing rooms.

"Something about respecting privacy. Yadda, yadda, yadda."

Quinn chuckled. "I know it seems extreme."

"No. More… mysterious."

"I get that." Setting down her bag, Quinn removed an impressive-looking camera. She changed lenses before adjusting several settings. "I can't say a lot. You understand."

She did? That was news to her. Colleen merely shrugged.

"When Zoe asked you about Midas?"

"Oh. That."

"Exactly." Quinn raised the camera, snapping a quick shot of Colleen. "Sorry. I tend to do that."

"Okay." Colleen didn't mind having her picture taken. The walk down the red carpet had told her that. It was the suddenness of Quinn's movements that threw her off.

"It isn't secrecy," Quinn continued. "Not really. As a group, they share more than any people I've ever known. Nor are there any major skeletons lurking in anybody's closet."

"You're positive about that?" Colleen didn't believe in open books. They didn't exist. Along with life, liberty, and the pursuit of happiness, everybody had the right to keep a few things to themselves. If that weren't in the constitution, it should be.

"I said *major* skeletons. There *is* a difference." Quinn lowered the camera. "The band has few rules. Don't talk to the press comes in first,

175

second, and third on the *hell no* list."

"Is that a warning?" Colleen would have expected it from Zoe. Quinn seemed too easy going. First impressions. To some extent, they always needed revising.

"Only because I like you." Quinn's easy-going smile was back in place. "You do understand?"

"Feel free to call me Schultz."

Momentarily confused, Quinn's frown slowly lifted. She snapped her fingers. *"Hogan's Heroes."*

"I see nothing." Colleen did her best exaggerated German accent. "I know nothing."

Quinn took another picture, laughing when Colleen pushed out her chest in an exaggerated cheesecake pose. "I knew I was going to like you."

MESMERIZED. THAT WAS the only way to describe it. Colleen felt drained and invigorated at the same time. A night of magic will do that to a person, she supposed.

The concert started on a high note. *The Ryder Hart Band* took the stage to a chorus of frenzied screams. From the first note, the energy was electric. Colleen watched Ryder as he sang lead on a song she knew very well. *Under a Blue Moon.* How many times had she played that tune while draining an oil pan or rotating a set of tires? Countless. It seemed impossible that she stood only a few feet away. Watching as they played it live. Stranger yet? She knew the band. It was crazy.

Ryder gave new meaning to the word dynamic. Zoe? What else. She was a badass on lead guitar. And Ashe sent shivers down her spine when he wailed on the saxophone. Yet it was Dalton she couldn't stop watching. Non-stop, he didn't keep the beat—he lived it. The others followed him. Who wouldn't? When a woman in the audience yelled out his name, swearing her undying devotion, Colleen didn't blame her a bit. All she could think was, *I'm right there with you, sister.*

When the song ended, there was no downtime for the band. They didn't do interviews, but as one of the organizers, there were photos to be taken with donors. All the money from the benefit went to children's organizations throughout the city. The proceeds helped set up shelters with clean, warm beds, hot meals, and counseling.

Colleen knew why this charity was so important to the band. Ryder and Zoe grew up with an abusive father. That was common knowledge. It could be a vicious cycle—one that the Harts thankfully avoided. Stopping the abused from becoming the abuser. Dalton and Ashe supported the cause all the way.

"This will take a while." Dalton had a towel wrapped around his neck, using another to wipe the flow of perspiration from his face. His t-shirt was soaked through. Drumming was a workout and a half. In deference to Colleen's pristine appearance, he merely brushed her cheek with his lips. "Will you be okay?"

"Bruce Springsteen is down the corridor. Word has it Madonna is in the building. Not to mention Beyoncé and Jay-Z. I think I'll muddle through."

"Keep an eye on her," Dalton said to Quinn. "Some of the musicians can get pretty handsy."

"Who is going to watch out for me?" Quinn called after him.

"They know you're mine." Ryder smoothed a hand down Quinn's hair. "If anybody touches you, they know damn well I'll tear them a new one."

Quinn stared him down. "Excuse me?"

Lips twitching, Ryder shrugged. "*You'll* tear them a new one?"

"That's better. For a second there I thought a stage light must have fallen on your head." Quinn slid her hand around Ryder's neck, pulling him close so only he heard what she said next. Whatever she said brought a huge grin.

"I think that can be arranged." The kiss they shared was searing, giving Colleen an, *oh, my,* moment.

"Should I ask what you said to him? Or is it too personal?" Colleen asked as Ryder and Dalton exited to their dressing rooms.

"I told him that caveman routine might be fun. Later. When we're alone." Quinn sighed. "Ryder is such a lovely combination of sexy alpha and sweetheart."

"You love him very much." Colleen wasn't asking. What Quinn felt—what Ryder felt in return—was obvious. And enviable.

"I do." Quinn didn't hesitate. "Does that surprise you?"

"*Love* surprises me."

Where did that come from? Colleen wondered. Funny. She hadn't realized she felt that way. Not really. True. She always found love to be a strange concept. In high school, her friends seemed to fall for one boy or another every other week. Some were still following that pattern. Through her mother's unfortunate second marriage and the current one that worked so well, Sherry claimed both men were the loves of her life—after Colleen's father.

Perhaps Colleen would understand love a bit more if she had felt its effects. Just once. Like? Absolutely. But love? Her feelings for Dalton were messing with her brain. For the first time in her life, she *wanted* to be in love. For the first time, she thought she might be capable of the emotion. What if that twisting in her gut—the squeezing in the vicinity of her heart—was merely once in a lifetime lust?

"I understand what you mean," Quinn nodded.

"Great. Can you explain it to me?"

"Can I explain love? Sorry." Somebody bumped into Quinn, sending her tripping toward Colleen. "Let's find someplace out of the crazy zone. One of the dressing rooms should be free."

Taking her camera bag with one hand and Colleen's arm with the other, Quinn led them down a busy corridor. Each door had a card taped to the front. When they reached the one that read Ryder Hart, they ducked inside.

"Did I say crazy?" Quinn laughed, pushing her hair back. "Between the talent and their entourages, it's chaos."

"You sound like that's a good thing." Colleen took a seat. The green sofa looked worn but clean. Before joining her, Quinn took two bottles of water from the small refrigerator.

"I love the energy. Getting a job covering *The Ryder Hart Band* was my big break as a photographer. If I had any hint that I would fall in love with their lead singer, I would have run for the hills. Ryder was not part of my plans."

That, Colleen could understand. "Are you sorry?"

"Ryder Hart is the finest man I've ever known. Every morning I wake up in his arms. Every day, he tells me he loves me. More important? He *shows* me."

There it was again. Quinn's words gave her that twisty feeling in the vicinity of her heart. Unconsciously, Colleen rubbed the left side of her chest.

Seeing the gesture—and understanding—Quinn smiled. "I suppose love is about taking a chance. The path I had chosen was straight and clear. My choice was simple. Stay the course or veer into the unknown. Admittedly, I jumped a little sooner than Ryder. Luckily, he wasn't far behind."

"I'm not in love with Dalton." Hearing the words didn't help. If anything, the twisty feeling intensified. "It's too soon. Isn't it?"

"You want to put a timetable on love?" The question seemed to amuse Quinn. "That's fair. How long. A month? Six? A year is a nice round amount."

"A week?" Colleen would have been the first to admit that it was a ridiculous situation. However, she couldn't find anything to laugh about.

"An intense week." Sympathetic, Quinn tempered her words. "Let me ask you this. When you take on the job of refurbishing an automobile, what do you look for?"

"A solid frame." Quinn's point clicked. "You think that Dalton and I have

179

a good foundation to build on?"

"What do you think?"

"That I can't move ahead unless Dalton wants the same thing."

"And you can't ask?"

Wide eyed, Colleen stared at Quinn as if she had grown a second head. "Would you?"

"After a week? Not on your life." Quinn took a sip of water. "Is there anything stopping you from staying in Los Angeles?"

"My plan was to leave Midas next spring. Los Angeles was on my short list of destinations. "I love it here. But..." Would it look desperate? Colleen wondered. As though she was setting her sights on the *big prize*?

"If things with Dalton blew up tomorrow, would you still want to move here?"

"Yes."

"There's your answer. You shouldn't change your life because of Dalton. That said, if you are in the same city, at the same time? The timetable for falling in love becomes infinite."

"We could date. Like normal people." As soon as the words came out of her mouth, Colleen knew how ridiculous they sounded. She burst out laughing. Quinn was right with her.

"Normal is relative when you are involved with a rock star."

Colleen had a lifetime of normal. She wanted more long before Dalton Shaw and his sputtering Porsche drove into her life. Changing her plans for a man? Even one that—if she were completely honest—already owned a piece of her heart? Absolutely not. That didn't mean she couldn't take a page from Quinn's book. For so long, she had been on the same boring path. Dalton made her swerve. And, Colleen realized, that wasn't such a bad thing.

"I can speak from experience," she said with a grin. "Normal is overrated."

CHAPTER SIXTEEN

SOMETHING WOKE COLLEEN at the break of day. To say she resented the interruption put it mildly. Slowly, reluctantly, she opened her eyes. What she saw almost made the effort worth it. Blinking once, she looked again. Naked Dalton. On his stomach. His face turned toward her. That sexy body, covers pushed off, stretched out on the bed less than an arm's length away. It would be like visiting the Louvre, ending the tour just before she got to the Mona Lisa.

She could sleep anytime. Beauty should never be ignored.

Warm and relaxed, Colleen pulled the sheet under her chin. They weren't at Dalton's house. It was a nice room. Luxurious. The penthouse suite in one of Los Angeles most exclusive hotels. The band's manager, Alden Christopher, had booked them the penthouse suite in one of the most exclusive hotels in Los Angeles. Since the after-concert reception was to be held in the hotel's ballroom, it made sense. Instead of worrying about dragging themselves to their separate homes, they could crash up here anytime they wanted.

Four bedrooms connected by a huge common area. Colleen hadn't seen a lot of it. She entered the suite slung over Dalton's shoulder after a heated make-out session on the elevator ride. But she was certain she would have plenty of time to explore before check-out time. The huge balcony she glimpsed before Dalton shut the bedroom door would be the perfect place to eat breakfast.

Dalton sighed, his hand brushing Colleen's. Holding her breath, she waited, but he didn't open his eyes. Not that she was surprised. The massive amounts of energy he expended on stage, the endless publicity pictures, followed by a reception where Colleen discovered Dalton could schmooze with the best of them—and slow dance to perfection.

A night like that would have knocked out anybody. Somehow Dalton managed to save the best for last. He pleasured her with so much care, it brought tears to her eyes. Over and over again. With his hands. His

181

mouth. His body. Making certain Colleen found her release before taking his own. If Dalton stirred before noon, she would be surprised. He more than earned the rest.

No sooner had Colleen finished the thought than her phone chose that second to buzz, signaling an incoming call. Cursing, she snatched it from the nightstand. Having adjusted the settings before the concert, she said a silent thank you that it was still on vibrate.

Colleen checked the screen. *Mom.* Careful not to disturb Dalton, she eased out of bed, grabbed her robe, and took the phone into the other room. Her mother was not an early riser. As Sherry often said, one of the benefits of owning her own business was the fact that she could get somebody else to open the salon. The sun wasn't visible, its light barely beginning to light the sky.

Concerned, Colleen hit the voicemail key. If her mother was calling at this hour, it had to be an emergency.

"Colleen!" Sherry sounded breathless, her voice vibrating with barely concealed panic. "This is an emergency. Call me immediately."

Any other time, Colleen might have laughed. She knew her mother. Sherry loved to draw out the drama. However, when the situation was truly serious, Mom understood the importance of brevity. Surprised to find her hand shaking, Colleen hit speed dial.

"Thank God," Sherry said. As greetings went, it did nothing to allay Colleen's anxiety.

"What's wrong, Mom? Is Rick okay?"

"Yes, honey. We're fine."

Relieved, Colleen filled her air-deprived lungs. Finding out nobody was hurt meant she could start to breathe again.

"You didn't call to say hello. What happened?"

"There's been a fire. Don't panic. Nothing more than some property damage."

"Your salon?" Colleen hated to think of her mother's business going up

182

in flames. But she was fully insured. Lives were what mattered. Things could be replaced.

"No. Not the salon." Sherry paused. "It's your car, Colleen."

"My Thunderbird?" Colleen slowly sank onto the sofa.

"There's nothing left but a shell. And Colleen? The police say it wasn't an accident."

COLLEEN DIDN'T BOTHER to pack. Jeans, a t-shirt, some clean underwear. Followed by a pair of sneakers, her jacket, and her purse. That was all she needed. The entire time she gathered her things, she kept an eye on Dalton. The last thing she needed was for him to wake up. To her relief, he didn't stir, his breathing steady. Pausing, Colleen blew him a kiss before slipping from the room. Dalton wouldn't support her decision. He would insist on returning with her to Arizona. Since Colleen's response to that would be, *over my dead body*, she thought it best to save them both the aggravation.

"Did you at least leave him a note?"

Stifling a yelp, Colleen whipped around, knocking her shin against the edge of the glass coffee table. Out of the shadows walked Zoe, eyes narrowed, her arms crossed over her chest.

"Of course, she left him a note. Right, Colleen?"

Colleen looked at Quinn then Zoe. Both women were fully dressed in workout clothes. At this hour of the morning? They couldn't have gotten more than a few hours of sleep. A healthy body was one thing. This was ridiculous.

"Keep your voices down." Furtively, Colleen glanced toward the bedroom.

"Nobody is up but us."

Zoe took a step closer. Her hair was pulled back. She wore no makeup. With little or no sleep, she looked fresh. A freaking natural beauty. Under different circumstances, Colleen would have taken the time to hate her—just a little.

"Want to tell us what's going on?" Quinn asked, standing shoulder to shoulder with Zoe.

"No." Without another word, Colleen turned to leave. One step and she stopped. The point was to get as much distance between herself and Los Angeles before Dalton knew she was gone. Unless she gave them some explanation, she couldn't count on Zoe and Quinn to keep her departure under wraps.

"I'll tell you. If you promise not to say anything to Dalton."

"No." Zoe's answer was quick, short and emphatic.

"I'm with Zoe," Quinn nodded. "Dalton is family, Colleen."

That said it all. Colleen had never met such a tight-knit group. She couldn't expect Zoe and Quinn to side with her. Taking a breath, she realized there was only one way. Colleen didn't have time to go into detail. But she could tell them her motivation. Hopefully, it would be enough.

"Dalton can't go back to Arizona. I have to. You have your car here, right?"

Zoe gave her a brief nod.

"If you will drive me to the bus station, I'll fill you in on the way."

"Let's go." Without further preamble, Zoe headed for the door.

"You heard her."

For some unfathomable reason, Quinn grabbed her camera bag before pushing Colleen into the hall. The elevator dinged, doors opening, just as they reached it.

"Okay." Zoe hit the button for the lobby, pinning Colleen with her sharp, blue gaze. "Start talking."

Colleen gathered her thoughts, took a deep breath, and plunged in.

"Somebody torched my T-Bird, and it has the stench of Collier Langley written all over it."

DALTON WAS DISAPPOINTED when he found the other side of the bed empty, but not alarmed. Squinting at the bedside clock, he groaned. Ten-thirty? Damn. He would have stayed in bed much longer. *If* there had been a warm, sweet-smelling woman to cuddle with.

Instead, he rolled to his feet, stretching his arms over his head as he slowly made his way to the bathroom. A hot shower wasn't the perfect substitute, but it would have to do. He would take his time before joining Colleen. He smiled, picturing her on the balcony she found so intriguing.

Twenty minutes later, he stood in front of the mirror. With a final swipe of his razor, the last of yesterday's stubble disappeared from his face, swirling down the drain. It had become a daily routine, one he did without thought or hesitation. For a man who had always hated to shave, it was telling. Colleen was a part of his life. A big part. If he had his way, a permanent part. He would do whatever it took to make her feel at home in his world. Protecting her delicate skin might seem like a strange way to go about it. It was a small step in a longer process.

How to woo a woman by Dalton Shaw. Grinning, he wiped the last of the shaving cream from his face. No. Not *a* woman. A very specific one. Colleen McNamara. Some of it would be work. Some might not. As corny as it sounded, Dalton wanted all of her. Body, heart, and soul.

Picking up his pace, Dalton threw on his clothes. As he expected, there was activity in the other room. Ashe was catching up on last night's baseball scores while Ryder's fingers flew over the keyboard of his laptop.

"Too much testosterone." Passing by, Dalton slapped Ashe on the shoulder. Finding the balcony empty, he called out, "Where are the women?"

"Before we fell asleep, Quinn mentioned that she planned on joining Zoe in the gym. I assume they took Colleen with them."

It sounded reasonable. Except for one thing. Zoe always worked out at the crack of dawn. No matter what.

"How long have you been up?"

Annoyed by the distraction, Ryder shifted his focus to the timestamp on the computer screen.

"Eleven o'clock? That can't be right. I was fiddling with this new music program and lost track of time. Ashe? Do remember what time I started?"

"Nine thirty. Don't panic." Ashe sounded like the voice of reason, but he was the one jumping to his feet. "When did Colleen leave?"

Frowning, Dalton shook his head.

"Ryder? Did you see Quinn this morning?"

"She was gone when I woke up."

"Check Zoe's room," Dalton called to Ashe, already headed to his.

Nothing was missing. Colleen's suitcase was in the closet. The dress she wore last night, flung over the chair where it landed after he pulled it off her. He tried to remember what she had packed. Not much. They weren't staying more than one night. Jeans? Sneakers? They were gone. So was her purse.

Ashe returned to the living room, shaking his head. "Zoe's room looks like it did when we checked in. I swear. That woman is freakishly neat."

"Quinn's camera bag is gone. Nothing odd about that. She takes it everywhere except the bathroom. Clothing wise, her workout stuff is all that's missing."

"Call them."

"Are we overacting?" Ashe asked, dialing Zoe's number.

"Better safe than sorry is a cliché for a reason." Dalton paced as he listened to Colleen's phone ring. He stopped when it went straight to voicemail.

"Hey, Red. Just checking in. Give me a call as soon as you get the chance."

Ashe hung up after leaving a message for Zoe. "Considering the way you're clutching your phone, that sounded impressively calm."

186

"Ryder?"

"Same here. Voicemail."

Ryder picked up the hotel phone. Just his luck. The night staff working the front desk went off shift at nine o'clock. The woman currently on duty was certain the women hadn't passed her way. She was a huge fan. If Zoe Hart were nearby, she would have noticed.

"Can you check to see if Zoe's car is still in the parking lot?"

"Right away, Mr. Shaw." There was a short pause while the woman used a different line. "According to our records, she had the car brought around just before six this morning."

"Five hours ago."

Dalton hung up. He had tried to tell himself that Ashe was right. In all likelihood, they were overreacting. So what if all three women were out. And not answering their phones. Or had bothered to leave a note. Zoe driving off in her car was no big deal. But at six in the morning? Damn it. What was going on?

A familiar ringtone filled the room. The opening notes to the song Ryder wrote for Quinn. Relief showed on Ryder's face as he answered.

"Hello, beautiful." Dalton admired his friend's ability to play it cool. "I missed you this morning." There was a long pause. Ryder's expression quickly morphed from relief to disbelief. "Are you out of your mind? Why would you do that?"

"Do what?" Dalton demanded. "Is she with Colleen and Zoe?"

"They are in Arizona."

"What the—" Dalton snatched the phone. "Let me talk to Colleen."

"She's fine, Dalton." Quinn sounded breezy, as though this was a conversation they had every day. "A bit of business popped up. Rather than bother you, Zoe and I offered to keep her company. Sort of a girl's day out."

"In Midas, Arizona? You know that isn't going to fly, Quinn. Where is

187

Colleen?"

"Talking with her mother. Lovely woman."

"You are *in* Midas?"

Ashe cursed. Ryder paced. Dalton wanted to smash something into a million pieces. *This* was why he took up the drums.

"We made excellent time." Quinn tried to keep it light, but she was starting to rush. "Zoe and her heavy foot. Somehow, we sailed through without getting stopped. Colleen called it good karma. I have to go, Dalton."

"Quinn. Don't you dare hang up."

"Tell Ryder I'll talk to him soon. We may stay overnight. Bye."

"Son of a bitch."

Handing Ryder the phone, Dalton opened the balcony door, walked to the rail, gripping it tightly with both hands. Taking a deep breath, he let out a blood-curdling yell. Finished, he breathed in and out before returning to the hotel room.

"Feel better?" Ashe asked.

"Not even a little. I never thought I would say this again. I need to get to Midas. Right away."

"The plane will take us to Phoenix. Less than an hour." Ryder checked his wallet before placing it in his back pocket. "I called Alden. All I said was that we would be out of town for a couple of days."

"That must have gone over well." Their manager was notoriously overprotective. Especially where Ryder was concerned.

"Alden's hurt feelings are the least of my worries."

"I can't believe they drove to Midas. And without letting anybody know." Ashe shook his head, right beside them as they left the hotel room.

Dalton didn't ask if Ashe was coming. It didn't occur to him. It was what family did. The elevator descended quickly, stopping once to pick up a man and woman. They were almost to the lobby when his phone rang. Praying it was Colleen, he looked at the screen. *Well, shit.* Definitely not Colleen.

"When it rains, it pours."

"Who is it?" Ryder glanced over Dalton's shoulder.

"My sister."

Any other time, Dalton wouldn't have bothered. The last thing he needed was another tear-filled plea for mercy. Or an attempt to lay on a thick layer of guilt. Maggie was in Midas—so was Colleen. It was the only reason he answered.

"Dalton? I need you."

"I don't have time for this, Maggie. Have you seen Colleen?"

"Dalton. I—" There was a catch in her throat. One Dalton had heard a thousand times. "He hit me."

"Your husband?" Dalton found that hard to believe. He found anything Maggie said hard to believe. But he couldn't ignore what she was saying.

"Not Norris. He would never..."

The elevator doors opened. Following Ryder and Ashe through the lobby and out the doors, Dalton slid into the back of Ryder's waiting car.

"Who hit you, Maggie?"

That got his friend's attention. Ryder glanced back as he hit the gas. From the front seat, Ashe sent him a worried look.

"It was Collier Langley."

Dalton closed his eyes, running a hand over his mouth. It just got shittier and shittier.

"Are you at home?" Dalton had no idea why he sounded so calm. How he was holding it together.

"Yes."

"Stay there. I'm on my way."

189

"What the hell?" Ryder zipped through traffic with the skill of a trained stuntman. "Do you believe her?"

"Do I believe somebody hit Maggie? Yes."

"Collier?" Ashe looked as sick as Dalton felt.

Dalton thought about it. He couldn't rule out that Maggie was telling him the truth. *Why*, was another matter. It felt wrong. Too convenient considering the history between him and Collier Langley.

"I guess we'll find out." Dalton took a deep breath, pounding his fist into the seat. "Goddamn Midas, Arizona."

WINCING, COLLEEN HELD the phone away from her ear. Modern technology had its upside. Getting a tongue lashing over voicemail did not qualify.

"Wow," Zoe said, swallowing her bite of greasy hamburger. "I don't think I've ever heard Dalton go off like that. His temper tends to be a bit more controlled."

"This town has that effect on people." Colleen sighed. She knew she should call Dalton. Even a text would be a step in the right direction. Instead, she put her phone back into her purse. Out of sight, out of mind. *My ass.*

"It isn't Midas that has him bellowing like a blue-balled bull. Take credit where credit is due, Colleen."

"Blue-balled bull?" Quinn snorted as she covered her fries in a layer of salt and pepper. "Good one, Zoe."

With a self-satisfied smile, Zoe took a sip of Coke. The hard stuff. No diet or caffeine-free for her. "I liked it."

"Dalton is pissed." Colleen felt too justified in her motivation to feel an ounce of guilt. However, not being a fool, she wasn't looking forward to their next meeting.

Quinn looked at her watch. "I give them an ETA of between three and four o'clock."

"That soon?" Colleen finished off the last of her turkey club.

"Delays happen. Don't bank on it."

Nothing out of the ordinary had occurred since they arrived in Midas. Colleen didn't know what she had expected. Booby traps around every corner. Collier Langley—or some goon he hired to do his dirty work—firebombing Colleen's car? Nothing. Unless she counted waiting at the police station while the paperwork concerning her burned-out car was ready to sign.

"I appreciate the company, but the two of you could have saved yourselves a trip. This looks like it is going to be pretty routine."

"Maybe it's routine *because* we are with you?" Quinn wiped her mouth, tossing the napkin into the trash can across the room. *Swish. Nothing but net.* "If the point was for you and Dalton to ride into town alone, Zoe and I put a major crimp in the plan."

"And if burning my car was nothing more than childish retaliation?"

"I get the chance to see Midas and find out what all the fuss is about."

Colleen waited, eyebrows raised. Quinn shrugged.

"I don't get it. I've driven through dozens of towns just like this one. The vibe is the same. It's a small town."

"You know the term walk a mile in my shoes? Try living here for over ten years. There is an undercurrent that can't be picked up in a few hours."

"We stayed after Dalton was arrested." Zoe tapped her foot, the toe of her bright blue running shoe knocking against the metal desk they used as a dining table. "Colleen is right. This town is creepy weird."

"Everybody looks so normal."

"Exactly." Colleen and Zoe answered at the same time with the same word. Eyes meeting, they laughed. Quinn joined in.

"Now isn't that a nice sound." Sheriff Gil Lott sauntered out of his office.

191

Middle aged, with a full head of artificially enhanced jet black hair and an increasing waistline, the sheriff liked to think of himself as a lady's man. There were ladies in Midas who would agree. Others, including Gil's wife, had a less favorable opinion. "I can't recall ever hearing you laugh, Colleen. These lovely ladies must be a good influence."

"You don't walk around town yucking it up?" Zoe's blue eyes were cool as she spoke to Colleen but looked at the sheriff. "Shame on you."

"Gil Lott." All smarmy charm, he took Zoe's limp hand in his, raising it to his lips. Zoe tugged free before he could complete the kiss. Undeterred, Gil's smile didn't slip. "And you are."

"Zoe Hart. We've met."

Without being asked, Quinn handed over a tube of hand sanitizer. Zoe squirted a large portion into her palm. Holding the sheriff's gaze, she deliberately rubbed in the clear liquid, concentrating on the patches where his fingers touched hers.

Gil either didn't understand the insult or was too busy trying to figure out how he and Zoe were acquainted.

"Hart?" Gil frowned. Suddenly, the confusion in his expression cleared, replaced by a trace of unease. "As in..."

"You interviewed me after the unjustified arrest of Dalton Shaw. Though at the time it was Deputy Lott. Nice promotion."

Gil retreated several steps. He looked nervous. "He was convicted of the crime."

"You say potato... I say railroaded."

"Now, see here—"

"Sheriff."

Colleen stood, putting herself between what was gearing up to be a battle of words. Zoe was packing all the ammunition, but it was a war she couldn't win. Like it or not, ten years ago the court sent Dalton to prison. There was no changing the past. Pissing off a man who carries a gun— and was authorized to use it—was not the best use of their time.

192

"Why are you here, Colleen?" Gil kept a wary eye on Zoe.

"My car was set on fire. Remember?"

"That hasn't been determined. The investigation is ongoing."

"Somebody broke into the garage attached to my apartment. Hauled my car away. And what? It magically caught on fire while sitting in the grocery store parking lot? I saw what was left of it, Sheriff. That was no accident."

"Perhaps you aren't as great a mechanic as you like us all to believe. Faulty electricals could be the cause. Either way, it will be several days until we can say for sure."

"That isn't what Officer Brinkley told my mother. Or me when I called from her house. I was told the paperwork for me to give my insurance company was ready for me to sign." Colleen looked at her watch. "That was over an hour ago."

"You were misinformed. Go home. Someone will call you."

With one last slit-eyed glance at Zoe, the sheriff strode into his office, shutting the door with a decisive click.

"What do you want to do?" Quinn laid a hand on her shoulder. "Head out or wait for the guys?"

"Leave."

"But?" Zoe stood, adjusting her purse across her body.

"I feel like something is in the air. Besides the usual miasma of sweat and discontent."

Quinn breathed in as they left the police station. "That's a charming—and sadly accurate—description."

"I hope I'm wrong. But if there any is any information to be had, there's only one place in town to go."

"Where is that?" Zoe hit the remote, unlocking the car.

"Get ready to be buffed within an inch of your life. Next stop, gossip

193

central. Or as my mother likes to call it, *The Curl and Swirl.*

"Lord help us," Zoe muttered.

With a slightly concerned frown, Quinn checked her cuticles. "Amen to that."

THE FLIGHT TO Phoenix gave Dalton plenty of time to brood. And think. Logically, he understood what Colleen was doing—with the help of Zoe and Quinn. She wanted to protect him. Which meant she cared. If they were in Los Angeles, he would be celebrating.

That was where logic ended, and the unreasonable Neanderthal that lurked inside of every man took over. Colleen attempted to flip the natural process of things. Dalton did the protecting—the saving. Not the other way around.

"Do you ever wish women were less...?"

"Let me save you a shitload of grief, my brother. Never think, let alone speak that sentence again. And whatever you do. Never, ever finish it." Ryder laughed at Dalton's sour expression. "Ignore my advice and spend the rest of your days taking solace in the arms of lesser women. A strong woman is the only way to go. Frustrating? Sure. Worth it? You bet your ass."

"What are you smirking for?" Dalton tossed his empty water bottle at Ashe who easily swatted it away. "Just wait. Your time will come."

"Bimbos, my friends. They are tons of fun without the work."

"When did you ever date a bimbo?" Dalton got past Ashe's defenses with a wadded napkin. Bam. Right in the kisser.

"When did he ever date?" Ryder asked, crossing his arms.

"None of us date."

There was no comeback for that. Ashe was right. Until Quinn, Ryder's relationships rarely lasted more than a long weekend. Dalton couldn't claim anything different.

"I guess there wasn't time." Dalton hadn't thought anything of it before now. "We were building our careers. Either on the road or in the studio. Downtime meant fun and games."

"I'm happy for you. Both of you." Ashe looked at his friends with complete sincerity. "Do me a favor? Don't turn into *those guys*. Now that you are happy and settling down, don't start pushing me to do the same. If the day ever comes when I meet the love of my life, let it happen naturally."

For the first time that day, Dalton laughed. It was more of a surprised bark, but it qualified.

"Care to share the joke?" Ryder asked.

"You won't like it."

"When has that ever stopped you?"

"Fine." Dalton shrugged. "What about Zoe's love life?"

Ashe's snort turned into a cough when he met Ryder's glare. "It's a fair question, Ryder. We talk a lot about women. The ones we *have* slept with. *Are* sleeping with. *Want* to sleep with. I know she's your sister— *our* sister. But all this conversation about Quinn, Colleen, and my *maybe* sweetheart? Not one of us thought about Zoe finding a man."

"I want Zoe to be happy," Ryder insisted. "Her love life is not something I want to think—or talk—about."

Dalton agreed. Still, Zoe listened to their crap, but who listened to hers? In all the years they had known each other, he was embarrassed to say this was the first time he had contemplated the question. She was so self-sufficient. Strong. At least, that was how it seemed.

"Zoe would tell us if she wasn't happy. Right?"

"Yes," Ryder said firmly. When he met Dalton's gaze, there might have been a touch of doubt.

The pilot's voice filled the cabin, letting them know they were minutes from landing.

"Zoe is fine." Ashe buckled his seatbelt. "She dates. More than we do. Like us, she hasn't had time for anything long-term."

"I suppose you're right."

"Ask Quinn," Ashe suggested. "They've been spending more time together."

"That's true." Ryder perked up.

"Zoe *does* have somebody to confide in." Feeling better, Dalton picked up his phone, checking his messages—again. "Finally. Colleen left a text."

"What does it say?" Ashe leaned closer.

"Meet us at the lake."

CHAPTER SEVENTEEN

AFTER HOURS OF silence, Dalton had expected more than four words from Colleen. As they drove from Phoenix to Midas, he wondered what the hell was going on. She still wasn't answering his calls. Neither were Quinn and Zoe. During the twenty-minute trip, Dalton fluctuated between anger and relief. At least she was capable of texting him. For now, he would console himself with the knowledge that Ryder was just as pissed as he was.

"Damn it, Quinn," Ryder growled into his phone. "Never again. Understand?"

"I'm certain she's quaking in her boots." Ashe occupied the backseat this time. Dalton drove the rented SUV while Ryder rode shotgun. "It isn't informative, but at least Zoe's text is colorful."

Dalton breathed a little easier as Midas came into view. *Jesus.* He never thought *that* would happen. "What did she say?"

"We can take care of ourselves. Stop calling every five seconds, asshole."

"That's my little sister," Ryder chuckled, pride mingling equally with exasperation.

Ashe looked out the window, his grin fading. "Is it possible that this town is more depressing than it was seven years ago?"

"Sad." Ryder perused the landscape. "It's hard to believe Colleen came out of this."

"She had the benefit of not being born here. Though I think Colleen would have turned out the same no matter the setting."

"Ah." Dramatically, Ashe clutched at his heart. "Tell me, Dalton. How do you know if it's love or a bad case of indigestion?"

Since he was still trying to figure that one out himself, Dalton let the jab pass without comment. One minute, he was certain he knew how he felt. Then Colleen made him so angry, he questioned how he could love her *and* want to strangle her at the same time.

Taking the turnoff to the lake, Dalton had to slow the SUV over the bumpy, unpaved road. The last two hundred yards seemed to take an eternity. Finally, he caught sight of Zoe's car. The cobalt Ferrari was parked in front of the cabin. Pulling to a stop, Dalton scanned the area as his feet hit the ground.

"Over here."

Colleen. Her red hair gleamed in the afternoon sun as she walked toward him. The second Dalton saw her, he had the answer. Loving someone and wanting to strangle them? As crazy as it sounded, not only was it possible, it was inevitable.

Meeting her halfway, Dalton opened his arms. Happily, Colleen walked in.

"Are you angry?"

"Yes."

"Want to yell at me?"

"Later."

Dalton took Colleen's mouth with his. He was rough to start, his pent-up emotions too deep to temper. Instead of pulling back, Colleen met his kiss head on. Her hands clasped the sides of Dalton's face as though afraid he would disappear if she didn't hold tight.

Next to them, Quinn and Ryder were clasped in a similar embrace. Less desperate, but no less intense.

"Don't even think about it," Zoe warned when Ashe met her gaze. Laughing, she accepted his hug. She gave in, relaxing in his arms. She felt the warmth of love—different than the kissing couples—but no less real.

"Everything okay, kid?" Ashe kept an arm around her shoulders.

"You won't believe the shit that is going down, Ashe."

"Shit?" Dalton glanced at Zoe.

"A massive pile. And it's growing as we speak." Colleen took Dalton's hand. "I won't apologize for trying to keep you out of it. You were worried?"

"That's one way of putting it." Dalton's response was as dry as the Midas air. Colleen had the good grace to wince. "Tell me what happened."

They gathered around the picnic table, listening closely. Colleen started with the phone call from her mother.

"We couldn't let Colleen come to Midas alone," Quinn explained. Before Ryder could blast her, she added, "You would have told Dalton. The whole point was to keep him out of it."

"You think that's a good excuse?" Ryder's eyes narrowed.

"That look isn't as intimidating as you think," Zoe told her brother. "And it isn't an excuse. Quinn was simply stating a fact. Our intentions were noble. We would do it again. End of discussion."

"I don't think so. However, that can wait until we get back to Los Angeles." Ryder shot Zoe a look that made her chin go up, and her shoulders straighten. "Go on, Colleen."

It didn't take long for Colleen to explain. The burned-out car. The runaround at the police station. It was pretty straightforward.

"I'm sorry about the Thunderbird." Dalton rubbed Colleen's arm. "You're right. It has Collier's petulant fingerprints all over it."

"I burned off my angry before we got to Midas. I'm grateful whoever did the job didn't start the fire in the garage. Somebody could have been killed."

"That's it?" Ashe looked from face to face. "You collect the insurance and Collier Langley walks away unscathed? Again?"

"I still have to deal with my sister," Dalton reminded Ashe.

"About that." Colleen hesitated.

"Do you know something about Maggie?"

"Tell him, Colleen," Zoe urged. "Dalton has few illusions left when it comes to his sister."

"Zoe is right." Dalton was prepared for the worst, but he couldn't help the feeling of dread. He had the feeling his last shred of hope for Maggie was about to be blown out of the water.

"Maggie is sleeping with Collier Langley." When Dalton didn't react,

Colleen frowned. "Did you hear me? Your sister and Collier."

"I already figured that out. Maggie's tearful phone call telling me Collier hit her? I don't think she lied. We know Collier likes to hit his sexual partners. It was the only thing that made sense."-

"There's more." Quinn took Ryder's hand.

"There always is." Dalton sighed, looking Colleen straight in the eyes. "Enough of the bits and pieces. What is going on?"

"We heard all of this from the woman who does Maggie's hair. It seems your sister isn't terribly discreet. Still, it is secondhand information. It made sense to get some reliable corroboration."

"Who—?"

Dalton broke off as a car came into view. The tan Ford Focus stopped a few feet away. As the door opened, a thin man with sandy-colored hair got out. He had changed, but Dalton recognized him immediately.

"Norris."

Maggie's husband, his shoulders stooped with what might have been the weight of the world, nodded.

"Hello, Dalton. It's been a long time."

NORRIS TOLD HIS story haltingly, sweat glistening on his upper lip. Listening to the tale of deception, tears, and woe, Dalton had little sympathy for his brother-in-law.

"I should have put a stop to it long ago," Norris sniffled, pulling a wrinkled handkerchief from the back pocket of his brown polyester slacks. "But she has a way about her, you know? I was dazzled from the moment we met. I loved her, Dalton. I wanted to make her happy."

Maggie used her husband as she used everyone. And he let her. Norris hadn't sold the story about Dalton to the tabloids. It was Maggie's idea. Norris didn't know where the money went. He let her take care of the finances. Moving to Midas had been Maggie's idea—though Norris admitted, he was out of work.

"I was never much of a businessman."

"What about Maggie and Collier?" Dalton felt a layer of dirt settling over him. There would be no washing it off until he had all the gory details—and was far away from Midas.

Norris kept his eyes on the table, his hands nervously fidgeting on his lap. "They were friendly before. Seven years ago."

Dalton discovered Maggie had a few surprises left for him. The affair with Collier began during Dalton's trial, lasting until the guilty verdict was handed down. That was when Maggie latched onto Norris, convincing him to move to New York. Buffalo wasn't ideal, but Norris had friends who could help them get started.

"Maggie was never faithful."

"I don't care, Norris." Jesus. The man was a quivering wimp. Dalton took a deep breath. "Keep the story to present day."

Sensing Dalton was losing patience quickly, Colleen touched Norris on the shoulder. "Did you bring the flash drive?"

"Right." Norris took it from his shirt pocket. "Sylvia set it up. She's the best."

"Sylvia?" Dalton exchanged confused looks with Ryder and Ashe.

Colleen plugged the drive into her phone. "Sylvia and Norris are going to get married as soon as his divorce is final. She works at my mother's beauty salon. Head beautician. It was her idea to put a camera in Maggie's bedroom."

"Evidence for a no-fault divorce." Norris frowned. "I think that is how Sylvia put it."

The picture was surprisingly clear. High-definition, Norris informed them proudly. It seemed Sylvia's second husband worked for the local cable company. She learned quite a lot in the six months they were married.

"I don't know who the bigger idiot is." Dalton shook his head as the screen went blank. "Collier. My sister. Or me."

"Don't you dare lump yourself with them." Colleen's green eyes contained a fierce glow. "*They* belong in the idiot's hall of fame. Your only crime was trying to find enough good in your sister to justify helping her when she asked."

"Colleen is right." Ryder looked like Dalton felt. Shell-shocked. "Nobody in their right mind thinks the way Maggie does."

"Except Collier." Ashe's eyes contained a slightly glazed-over expression.

"You'll take care of everything?" Norris stood, inching toward his car. "Sylvia said you would."

"Leave it to us, Norris."

"Was he always so twitchy?" Zoe asked Dalton, watching Norris drive away.

"I don't remember him that way."

"Seven years of Maggie." Ashe shuddered. "How scary is that?"

"What now?" Quinn sat with Ryder's arm around her. Like everyone, she was trying to process all the information. And the implications.

Dalton didn't have to think about it for long. There was one way to end it. Here and now. A solution that would put a big, flashing exclamation point on this mess and the one he got himself into seven years ago.

"It's okay, Red." Dalton kissed Colleen's worried brow. Picking up his phone, he hit speed dial.

"Dalton. Are you still in Midas? Please tell me you aren't in jail."

"Not this time, Alden." Dalton smiled. Leave it to their manager to unknowingly lighten the moment. "I need you to do me a favor."

"Name it."

THE GATES SLOWLY opened allowing Dalton to drive through. It was a different world. All green lawns and shiny windows. It gave Dalton the creeps. All he could think as the SUV's tires passed silently over the paved street was that fate had to be laughing her ass off. Not only was he willingly on his way to the home of Judge Manfred T. Langley, the visit was by invitation. Issued by the man himself.

Not that Langley had a choice. Alden used his contacts to make it clear. Either he play host to Dalton or, within hours, find his son's latest screw up blasted all over the internet.

Dalton made a right turn, pulling into a long, circular driveway. "I have to hand it to our manager. Alden moved fast. Without his usual endless questions."

"Is it just me, or does this place give off a creepy vibe?" Ashe asked, peering out the window as Dalton stopped in front of the Langley mansion.

"It's not you," Zoe and Quinn answered simultaneously.

"I thought the same thing," Ryder remarked, helping Zoe from the SUV before taking Quinn's hand.

"Me too."

"Me three." Dalton laced his fingers with Colleen's. "Safety in numbers."

"You have truth on your side," she reminded him.

"I had that seven years ago and look where it got me."

"This time, all the witnesses are on your team. Langley can't pay us off."

Ryder was right. Tonight, Dalton had all the power. Keeping Colleen close, he raised the ornate brass knocker, banging it twice. One last surprise. Instead of a servant, Judge Langley was the one who opened the door.

"I expected you to come alone."

"My game, Judge. My rules."

Nodding his head, the older man let them enter. Dalton didn't spend time taking in his surroundings. Luxurious furnishings that screamed rich. He had seen it all before. It was Langley who interested him. They had never met. Not officially. Dalton had wondered what it would be like to stand face to face with the man who had changed the course of his life.

"I thought you would be taller."

And bigger, Dalton thought. Manfred Langley turned out to be an average man. In height. In build. He wasn't handsome or homely. His silver hair wasn't thick or excessively thin. Average. Monsters, it seemed, came in all kinds of packages.

"Excuse me?" Judge Langley's gray eyebrows raised in surprise.

"Nothing." Dalton shook his head. "Just a random thought."

"We might as well get this over with. Follow me."

"There's no point. I'll say my piece and leave."

"This isn't about money?" Langley frowned, obviously thrown by the discovery.

"Blackmail, Judge? Not my style." Dalton took the flash drive, setting it on a small marble-topped table near the door. "Collier conspired with my sister to set me up. You know the routine. He hits Maggie. I knock the shit out of him. Police. Handcuffs. Jail. Perhaps a convenient witness or two. You get the idea."

"I'm certain you're mistaken." Langley had a fine poker face. It didn't matter. This time, Dalton had a straight flush, ace high.

"It's all there. Recorded for posterity."

To his credit, Judge Langley understood when he was beaten. Head held high, he met Dalton's gaze head on.

"What do you want?"

"Simple. Collier's political aspirations are over. If I get a hint that he's considering running for elected office, I won't hesitate to release his latest folly to the public."

"What about your sister?"

Without the slightest hesitation, Dalton simply said, "What about her?"

No one spoke as they left the house. They loaded into the SUV. Before they were out of the driveway, Zoe closed her eyes, snuggling down with her head resting on Ashe's shoulder.

"Forget driving back to Los Angeles. I'll hire somebody to do it for me."

"Sounds good to me." Quinn yawned.

"If I never see Midas again, it will be too soon," Ryder declared. Making certain Quinn was buckled in, he put on his seatbelt.

Ashe let out a long, loud sigh. "Amen, brother. By now, those words should be indelibly branded into our brains."

"How about you?" Dalton asked Colleen.

"I'm through with Midas. I'm with Ryder. Never again."

Words that were the cherry on top of an unbelievably satisfying evening. Colleen hadn't exactly made a declaration of her undying love. If she planned on living in Los Angeles, Dalton saw his chances as mighty fine.

Just to be certain, Dalton decided to play devil's advocate. "You have an apartment full of stuff. And what about your mother?"

"For a few beers, Rick can get his buddies to clean out my apartment. As for Mom?" A smile flitted across her lips. "She will love Los Angeles. I won't have a problem getting her to visit."

That settled, Dalton headed out of town. Nobody looked back when they passed the sign that read Leaving Midas.

"I live in Los Angeles."

"I'm aware."

"Colleen—"

"I think we should date."

Suddenly, you could hear a pin drop. It wasn't the audience riding in the back that made Dalton choose his words carefully. This was his future hanging in the balance. His happiness. The last thing he wanted was to say the wrong thing when the woman he wanted was so close to being his.

"Date? As in dinner and a movie? Walks along the beach? A weekend in the country?"

"Sounds perfect."

"Are you thinking about getting an apartment?"

"Zoe offered to let me stay with her. At first."

"Did she?" Looking in the rearview mirror, Dalton swore he saw Zoe's lips twitch. Since Zoe's house was less than a ten-minute drive from his, he decided he could live with that. For now.

"I need to find a job."

"You should be restoring cars. I can lend you start-up money."

"You could," Colleen nodded. "How long until I have to pay you back?"

"Take all the time you need. Five, ten years?" Dalton liked the sound of that. A long, drawn-out contract.

"You realize that if I take your money, we can't have sex until I pay back the loan."

Ashe found Colleen's declaration hilarious, making no attempt to temper his laughter.

"How about a bank loan? I could co-sign."

"Same principle," Colleen told him firmly. "You can help me, but I become a no-sex zone. At least where you're concerned."

"Who else do you plan on having sex with?" Dalton had no idea how he had dug this hole, but it seemed to be getting deeper.

"My plans only involve you."

"I like the sound of that."

"As long as you drop all talk of money." Colleen smiled when Dalton silently crossed his heart. "There are several businesses in Los Angeles that specialize in classic car restoration. I know the owner of one. He was a big help when I hit a snag in the middle of fixing up the Thunderbird."

"You've met?"

"E-mail buddies. However, he told me if I ever moved to Los Angeles, there was a job waiting."

"You didn't tell me that."

"I'm telling you now." Colleen's hand came to rest on his thigh. "In a few months, who knows how you'll feel. How I'll feel. We have time to find out."

Dalton drove into the night. Turning on the radio, he chuckled when the band's latest hit song poured through the speakers. *Time Is On Our Side*. Hearing Colleen's answering laugh, he placed his hand over hers, relaxing. The lights of Phoenix burned brightly in the distance. No more looking back.

They *did* have time. All the time in the world.

EPILOGUE

SIX MONTHS LATER

"DON'T TOUCH ME!"

"Those are the words every man longs to hear from the woman he loves."

"This woman is a dirty, sweaty mess. But she loves you, too."

"*That*, I definitely want to hear."

Dalton gladly accepted Colleen's quick kiss, understanding why she leaned in, keeping her body as far from his as possible.

"If I don't hop in the shower, we'll be late meeting everyone for dinner."

Colleen rushed up the stairs, pulling her shirt over her head as she went. Enjoying the view, Dalton trailed behind. He liked this arrangement much better than the one they had the first few months after Colleen moved to Los Angeles. She and Zoe turned out to be surprisingly compatible roommates. For a while, Dalton worried about prying her loose. He wanted her with him. Not living the single life with her new BFF.

Dalton had nothing to worry about. Between her new job at World Restorations, and acclimating to city life, Colleen had little time for anything else. She settled in nicely. He soon realized his worries were without foundation. Work during the day. Dalton at night. Before long, Colleen spent more time in his bed than the one in Zoe's guest room.

It was during one of those sleepovers after he had shown her with his body how much he loved her, that she said the words. *I love you*. Dalton hadn't hesitated to tell her what he had known almost from the beginning. *I love you, Colleen*.

Colleen had said it hundreds of times since that first time. However, it hadn't lost its impact. Dalton was certain it never would. Tonight, in front of their friends, he planned on asking her to spend the rest of her life with him. It was a big step. Before Colleen, he would have sworn it was a step he would never take. Crazy as it sounded, the cliché was true. All it took was the right woman.

Dalton quickly removed his clothing. Sharing a shower with Colleen was one of life's great pleasures. He would be a fool to pass up the opportunity.

"You know where this will lead."

"I can only hope."

Turning, Colleen wrapped her arms around his waist. The water had turned her hair a deep auburn. In Dalton's mind, red was red. Beautiful no matter the shade. He squirted a dollop of her favorite shampoo into his palm, running his fingers through the thick locks until her head was covered in citrus-scented lather.

"Mm." Closing her eyes, Colleen's turned her face upward, her lips curving into a smile. "You are so good at that."

"Aren't you glad you agreed to move in?"

"You do come in handy." Colleen wrapped her fingers around his erection. "For so many things."

"We'll be late," Dalton warned, not giving a damn.

"You can blame me."

Dalton covered Colleen's mouth with his. Had he been happy before her? Yes. A different kind of happiness. This was richer. Deeper. The kind that could only grow brighter with each passing year.

"I love you, Colleen." When she didn't answer, Dalton dipped his head, looking into eyes that sparkled like brilliant emeralds. "Tears?"

"I can't help it," Colleen brushed her lips against his. "Those words get me every time. I love you."

Dalton didn't cry. He was too happy. But he understood. Those words. *I love you.* When Colleen said them, they got to him. Every time.

COMING SOON

Flowers Are Red

Hart of Rock and Roll Book Three

AFTER THE RAIN
(One Pass Away Book One)

PROLOGUE

LOGAN. LOGAN. LOGAN.

Logan Price closed his eyes, taking it all in.

"Hear that, kid?" Starting quarterback Gaige Benson slapped him on the back. "Two games under your belt and you're a star. Now let's go out there and add super to the front of it."

The announcer for the team set them in motion down the tunnel with his familiar introduction.

"And now, let's hear it for your division champion *SEATTLE KNIGHTS*."

The roar of the crowd. There was nothing like it. A packed stadium. Fans chanting his name. Few people would ever experience what it was like to take the field in a professional football game.

Logan Price had been working for this his entire life. He could still remember in exact detail the first game he ever saw. Too small to climb onto the stool in his father's bar by himself, his old man had lifted him onto the seat.

Stay and be quiet.

Not an easy order to follow for an active, inquisitive little boy. One look at the game and for once, Logan had no problem following his father's command. The old TV transported him to a foreign world filled with bright lights and shiny helmeted warriors. Logan didn't know what he was watching. He did know he wanted to be one of those men.

A Sunday afternoon in rural Oklahoma. *Lefty's Pub* was filled with after-church drinkers who figured they had done their duty to God and family. The rest of the day was their time. A beer. Or two. Or six. Cronies who understood a man's need to unwind before the start of another workweek.

And football.

If the Friday night high school game was their true religion, the Sunday afternoon games were a close second. As Oklahoma boys, they hated anything Texas. The men of Denville gathered every week to root for whichever team was playing the Dallas Cowboys.

No matter how the games ended. Whether the crowd was happy or disgruntled. It meant more drinking. Hours later, husbands, boyfriends, and sons would stumble out, pile into beat-up trucks, and weave their way home to frustrated wives, girlfriends, and mothers.

As he grew older, Logan's view changed. He moved from the stool to behind the bar. And he promised himself one thing. He would never become one of those men. He wouldn't spend the week at a job he hated. His home wouldn't be a semi-wide trailer filled with hand-me-down furniture and a wife to whom he couldn't face going home.

His Sundays were going to be spent playing football, not watching it.

"Ready to take down this vaunted Arizona defense?" Gaige yelled at him, butting helmets.

Vaunted. Good word, Logan thought. His QB liked to use what his granny called highfalutin talk. Must have been that Ivy League education. He knew that Gaige Benson didn't grow up with a silver spoon in his mouth. He came from the mean streets of Brooklyn. He had the scars to prove it.

Like Logan, Gaige had vowed to get out of the life into which he was born. In the process, he polished himself up like a new penny. He took advantage of his full-ride scholarship to Yale. He didn't spend all his time on the football field. Fancy vocabulary. Fancy clothes. Fancy women. They were all part of the package Gaige purposefully fashioned for himself.

Seventeen years after clawing his way out of the tenement that he grew up in, very little of that borough-rat remained. Until game time. No one was tougher than Gaige Benson. Three-time league MVP. Considered one of the best ever to play the game. No one stood in his way when he was playing the game. He had the scars to prove it.

"Gather round."

Knights head coach Harry Coleman gathered the team close. He had to yell over the crowd, but he had the voice to do it. Booming was putting it mildly. The first time Logan heard it, he stood right beside the man. The ringing in his ears didn't go away for three days.

211

"Divisional game. If I have to say any more than that, you shouldn't be out here. Go kick some ass."

The defense took the field to start the game. Arizona had a rookie quarterback drafted in the second round from a small college in the Midwest. The only reason he was out there was because the regular starter suffered a concussion in last week's game and the regular backup had food poisoning. Thrown into action at the last minute, Logan swore he could see the guy's hands shaking before he took the first snap. When the ball went sailing between his legs, Logan shook his head.

The moment was too big for some people. For Logan, it wasn't big enough. He aimed for the biggest stage of all. The Super Bowl. It wasn't a matter of *if* he would get there, but when.

"Three and out." Gaige grinned, pulling on his helmet. "Come on, kid. Let's go show them how it's done."

Logan ran onto the field. *Kid.* He shook his head, grinning. From the first day of training camp, Gaige had hung that moniker on him. Ironic since he was almost twenty-five, a good two years older than most of the other rookies. However, he supposed when someone had been in the league as long as Gaige, all the new guys seemed like kids.

"We're starting on the ground," Gaige instructed them in the huddle. "Sweep out left. Basic. Got it?"

Lining up as he had a thousand other times, Logan checked the defense. He knew he was fast. One of the fastest in the game. What set him apart was his anticipation. He had the uncanny ability to read the guy covering him. He knew when to fake left or when to fake right. Stutter step or flat out, in your face, catch me if you can.

His speed got him out of Denville, Oklahoma. His brains and determination got him to the NFL.

The sounds of the game were as familiar to Logan as the back of his own hand. The call from scrimmage. Each quarterback had his own unique cadence. Gaige was a master of mixing his up. Study him all you want. Good luck figuring it out. His teammates knew. A signal just before they broke the huddle.

Pay attention, you were golden. Slack off even once? Gaige could ream a guy out with the best of them. And he had no problem doing it in the middle of the game.

212

An entire YouTube channel had been devoted to Gaige and his rants. They were as legendary as the man himself. With a ball in his hand, he was cool as ice. The rest of the time, watch out.

No one would ever accuse Logan of lacking focus. Today was no exception. They were driving down the field. First and ten from the Arizona twenty-yard line. He already had three carries of thirty-five yards. It was going to be a good day.

"Ready to take it in?" Gaige asked.

"Always."

"Then show them what you've got."

A quick snap later, Gaige handed the ball to Logan. The offensive line created a seam. Not a big one. Just big enough. Using the push of his powerful legs, Logan surged through. One more step. They wouldn't catch him. No one could.

Like everything connected with the game, Logan heard the snap of the bone with total clarity. The agony that surged through his body was so intense he almost passed out. In the next few minutes, he was going to wish he had.

"Get back." Logan heard Gaige through the haze of pain. "Goddamn it. Move the hell off."

The three-hundred-and-fifty-pound linebacker didn't get off by standing. He rolled. Crushing Logan's broken leg as he went. He would never know if the move had been deliberate. Now, it was the last thing on his mind. He only cared about two things. How bad was the injury and when would he be able to play again.

"Hold on, kid." Gaige took his hand. "They're bringing the stretcher."

The team doctor checked his eyes. Logan knew he was asked some questions. What they were and how he answered, he would never remember. By the time they carted him off the field, Logan knew the break was bad.

"Gaige." Logan reached for him.

"I'm here, kid."

"Is it over?"

"The game?" Gaige walked with him, his head bent toward Logan. "No. But I promise we're going to win the bastard."

213

They loaded him onto the open cart. They had him secured and the vehicle rolled away before Logan had his answer. He wasn't wondering about the game. It was his career.

To no one in particular, he whispered the question again.

"Is it over?"

CHAPTER ONE

LOGAN SAT UP in bed, his body covered with a fine coating of sweat.

He glanced at the clock. Three in the fucking morning. On the one night he managed to get to bed at a reasonable hour, he was plagued by the nightmare that had haunted his dreams for the past two years.

Running his hand through his long, damp hair, Logan fell back onto the mattress. His sheets were as wet as he was. With a grimace, he rolled onto the floor. Flexing his stiff knee, he stripped the bed, tossing everything onto a pile of dirty clothes he planned on taking to the laundromat on his day off.

There was an alternative. He could always take Linda Sue Hemmings up on her offer. She would do his laundry anytime. Payment. On-call stud service whenever her husband Darryl was out of town on business. As much as Logan hated folding socks, he decided the price was too high. He had lost a lot in the last few years. He still held onto his dignity. Just barely.

Still groggy, Logan shuffled to the bathroom. Flipping on the light, he grimaced at what the mirror reflected.

Too many late nights followed by not enough sleep. As patterns went, it wasn't a healthy one. Perpetually bloodshot eyes. Dark circles on his dark circles. He needed a haircut. Logan ran his hand over his face. Even more, he needed a shave.

He had to hand it to himself. When he let himself go, he went all the way. All he had to do was stop showering. If he wasn't worried about driving the customers away with his smell, he might have considered it.

The old plumbing rattled with protest when he turned on the faucet. It wasn't a bad place. There were worse. Logan splashed some cold water on his face. He didn't bother with a towel. It would dry soon enough on its own.

He had two choices.

Toss and turn for a couple of hours on the unmade bed – he really needed to get more than one set of sheets.

Or lose himself with an old friend.

Sleep wasn't coming which made the choice an easy one.

Logan pulled on a pair of old shorts, a faded t-shirt and sweatshirt that was too ratty to be called anything as fashionable as a hoodie. After lacing up his sneakers, he hit the road. When he was a kid, he ran for the fun of it. In high school and college, it strengthened his legs and improved his stamina. Now, the only thing it accomplished was getting him a reputation as that half-crazy Price boy. Running the deserted streets at all hours? Maybe his head had been permanently injured along with his leg.

Logan jogged past *Lefty's Pub*. The place where he spent most evenings tending bar. The day he left for college he swore to anyone who would listen that he had served his last beer. Eight years later, here he was, washing glasses and putting up with not so subtle jabs about how the mighty had fallen.

Coming back to Denville was more of an adjustment than Logan anticipated. He expected the cracks about his failed NFL career. Any kind of success tended to breed a certain amount of jealousy and resentment. There were those who reveled in his injury.

Logan Price always thought too much of himself. Denville wasn't good enough for the high school's star running back. He forgot all about us when he made it big.

The sound of his feet pounding on the unpaved side street couldn't keep the usual thoughts from creeping back. Some of what those people said was true. He had been full of himself. At seventeen, one wasn't written up in national magazines without it going to his head.

Logan never tried to hide his plans. A full-ride scholarship to the college of his

216

choice. Then the pros. MVP awards. Super Bowl rings. The cocky attitude of a teenager wasn't any easier to take than if he had been an adult. Most of Denville embraced their golden boy.

AFTER ALL THESE YEARS

(One Pass Away Book Two)

PROLOGUE

SEAN McBRIDE WOKE up with a smile on his face. It happened a lot lately. And he thoroughly approved.

He stretched his long, athletic body. Some mornings every inch of him ached. Such was the life of a professional football player. Everything was about preparing for the game. Focus. Concentration. The goal was to be ready for game day.

He had to hold it together for sixty minutes. Pull out a win any way possible. Sacrifice his body to the football Gods and pray he walked away healthy enough to do it all again next week.

Sean dreaded the day after the game. The adrenaline had long ago worn off and he felt all of his thirty years. There were degrees of bad. Sometimes he shuffled to the shower, the aches and pains palpable, but mercifully bearable.

Then there were the bad days. After a day of three-hundred-pound defensive backs using him as their own personal punching bag, he didn't get out of bed— he crawled.

Bruised from top to bottom, his joints creaked and his muscles protested like screeching banshees. Those were the times he wondered why he did it. He could have been a doctor. Or a lawyer. He could have taken his father's advice and gone into the family business. No seventeen-year-old with dreams of glory in the NFL wanted to think about becoming a butcher. But damn. Cutting meat sounded good on those mornings.

This was a good Monday. His body felt lithe—limber. The bruises were there. That was part of his life. However, yesterday had been one of those rare games when every moment fell into place. From the kickoff to the final whistle, the outcome of the game was never in question.

Sean caught every ball thrown his way. He evaded the defense. Fast as the wind. Three touchdowns. One hundred and eighty-two total yards. A damn good day for any wide receiver. He would have had more if Coach Coleman hadn't taken him out of the game in the fourth quarter. With a big lead, there was no reason to risk injury when he wasn't needed.

The after-game celebration moved from the locker room to one of the team's favorite hangouts. Naturally the atmosphere was raucous. Cautiously so.

The Knights were having a stellar season. Ten wins, two losses. Sean and his friends had enough games under their belts to understand how quickly that could turn. Injuries tended to come in bunches. So far, they were healthy. However, that was bound to change. The hope was to get to the playoffs with all their major players on the roster.

After the game, they had a few drinks. Three was Sean's limit these days. A few years ago it was a different story. He would have closed the place down after a win. He and his bed partner of the moment would have moved on to someone's apartment, partying until dawn before going back to her place and fucking like demented rabbits. Then he would go home alone and catch a few hours sleep until it was time to grab a quick shower before heading to the Knights' headquarters to review film from the game.

Those days were over. Sean wasn't a kid anymore, high on his own press clippings and more testosterone than brains. Not that he had settled down completely. He could still party with the best of them. However, he chose his moments—ones that never took place during the season.

Women were another matter. Sean liked sex. Always had. If there were a God, he always would. While his bed partners weren't as varied, they were almost as frequent.

Sean knew players who abstained a few days before the game, saving their *juice*. He wasn't one of them. Sean had plenty of juice, thank you very much. Sex was necessary for a happy and healthy mind. For *his* happy and healthy mind.

A big plus to having sex at night was sex the next morning. It was one of his favorite things. A partner, warm and willing.

The perfect way to start the day.

Speaking of which. Smiling, Sean turned over. His hand reached out, expecting to find a soft, sweet woman. Instead, he found cold sheets. Sitting up, he looked around the room. Like the bed, empty. The bathroom door was open and the light off.

Not bothering to cover up, Sean jumped out of bed. Buck naked, he searched the house. She wasn't in the kitchen. Why would she be? She didn't cook, not even coffee. She was on a first-name basis with half the baristas in Seattle.

Was that it? Would she be back soon with two cups of steaming black caffeine and his favorite muffins? Sean was talking himself into that scenario when he saw the note.

He picked up the paper that had been propped against the lamp by the front door.

Sean.

Thank you for the past few weeks. After years of building it up in my mind, I was worried that it couldn't live up to my expectations. I should have known better. It was everything I had hoped for—and more.

We didn't make any promises. No strings were attached that need to be broken. After all these years, you can finally breathe easy. It's over. We are now friends without the expectation of benefits.

When we see each other, it will be as if it, we, never happened.

Sean read the note. Then read it again.

What the fuck? What was in those drinks?

Sean searched his memory for some kind of clue. The bar. His teammates. Then she was there. They laughed. Everything was smooth and easy. They seemed to be developing a rhythm. In his mind, they were together. Not a man and a woman—a couple.

It sounded good to him. He would have sworn she felt the same. He didn't want another woman. He wanted her. In his arms. In his life.

No expectations? Hell. He woke up with plenty of them, only to find out he was alone. Alone in bed. Alone. Period.

Sean scrubbed a hand over his face. He remembered the way she tasted. The way she melted into his arms. The curves of her luscious body pressed against his. Her sighs. His belief he would never get enough of her.

Crumpling the note into a ball, Sean tossed it across the room. Suddenly he felt every ache. His legs felt like lead. Slowly, he shuffled toward the bathroom. He needed a shower. Long and hot. Determined not to look at the bed, Sean's peripheral vision wouldn't let him off the hook that easily. It captured everything. The rumpled sheet. The pillow still holding the imprint of her head. A slash of red on the floor.

Frowning, Sean picked up the scrap of silk. So small he wondered why she had bothered. The image of her standing in nothing but her heels and the panties popped into his head. Unconsciously, his body tightened with desire.

Right, that was why.

Sean ran the smooth material over his cheek, feeling it catch on his morning stubble. He breathed deeply. He smelled vanilla and spice. Her essence. He would never forget it. As long as he lived, he would be able to close his eyes and conjure up her scent. Her taste.

His eyes popped open. *Friends? Nothing more? Bullshit*!

Keeping the panties in his hand, Sean headed for the shower. This wasn't over. Not by a long shot. It was just the beginning.

AFTER THE FIRE

(One Pass Away Book Three)

PROLOGUE

SHE HAD ONCE asked him if he believed in a higher power.

God? Buddha? Fairies dancing around a blazing fire late at night? Something. Anything bigger than us.

Gaige Benson hadn't known what to say. Not then. But as he stood in the empty open-air stadium—the stars lighting the evening sky—he knew the answer.

Football was his religion. The field he played on and the building surrounding it, his cathedral. If a higher power had a hand in it, then his answer was yes.

He believed.

Walking to the center of the field, Gaige took it all in. He found football at the age of thirteen. A boy who saw his future mapped out. Working in a factory. Drinking away his salary. Divorce. Doling out child support without maintaining a relationship with his children. A weekend father, who half the time didn't bother to show up.

The first time Gaige picked up a football, he felt a connection. The first time he threw it, it wobbled with the grace of a drunk leaving his favorite watering hole on a Saturday night. But it didn't matter. He threw the ball again. And again. Until he taught himself to make it spin in a perfect spiral.

At the time, Gaige didn't know his talent could be useful. Where he came from, Brooklyn kids didn't dream of bigger or better. Most of them didn't dream at all. Gaige was no different.

One day he was passing a playground when a football landed at his feet. The boys on the field yelled for him to toss it back. Without thinking, Gaige sent it sailing, a perfect strike. Then kept walking. He was wary of the man who ran after him. Strangers were the enemy—according to his father. They either

222

wanted money or accused you of something you hadn't done.

Gaige took everything his father said with a big grain of salt. Don Benson didn't have a dime to his name. Why would anyone expect to get money from him? And if a man accused his father of something, chances were he was guilty.

But Gaige was a cautious boy. He fought when necessary and ran when he had no choice. The man trying to get his attention was big. His dark complexion didn't worry Gaige. In his experience, a man was either good or bad. The color of his skin had nothing to do with it.

It turned out that this man wasn't simply good. He was the best thing that ever happened to Gaige.

Terrance Aldridge coached the local Pop Warner football team. A boy with an arm like Gaige's shouldn't let his talent go to waste. Gaige listened. Play football? On a field? With other boys? Was such a thing possible? He didn't know if it were a scam—nor did he care. If there were the slightest chance, he would take it.

The only obstacle was getting a parent's permission. Terrance gave him the papers to be signed, telling Gaige to have his folks call him if they had any questions. Gaige didn't laugh aloud, but he wanted to. His mother never asked questions. Unless they were directed at his father. Wynona Benson hadn't made a move in fifteen years unless she received permission first.

His father was another matter. His word was law. Don Benson could do no wrong. If he drank too much and staggered home two days late, it was his right. If he backhanded his wife—just because—whose business was it? He earned the money. He made the rules. End of discussion.

Gaige hadn't asked his father because he knew what the answer would be. No! Not because he thought there was anything wrong with football. He watched it every Sunday—after laying down a bet that he never won. No, he wouldn't let Gaige play because he was a mean bastard who wanted everyone to be as miserable as he was.

Gaige got around it easily enough. He forged his father's signature. It wasn't the first time and it wouldn't be the last. There was no reason to think anyone would find out. His parents didn't care how he spent his days as long as the police didn't come knocking on the door.

He could steal. Lie. Cheat. Hell, his father wouldn't bat an eye at murder. *Do what you want as long as you don't get caught.* The mantra at the Benson house.

Gaige had no intention of his father finding out. He tried out for the team and made it. The money for equipment was another matter. Gaige didn't steal. Or cheat. Lying was a necessary evil. He would have done almost anything to play but it looked like his first and only dream would die before it had a chance.

Luckily, Terrance was able to dip into a discretionary fund to help boys like Gaige. It rankled to take charity. Especially when the other boys on the team had families to pay their way.

"Don't let it stop you, Gaige," Terrance told him. "Remember. And one day, when you have the means, pay it forward, son."

Twenty-five years later, Gaige hadn't forgotten that kindness and generosity. When he saw someone in need, he did something about it. Over the years, the *Gaige Benson Foundation* paid out millions of dollars to charities and individuals. He had filled the board with people he trusted and could count on to distribute the funds judiciously and without prejudice. The first man he had recruited was the man to whom Gaige owed everything—Terrance Aldridge. Friend. Father figure. Teacher.

"Hey, Gaige." Logan Price called out from high in the stands. "You coming? The guys are waiting to go to dinner."

"Five minutes."

Closing his eyes, Gaige breathed in the air. February in Texas. Tomorrow he would play in his first—and last Super Bowl. Win or lose, he was hanging up his cleats. He was thirty-eight years old. He had more money than he would ever need. He had won every award from Rookie of the Year to league MVP—four times.

This season he put everything on the line to get here—including the possibility that he had lost the only woman he had ever loved.

Gaige Benson was known for his razor-sharp focus. Any distractions off the field were left there as soon as the first whistle blew. It wouldn't be any different tomorrow. Nothing would get in the way.

His gaze drifted to the section where she would be sitting. If she showed up. Gaige planned on going out a winner. But what about the day after? Or the day after that? His future stretched out in front of him. He had plans in place. There were hundreds of options for him to consider.

Do you believe in a higher power?

Her voice and that question had haunted Gaige for almost sixteen years. If there were a God, he prayed the woman he loved would find it in her heart to forgive him. He had a lot of years left. He didn't want to spend them alone.

In his lifetime, Gaige Benson had dreamt of only two things. Playing football. And loving Violet Reed.

DREAMING WITH A BROKEN HEART

(Hollywood Legends Book One)

PROLOGUE

THE ROOM WAS dark. Too dark for Garrett's liking. A little stuffy, a slight antiseptic smell with an overlay of sex. That's what you got from a cheap motel and furtive lovemaking. Odors and memories you'd just as soon forget.

The sounds from behind the closed bathroom door indicated his partner was trying to remove all traces of their recent activities. It shouldn't hurt. This wasn't the first time, and damn his weak resolve, it wouldn't be the last.

If he smoked, he would have something to do with his hands. Watching his father struggle with lung cancer put the fear of God in him and his brothers at an early age. All four of them had their vices; smoking wasn't one of them.

Get up. Get dressed. For once, be the first to leave. Even if he could find the balls to walk out on her, he couldn't leave her alone at this time of night. In this part of town.

God, it was like a furnace in here. Despite having the AC wall unit on high, Garrett knew it must be hotter in here than outside. The sheet riding low on his hips was too much. Damn modesty. The room was too dark to see anything; if she didn't like seeing his naked body, she could turn away. Garrett whipped off the coarse cotton material at the same moment the bathroom door opened.

"You don't have to go," Garrett said to the shadowed figure.

"Yes, I do."

She always made sure the light was off. Her silhouette showed a tall woman, thin. Too thin. Even by L.A. standards. She was gaining weight — slowly. Garrett could attest to that. He knew it was a struggle. One she fought every day.

Garrett felt the anger drain from his body — his heart melt. Her demands were

226

not capricious whims. They weren't her attempt to gain the upper hand. Her goal was not to manipulate. She had her reasons. They were real. Legitimate.

"It's still early."

Garrett kept his voice low and even. Shouting didn't help. She never fought back. Retreat. That was her coping mechanism. The last time he blew up it was two weeks before she would take his calls.

"I..." she cleared her voice. "His flight gets in at midnight."

"Don't be there."

"You know how he gets."

Garrett knew all right. She was devoted to a man who treated her like crap, forgot her existence ninety percent of the time, yet expected her to be there when he decided to come home. His fists clenched the mattress. It was the only thing preventing him from grabbing her, begging her to stay. *For once, pick me.*

"I don't know when I can see you again."

I don't know if I ever want to see you again. Garrett thought the words. He would never verbalize them. She was his drug of choice. Weeks passed. The need for her grew. Outwardly, his life looked smooth as glass. Inside, the itch grew.

Garrett became an expert at compartmentalizing. His work never suffered. His family never suspected. No one had the slightest clue about what was raging inside of him. *She* knew. Because she shared his unbreakable habit. Enablers. That's what they were. It was sick. Sometimes, like tonight, he hated himself. He wished he could hate her. Then, maybe, he could walk away.

"I'll be out of town for the next month."

Garrett wished he could see her face. Was she sorry he'd be gone? Relieved? Would she miss him half as much as he was going to miss her?

"Take care."

Garrett waited a second, letting the motel room door close behind her. Jumping up, rushing to the window, he pulled back the thin, dingy curtain. He never walked her to the taxi. Even the minutest chance of them being seen was too much.

The ritual of watching until she was safely inside the vehicle, seat belt on, doors locked, was something he never ignored. Nothing bad would happen to her when he was around. It was when he wasn't there that trouble found her. One more frustration. It wasn't his place to protect her. Knowing that drove him crazy.

Garrett grabbed his jeans from a nearby chair, pulling them on. Unlike her, he wouldn't clean up before he left. He would carry the smell of her with him — let it fill the interior of his car. Tomorrow he would pretend it was still there.

Damn it. Enough. He deserved more than this. They both did. One month. When he got back, one way or another, things were going to change.

CHAPTER ONE

HOLLYWOOD. DREAMS FULFILLED. Dreams crushed. It happened every day. Wide-eyed kids still came hoping to be a star. More often than not, they went back home — a nobody. Iowa, Nebraska, Texas, Georgia. Insert state here. Small town, big city. It didn't matter. The movie industry seemed vast from the outside. In truth, it was the most insular of worlds. Making it took determination, perseverance, and a whole lot of luck. Talent was so far down the list it wasn't funny.

Connections. That was what got you through the door. If you had a recognizable name, the door swung wide, the smiles welcoming. If you couldn't pull your weight once you were inside, no one hesitated to kick you out. That famous name only got you so far. The rest was on your shoulders.

Sink or swim. No life preservers were thrown your way. If anything, you were fitted with cement shoes. The only thing this town loved more than a winner was the child of a Hollywood legend falling flat on his face.

Garrett Landis felt the weight of those expectations every time he stepped on a movie set. His father set the bar so high none of his sons was expected to reach his lofty heights. The fact that all four seemed well on their way to not only matching Caleb Landis' achievements, but surpassing them, caused quite a stir.

Resentment simmered under the surface of hearty backslapping and insincere ass kissing. Their father taught his boys many things. In this business, never turn your back on friend or foe. Treat everyone with respect, from the lowliest crew member to the head of the studio. The most important thing? In this business, trust no one — except brothers. Eight years after making his first low-budget independent film, Garrett followed those rules without question. The Gospel according to Caleb Landis. His father's words were his bible. His brothers were his rock.

Wyatt, the oldest, followed directly in their father's footsteps. He was a hard-ass, bottom-line producer. Nathaniel, Garrett's fraternal twin, was the daredevil of the bunch. He was the most in-demand stuntman in Hollywood. Baby brother Colton was blessed with movie star looks. His charisma leaped off the screen, pulling in even the most cynical audience member. Or so one critic wrote after seeing Colt's first movie. Individually, each Landis brother was formidable. Together, they dominated almost every branch of the industry.

229

"How can we be behind schedule when we haven't shot a single frame?"

"Welcome to the glamorous world of moviemaking."

Garrett grinned when he answered his assistant director, Hamish Floyd. This was their fourth collaboration. The first two made a nice profit. Number three broke box office records. Expectations for *Exile* went through the roof the second Garrett's name became attached. With Wyatt behind the scenes, the movie's success was practically guaranteed.

Garrett didn't believe in sure things. He worked hard on every project, no matter the size. Bigger budget, more potential headaches. That included a prima donna leading lady who couldn't get her ass on set at the designated hour. Garrett refused to start leaking money on day one.

"You want me to coax America's sweetheart of the week out of her trailer?"

"You'd never get past her PA," Garrett told Hamish. "Lynne Cornish thinks one hit movie and a few magazine covers give her the right to make her own rules. She's going to find out on this movie set, there is only one set of rules — mine."

"She has a contract."

"Wyatt's standard contract. She signed it. Her mistake if her lawyers didn't read the fine print."

Contracts were fluid. *Before* they were finalized. Each actor, depending on their box office leverage, could get their people to make demands, tweak the perks. The basics were non-negotiable. Under no circumstance, barring personal injury, a death in the family, or a genuine nervous breakdown, was an actor allowed to delay production. Once, you were warned. Twice, bye-bye. As far as Garrett's big brother was concerned, potential loss of a lead actor was the reason they paid huge insurance premiums. It hadn't happened to Garrett. Not yet. There was always a first time.

Tim Bodine, Lynne Cornish's PA, waylaid Garrett before he was halfway to her trailer.

"Lynne isn't feeling well."

"She was fine an hour ago."

When she was flirting with every man on the set. Apparently, Ms. Cornish could drag herself to any early breakfast if adoring men were present. She found out quickly that Garrett wasn't among them. Whether her sudden *illness* was a result of a hurt ego or plain laziness, he didn't give a damn. Starting right now, Lynne

230

Cornish needed to know who was boss.

"Does she need a doctor?"

"Nooo." Tim drew out the word.

The PA's lack of concern only ratcheted up Garrett's annoyance.

"Five minutes."

"What?" Tim yelled at Garrett's retreating figure. When there was no response, the man hurried to catch up. "She can't make it in five minutes. Lynne doesn't think today will work for her. At all."

Garrett rounded on the smaller man. He topped him by at least eight inches. Tim was slight, Garrett muscular. Yet that wasn't what had the PA stepping back several feet. It was the look in Garrett's steely eyes.

This man exuded confidence. Strength, both physical and psychological, radiated from his core. You didn't mess with Garrett Landis. Not if you had half a brain.

"She was looking a little better when I left her trailer," Tim said, clearing his throat. "She wanted to speak with you. *Privately*."

Well, shit. Garrett didn't see that coming. Lynne made it clear, early on –she was interested. He made it equally clear he wasn't. End of story. They would have a friendly, professional relationship. Finding out his beautiful leading lady was angling for more didn't hold the thrill it once had. It made Garrett... tired. His personal life was full of enough turmoil — he didn't need the added drama of an on-set romance.

"I don't have the time, or inclination, Tim."

To Garrett's surprise, the PA blushed. In Hollywood, that ability was knocked out of a person fast.

"I can't guarantee anything."

"Then Lynne will be out of a job. How long do you think you'll last after that?"

Tim Bodine looked like a smart man. One capable of cajoling his uncooperative employer. Garrett didn't care what it took to get his star in front of the camera as long as it happened. Immediately.

"Five minutes?" Tim asked, a little panicked.

"I'll give you ten."

Garrett wondered if it was too late to get out of feature films. Animation. That sounded good. No location shoots. Voice-over actors happy to skip wardrobe fittings and hours in the makeup chair. A little direction on his part. Mostly setting the scene. One or two takes. Right now, it sounded like heaven.

"What's the word?" Hamish asked him.

"Bitch?"

"Any chance she'll be joining us in the near future?"

"Your guess is as good as mine."

Garrett looked around. They were ready to go. Cameras primed, leading man looking as impatient as Garrett felt. At least he'd lucked out with Paul McNally. He was a professional through and through. No power plays. No outlandish demands. There was no propositioning the director. Paul's first job was a small part in a Caleb Landis production. He was a great actor. More importantly, he was a friend. Garrett felt lucky to work with him.

"Once again, you've lived up to your reputation," Hamish said with admiration. "You really are a miracle worker."

Garrett looked over his shoulder. Lynne Cornish. In full costume and makeup. A little pouty. He could work with that. It complimented the scene.

"Tell them five."

"We're shooting in five minutes, people," Hamish called out Garrett's directions. "Pee now or forever hold it."

Garrett moved over to camera A, checking the shot. Perfect. This was his world. He knew what he was doing. No one questioned his authority or failed to jump at his command. Unlike his personal life, his professional life stayed on a clear path.

232

DREAMING WITH MY EYES WIDE OPEN

(Hollywood Legends Book Two)

PROLOGUE

NATE LANDIS NEVER thought much about the way he looked.

Women seemed to like his face. That was genetics. He was the son of Hollywood royalty. Alone, they turned heads. Together, they dazzled. It made sense that they would pass some of that on.

Nate took it in stride. He was strong. Healthy. His body was trained to do what he wanted it to do, under what could only be called extreme situations. He ate right, worked hard, and played harder.

At some point, his lifestyle would catch up with him. Age would take care of that. Right now, he was in his prime. If he wanted to scale a mountain, that's what he did. Jump from a plane? A piece of cake. Race car driving. Deep sea diving. You name it; Nate was the first one in line.

When he was three years old, his mother called him her little daredevil. Fearless, she swore he gave her wrinkles for worrying what he would get into next. Nate would always laugh, peering closely at Callie Flynn's flawless complexion. What wrinkles? In her fifties, she was, and would always be, one of the movie industry's great beauties. Nothing he or his brothers did could alter that.

As Nate stepped to the edge of the cliff, he didn't think about the two-hundred-foot drop. He'd jumped from higher than this. It was what he did. And he did it better than anyone else. For some reason, today he thought about his mother.

Callie never discouraged him from pursuing danger, even though Nate knew she wished he had chosen a safer way to make a living. She didn't say so, but he knew she worried about his safety. It didn't stop him — he seldom thought about it. Until today. As he waited for the director to signal the camera was rolling, for the first time Nate let himself worry about his mother's reaction if something happened to him.

He shook off the morbid thought. Now wasn't the time. He needed to focus. Ninety-nine percent of the time, if something went wrong, it was due to a loss of focus. Nate took a deep breath. He cleared his mind. Three flashes of light. That was his signal. He squared his shoulders, coiled his body. And jumped.

Nate Landis was a stuntman. Some might say it was his calling. If a director needed it done big and done right, that person called him. Nate loved his job.

He let his body relax as he sailed through the air. The count in his head was precise. If he pulled the ripcord too soon, the shot would be ruined. Too late, he risked ending up a pile of broken bones.

Nate planned every stunt. He worked out the timing, the logistics, and the angles. He never let anyone perform a stunt unless he tested it. Over and over again. He refused to rush. Anxious directors. Bottom-line producers. Some tried to push him into cutting corners.

Few things made Nate lose his temper. His brother Garrett claimed Nate had the longest, slowest burning fuse in history. But he had his hot buttons. Endangering himself and his crew was one of them. Last year, a director, trying to save time, ran a stunt when Nate was away from the set. Poorly conceived and executed, two stuntmen went to the hospital with second-degree burns.

Todd Winesap went to the hospital with a broken jaw and a tarnished reputation.

It took a lot to make Nate mad. But watch out when it happened.

Nate ran the count through his head. Eight, nine, ten. He gave the cord a firm, steady pull. Smooth as glass, the chute opened. Even so, he traveled at a high speed. The parachute was safety measure number one. Number two was the large, air-filled target waiting below.

Having done this stunt hundreds of times, Nate knew what to expect and how it should feel. And he knew when something was wrong.

The air bag, that Nate had personally supervised the placement of, wasn't where it was supposed to be. He didn't have the time to wonder how that had happened. If he didn't act fast, he wouldn't be around to beat the shit out of the asshole responsible.

Grabbing the guide strings, Nate pulled a hard right with all his considerable strength — and prayed.

CHAPTER ONE

HOLLYWOOD WAS AN unforgiving town with a long memory.

Drugs could be forgiven. Drunk driving. Spousal abuse. Those things could be forgiven. In the movie industry, your worth was measured by one thing — box office returns. Three strikes, you're out.

Early in his career, Caleb Landis knew the meaning of holding on by his fingertips. He was young, inexperienced, and hungry. That meant working all the angles. No one opened any doors for a dirt-poor would-be producer. That was fine with him. He had no problem barreling his way in. His take no prisoners attitude earned him respect. And enemies.

Hard work. Long hours. Sacrifice. Eventually, it paid off. Caleb's career spanned over four decades. He had money and power. The shelves of his office were lined with every award the industry could give him.

When a movie had the name Landis attached to it, the world knew they were getting quality.

Sitting back, Caleb looked around the table with pride. His family. That was his greatest accomplishment. The fame and money meant nothing compared to the joy of knowing the most important people in the world surrounded him. The people he loved. The people who loved him.

It all started and ended with his Callie.

Screen goddess to the world. To him, protector of his heart.

He had no doubt the first time he saw her. He knew she was the woman he wanted to spend his life with. She was the only woman he would ever love. Their life hadn't been the fairy tale some people made it out to be. They had

236

their ups and downs. But through it all, one thing never changed. Their unshakable love.

His beautiful wife had given him four strong, healthy sons. Men a father could be proud of.

Wyatt was the oldest. Like Caleb, a producer. The difference was *he* trusted his gut. If a project felt right, he fought until he got it made. Wyatt was a thinker. His first concern was the bottom line. They had squared off more than once about artistry versus the almighty dollar.

The end was always the same. He and Wyatt were different enough that butting heads was inevitable. They had enough similarities to put those differences aside. The most important thing was the movie. Together they made art — and money.

Caleb's gaze moved to the other side of the table. The laugh he heard was a deeper version of his sweet Callie's. It made him smile. Colton. The youngest of his four boys. He was the only one to follow his mother's lead, stepping in front of the camera to make his mark. And what a mark it was going to be.

Colt had a face the camera loved. The first offer to put him in the movies came when he was only a year old. The offers kept coming. Callie didn't want any of her sons to be *child stars*. Caleb agreed.

Growing up was hard enough. In Beverly Hills, the temptations were magnified. Caleb and Callie did their best to give their children as normal a childhood as possible. Family dinners. Game night. Backyard barbecues. If that childhood included trips to Cannes and vacations on private yachts, so what? This was their version of normal. It wasn't perfect. But then, what was?

Colton was one of the biggest movie stars in the world. In public, that meant screaming fans and preferential treatment. At dinner with his family, he was expected to set the table and dry the dishes. It was true when he was ten. It was true now, even if his last movie *did* break box office records.

Then there was Garrett. Caleb sat back smiling when he heard his middle son complaining to his mother.

"What is the world coming to when a man's family takes sides against him?"

"First, Jade is your family. And ours." Callie patted Jade's hand. "Second. She's right. You're wrong. End of discussion."

"Hey." Garrett looked at the two women. His mother on his right. The love of his life on his left. There was no rock. No hard place. With a snap of his fingers, there would be a thousand men lined up to take his place. He was no fool. He knew he had it good. "I give up," he said, wisely conceding the point.

Dazzled by Jade's smile, Garrett melted. He tucked a lock of her long, silky red hair behind her ear. The unconsciously intimate gesture had his parents smiling with approval.

"A wise decision, son." Caleb nodded at Garrett with a wink. "When you realize your lady is the brains in the relationship, the sailing will be much smoother."

"Where are you on *Exile*?"

Garrett and Jade were just back from Vancouver where he had finished principal shooting on his current film. His last project had garnered him an Oscar nomination for best director. Caleb believed this one would win his son the statue.

"I'm in the studio next week. The soundtrack needs some tweaking, but the composer assures me it will be ready."

"It better be," Wyatt added. "The Los Angeles Philharmonic doesn't come cheap. You have them for a week. That's all the budget will allow. After that, I'll take it out of your salary."

"It's my own fault for working with family," Garrett sighed. "I could knock any other producer on his ass if he talked to me like that. Mommy would have a fit if I bruised her baby's face."

"Jade, you're marrying an idiot."

"Pardon my French in advance, Mom." Garrett gave Wyatt the finger, and then added, "Fuck you, Wyatt."

"Nice mouth, brother. You might think about washing it out with soap before kissing your woman." Out of Callie's sight, Wyatt flipped Garrett the bird.

"I just brushed. How about kissing me instead?"

"Nate!"

Callie was across the room in a flash. Instead of jumping into his arms, as was her custom, she held back. She knew the doctor said Nate's ribs were healed, but she was his mother. The thought of causing him the slightest pain was unthinkable.

"Where's your sling?"

"Gone for good. Thank God."

Nate's left arm was still in a cast. With little effort, he used his right to swing Callie in a circle. The comforting scent of roses and vanilla drifted around him. As always, it took him back to his childhood when she would tuck him in at night. Burying his face in her hair, he breathed deeply.

Mother. Love. Safety. From the time he was born, she had steered him with a gentle yet firm hand. There was a fine line between controlling and

239

supportive. Callie Flynn showed her sons by example that a woman could thrill the world with her acting and still be the best mother anyone could ask for. Nate affectionately kissed the top of her head. What would he have done without this woman?

"We didn't think you were going to make it." Callie took his good hand, leading him to the table. "Sit. I'll get you a plate. I swear, since the accident you've wasted away to nothing."

Colt snorted in disbelief. "How can you tell? The man is a freaking brick wall."

"Callie's right." Jade smiled at Nate. "You look thinner."

"I knew the woman couldn't keep her eyes off me. Tell me you've finally realized you picked the wrong brother."

"One more word and I'll forget you're my twin." Garrett turned to Jade. "I always felt sorry for him. I got the looks, the brains, and the charm. And Nate got the...? What did Nate get?"

"The ability to kick your ass?" Nate flexed his impressive biceps. "And more women than even Colton could handle."

"Hey," Colt interjected. "That's my reputation as a man-whore you're besmirching. What would the tabloids say if word got out that my brother was getting more women than I was?"

"Don't listen to him, Colt." Garrett loved jabbing at his twin. Just as Nate loved returning the favor. The sport never grew old. "He overcompensated for his shortcomings by living in the gym. I suppose some women find brawn over brains attractive."

"More than a few."

"Enough." Callie chuckled. She had heard this banter for years. "You," she said to Nate, "stop talking — eat. And you," she looked at Garrett. "Leave your brother in peace for five minutes."

Thanking her with a smile, Nate took the plate from his mother. It overflowed with roast beef, mashed potatoes, fresh green beans, all drowned in rich, brown gravy. Adding three fresh baked rolls from the basket on the table, Nate was a happy man.

The truth was, since the accident on the movie set last month, he hadn't been himself. It would be different if he could work. Keeping busy was the best way to calm his mind and body. Unfortunately, the injuries he had sustained kept him sidelined.

Too much time on his hands. Too much time to think about what had gone wrong. The botched stunt could have ended in tragedy. Thanks to his quick reflexes, physical strength, and determination not to end up in a heap of mangled bones, Nate walked away with a few cracked ribs and a broken arm. The only reason he stayed the night in the hospital was to appease his mother. The doctor assured her Nate didn't have a concussion. Callie didn't want to take any chances. One night of observation was a small price to pay for his mother's peace of mind.

It didn't hurt that his nurse was a curvy brunette with warm, soft hands.

"I know that smile." Wyatt shook his head. "Which conquest are you thinking about now?"

"You wouldn't give me such a hard time if you were getting laid more often." Remembering where he was, Nate gave his mother a repentant grin. "Sorry."

"Your brother's love life is his own business," Callie said firmly.

"Thank you." Wyatt gave Nate a *take that* glare.

"Though..."

"Ah, crap." Wyatt's head fell forward, his chin hitting his chest.

241

"Come on, Wyatt," Garrett laughed with delight. "Every man lives to have his mother discuss his sex life."

DREAMING OF YOUR LOVE

(Hollywood Legends Book Three)

PROLOGUE

LIGHTS FLASHED FROM every direction. It blinded and dazzled all at once.

Screams drowned out every other sound. This was Los Angeles. Busy streets in every direction. Jet patterns overhead. The excited—in some cases rabid—fans that surrounded the roped-off red carpet made it seem like nothing existed but them and the bright lights.

It shouldn't have been a pleasant experience. Alighting from the over-the-top luxury of a Rolls Royce into chaos and mayhem? No normal human being would willingly seek out such an experience.

However, Colton Landis was not a normal human being. He was an actor.

Colt turned his world-famous megawatt smile on the crowd, eliciting another deafening burst of heartfelt screams.

"We need to get inside, Colt. The movie starts in ten minutes."

"Relax, Deb."

Colt's publicist had been with him for five years. Deb Kline knew how to spin a press release like nobody else. They saw eye to eye on most things. Except how much he should expose himself to his fans. If she had her way, he would zip from point A to point B as quickly as humanly possible.

In this case, point A was the limo, and point B was Grauman's Chinese Theater.

243

"I'll relax when you are safely inside. Have you forgotten Dallas already?"

"Dallas was an anomaly."

Colt continued to wave and smile. Deb wanted him to curb his accessibility. She had always been cautious, but after a fan somehow breached security during a press conference to announce his next movie, she was particularly leery of events like this one.

"Colt."

"Don't go over there, Colt."

Deb knew the second Colt observed the waving autograph books, her words fell on deaf ears. He believed in giving his fans what they wanted. It was one of the things that made Colton Landis a huge movie star. He genuinely loved his fans. He loved meeting them, speaking with them, having his picture taken with them. Most of her clients searched for any reason to avoid these moments. Not Colt. He didn't have a public persona and a private one. What you saw was what you got—twenty-four hours a day, seven days a week.

Colt made her job as a publicist a dream. Keeping him safe was a nightmare.

He refused to have a bodyguard. Part of it was ego—and he had plenty of that. Many of his parts portrayed him as a big, macho, tough guy. How would it look if he had a bigger, more macho, tough guy constantly shadowing him? Not great for his reputation. He would look weak. And in Hollywood, perception was everything.

It was a valid argument. Not so valid? Colt believed that, for the most part, his fans were harmless. Not that he was a naïve Pollyanna. There was no need for Deb to point out the entertainment world's tragic examples of the heinous acts obsessive fans could commit.

Colt lived the life. He grew up watching his superstar mother traverse that fine line between making herself accessible to fans and maintaining some much-needed privacy.

However, he didn't have a family to consider. No wife. No children. His life was his own. A bodyguard would mean he was giving in. Turning his life over to fear instead of embracing every single moment of his fairytale existence.

"Ten minutes."

Deb didn't know if Colt heard her over the screams. Nor did she care. She was getting him into that theater if it meant grabbing his ear and dragging him along like an errant five-year-old. And wouldn't that make a great picture in *People* magazine? Okay. No ears. *Ugh. This man was going to make her old before her time.*

Colt held a woman's phone at arm's length, including himself in a selfie of her and her three friends.

"I love you, Colton."

Colt couldn't single out the speaker. The cry came from every direction. He waved and called out, "I love you, too."

He signed a few more autographs, moving along the line. Deb was right. He needed to get inside. It wasn't fair to keep everyone waiting. Ten more, he promised himself. It killed him to see the expressions on the faces of the fans who were left out.

"Thanks. See you soon," Colt called out to the crowd.

Handing her signed book to a dreamy-eyed woman, Colt gave the crowd a final wave.

"Ready?" Deb tried to maintain the *stern teacher* expression she had spent twenty years cultivating.

Colt had a way of making her professional mask slip. Thank goodness she was old enough to be his youngish grandmother. While his charm was undeniable, her age and experience allowed her to put the sexual pull that radiated around him into perspective.

Until he turned his smile on her. Full blast.

"Am I that big of a pain in the ass?"

There it was. That naughty twinkle in his deep blue eyes that made the world swoon. On screen, it was irresistible. Paired with dark hair and a tall, muscular frame, was it any wonder the camera loved him?

Reluctantly, Deb returned his smile.

Colt was her client. He was also her friend. She knew he wasn't trying to be difficult. He was being himself. For a man who was adored by millions, catered to on a daily basis, and could buy and sell two or three third-world nations without raising a sweat, Colton Landis was surprisingly down to Earth. And hard-headed. And opinionated.

On top of that? On occasions such as this one, a major pain in the ass.

Still, if she were honest, there wasn't a single thing about him that she would change. As movie stars went—hell, as human beings went—Colton Landis was a joy to be around. Not that she would ever tell him that. The last thing he needed was another person extolling his endless virtues. Colt hated that kind of treatment. One of the reasons they worked so well together was because Deb didn't kowtow.

Deb was about to hit him with one of the nifty sarcastic one-liners he loved, when a scream came from the crowd. Not a *we love you* cry, but one of terror. Before she could react, Deb saw a man jump over the velvet rope. He carried a knife.

Colt pushed her to the side, effectively putting himself between her and the attacker. *He isn't after me*, Deb wanted to protest. But everything happened so fast, she didn't have time.

In the blink of an eye, the man raised the knife and stabbed Colt.

IF I LOVED YOU

(Harper Falls Book One)

PROLOGUE

IT WAS SOMETHING out of a fairy tale.

Thousands of flickering lights dazzled her senses, almost as much as the tall, wickedly handsome man who so expertly danced her onto the shadowed balcony. The music that filtered from the nearby ballroom only added to the already magical atmosphere.

Women dreamed their whole lives of a moment like this — a prelude to a happily-ever-after ending. Ever so briefly, she let herself drift into that fantasy as if she was one of those women. For a moment, she let herself pretend that her childhood had been filled with the kind of whimsicality that allowed those fantasies to carry over into adulthood.

But no, she wasn't a romantic, hopeless or otherwise. She didn't want a prince to sweep her into his arms and carry her away on his faithful steed. She was more than capable of rescuing herself. She preferred it that way.

The stars were in the sky, not in her eyes.

"I'm glad you asked me to dance," her partner whispered, pulling her closer.

Suddenly, she was nervous. The champagne she downed earlier had completely worn off. No more floating on a cloud of false courage. If she was going to do this, she was going to have to do it on her own.

"Jack," she said. Damn, it was hard to sound seductive when your voice squeaked. "Jack." That was better, lower, and slightly husky. She'd read somewhere that guys liked husky voices.

"Rose."

"Yes?"

"Nothing, I just thought we were saying each other's names." He put his lips next to her ear. "I like the way you say mine."

"Jack." Good Lord, she had to stop repeating his name. "I need a favor, Jack. A big one." Or should she say, she hoped he *had* a big one. Rose groaned to herself. At least she hadn't said that aloud.

"I'll help if I can."

"You're the only one who *can* help." She took another deep breath. "I need you to take me home and screw my brains out."

www.ingramcontent.com/pod-product-compliance
Lightning Source LLC
Chambersburg PA
CBHW071143170626
46809CB00002B/751